THE BUTTERFLY

THE BUTTERFLY

Michael Rumaker

New York: Charles Scribner's Sons

TO MY FATHER AND MY MOTHER

THE BUTTERFLY

❧ THE MORNING GLORY

JIM HAD this tennis ball he found at the hospital, in the grass near the tennis courts. He walked around bouncing it off the sidewalks and off walls. He bounced it in the library and bugged everybody. He was wearing an imaginary baseball cap until he could get a real one.

He felt very thin and 17. Sometimes when he talked to Doctor Sylvan it was like in the movies, but very real. When things got very real for him it got to be like a play or a movie—or it got to be like a story and he wanted to write it. Right now the sun was shining and he was killing time before going back to the building for Group. Group was where everybody sat around a table and shouted at each other, and sometimes cried. Sometimes he cried. The ball was very important. He bounced it partly because he was afraid and partly because it was a way of telling everybody he was here. He bounced it very hard and furious sometimes just to let them know, and let himself know, too.

It was a bright sunshiny morning. He sat on a green bench under the cool shade of a tree. In the auditorium the patients were at services and the organ was playing, very muted and soft, as though far away. And not five yards away on another bench was a lovely blonde-haired girl, as fresh and soft as the morning. He couldn't go away from that place because he wanted to be near her. He kept stealing looks at her and felt incredibly gangly and foolish. She was writing in a tablet, a letter maybe, and she looked up now and then as though to think out what she was going to say next. Sometimes she looked at him and he tried to look into her face and not look away but his shyness got the better of him and he turned and looked up at the trees, looked anywhere, the sky, to hide his confusion. How beautiful she was! in a light green summer dress, and her full light hair.

Several times she had come into the library where he worked sometimes. He was afraid to look at her. He felt, as now, all arms and legs and the ugliest creature in the world with the thickest tongue and not a thought in his head and without the courage to even whisper hello.

She had an open and generous face. He had a fantasy she was from Western Pennsylvania, though why he didn't know: some sturdily built, honey-colored creature from the mining towns who had somehow gotten away and come to the hospital to study to be a nurse. The other day he passed her on the street on his way to the library. She was coming from the library with a girl friend and he cursed his luck for not having gotten there earlier so he could maybe sign out her books and find out what her name was. But as she passed him her eyes went to his feet—and his heart leapt up because he saw she was looking at his new shoes and her eyes traveled up to his face and he looked into her face and their eyes held for a moment in passing.

He was so afraid to speak to her, afraid he would say some dumb thing and get very awkward and stupid. Maybe even step on her foot or some 17 year old thing like that in his embarrassment and shyness. And what if she didn't like him! Well, he couldn't think about that. When she looked up from her writing he tipped his imaginary baseball cap over his eyes and pulled his legs up and clamped his chin on his knees and hugged his knees and looked away at some imaginary hummingbird tracing fantastic invisible patterns in the air, now here, now there, a kind of dizziness, the bird moved so fast, like his heart beating, with fear and desire.

A dumpy Puerto Rican, a patient, was hanging around her bench. Just stood there like a dumb piece of clay, waiting, Jim guessed, for her to look up and say hello and invite him to sit down. That pissed him off, that the man had the guts to go right up to her and hang around like that, these big clay hands stuffed in his pockets and him hanging near the bench—Jim knew what he was hanging there for but like looking off in the distance as though there was some fabulous thing he was looking at and not that every nerve in his body was attuned to the blonde sitting a couple feet away.

Jim cocked his baseball cap back on his head and thought, I'll just sit here and if that bastard tries to get wise with her I'll run over and knock his block off. Mainly, he was worried about this. Of course he was a big coward but you never know what you will do if somebody means so much to you.

He was a dumpy fat little Spaniard and it really got Jim hot under the collar when he just slid down next to her and sat there, his fat hands folded in his lap like a fistful of sausages. Jim could see he didn't know how to talk to this girl. He was a real lump and only knew fuck-fuck and that was all a woman ever meant to him, Jim could see that right off. But the blonde was very cool and went on writing and not paying any attention to him. He started whistling some dumb Puerto Rican love song —a rather nice one, too—but it didn't carry any feeling. He just didn't have it in his heart, it was all fuck-fuck to him. Jim had to admire his guts, though, that he could slide right down next to her that way and himself scared to death to even look at her.

The man just sat whistling like that and she went on writing. Then Jim heard her speaking to the man and her voice sounded very pleasant but he couldn't make out what she said, the wind carried her words away. A very sweet and pleasant voice she had. He thought she was being nice to the gook, a student nurse and all and taking her psychiatric training. Then all of a sudden, very distinct and clear, "Go, please, go!" His heart beat fast and he knew the man was really annoying her. He leapt up and as he was about to start over the blonde let the man have one square across the face. The man jumped up and made a beeline across the grass and disappeared around the corner of the auditorium. What a girl! The only thing was, she stayed only a few minutes after the Puerto Rican ran off. She gathered up her books and paper and pencils and got up and walked back towards the home where she lived.

Jim watched her go. He hoped the Puerto Rican hadn't spoiled her morning. It was a very cool bright green morning with the invisible birds up singing in all the trees and the light blue sky clean and not a cloud and the grass green at his feet and spreading out all around him.

He got up to go to Group. On the way he bounced his tennis ball hard on the walk. Behind one of the homes, up the wall, a morning glory peeped over: a magnificent broad-belled flower, deep rich blue with white creases and the blossom speckled with golden pollen. He ran over the grass and stood on tiptoe to pick it. An old patient, sweeping the flagstone walk, shouted and waved his broom at him, but he pinched the flower from the vine and ran off with it.

He ran back to the building and up the steps and rang the bell. An attendant unlocked the door and Jim showed him his parole card and the attendant let him in. He went down the hall to Group, holding the flower like some big bell, the throat of it silver and its petals flecked with golden pollen. He held the flower so, for everyone to see, as though to celebrate the day and the morning; the blueness of the flower deeper than the blue of the morning sky but as lovely and rich and clear.

As he walked down the hall, the morning glory swaying gently in his hand, attendants and patients and doctors turned to look at it. He stopped at the Supervisor's door and tilted it at the nurse sitting behind the desk and her hands moved to her cheeks for the sheer beauty of the flower.

Paul was waiting on the bench outside the door of the room where Group was held. Jim was early and he sat down beside Paul. Paul had a lean horse face and long yellow teeth. His face had a tic that made him always look like he was cracking nuts. He admired the flower and took it in his hand. He had a real sense of morning-gloryness because he didn't put it to his nose to smell it. Its beauty was so delicate it was as though the slightest breath would begin to wilt it. Paul held it to his face and looked into it.

"I should get something to put it in," Jim said. "With water. But I don't see anything around."

Then he snapped his fingers and reached in his pocket but only found a nickel. He asked Paul if he had a nickel and Paul brought one out and gave it to him. Jim went to the coffee machine and put in the nickels and got a cup of hot chocolate and drank the chocolate and then went to the water fountain, rinsed out the cup, ran water in it and put the morning glory in that.

The psychiatrist arrived with the patients from the closed wards. He unlocked the door of the room and everyone went in and sat down around the big square table. Doctor Sylvan was a dark man with dark, warm, intelligent eyes that sometimes filled with tears but most often had a mischievous glint. He had very black curly hair which glistened with pomade and shiny white teeth which showed quite a bit because he smiled a lot.

Jim sat down directly across from him and inched the morning glory across the table and told the doctor it was for him.

Doctor Sylvan's eyes shone as they did when he was moved and he smiled and bowed his head, thanking Jim, then put the flower in the center of the table for everyone to see.

Everyone was pleased with the morning glory and leaned over to look at it and smell it. Frank, who was long and thin and tense and who was sitting next to Jim, his arms folded tightly and pressed against his chest, he didn't like the flower. His eyes were hard and fixed against it.

Jim had the sudden impulse to move the flower close to himself, to protect it in some way, or to move it toward the doctor, away from Frank. Suddenly Frank lifted the flower from the cup and stuck his nose directly into the throat of the flower. His breath made the broad petals of it flutter against his cheeks as though trying to pull away from him. He sniffed strong at it two or three times and the flower began to wilt. When he put it back in the cup his breath had left streaks across the blossom and it had almost imperceptibly begun to droop.

Jim looked at Frank's hands and he wondered that such slender fingers, fingers that looked so sensitive, could have no sense of the morning glory.

"Okay," said Doctor Sylvan, "let's get started. Who's got anything to say?"

The Group quieted down. There was silence. John, a tall

well-built boy, got up from his seat and went to the heavily
screened window and stood there silently, staring out. Frank
began his little game of gathering what packs of cigarettes there
were on the table and stacking them and packs of matches on
top of one another, as a child with blocks. He began to talk
loudly and angrily, his anger chronic and persistent, torn from
him in furious snatches only to withdraw again and hide in him.
While he was balancing the cigarette packs and matches on
top of one another he railed, red-throated and swollen-veined,
like a puffed-up turkey, at the others in the Group. He was
building his little tower close to the morning glory and Jim's
hand slipped up from his lap; he wanted to move the flower
but he held his hand back, waiting, watching Frank making
the structure. All the time Frank shouted at them, trying to
make them understand that it was no good to hide and bottle
up one's feelings. He tried to make them see what it had done
to him.

"Look at me!" he shouted. "At what all that tying away
of feeling has done. You see me all choked and enraged and
persistently angry at everyone and everything. Because I didn't
let it out and it grew and accumulated over the years, smother-
ing out all other areas of feeling—till you see me now this rag-
ing thing who no longer remembers what he's angry at!"

His hand cut down to the base of his cigarette pack tower
and sliced at it. The tower toppled. Jim held his breath. The
tower fell on the morning glory, tearing the thin skin of the
blossom. The flower began to lose its rich blue color, its color
faded, as though it were bleeding, invisibly, and the edges of
the flower began to curl and turn inward.

It was as though Jim himself began to close, watching the
flower close and listening to the harsh, high-pitched anger of
Frank crying across the room. He began to close up and withdraw, feeling a chill in the room as though some murderous

frost had entered there. He was with his father then, back there, at home, remembering his father's anger, like Frank's; anger which he didn't understand, anger which never seemed of the moment and for some definite palpable reason but seemed always to do with something else. How often it seemed to him he was the scapegoat, the target, of his father's anger, and how, like the morning glory, he would turn inward and withdraw, chilled and bewildered, not understanding his father's anger toward him or why he was angry.

The morning had begun so well. He had felt as bright and clear and alive as the morning. But Frank's anger was like a frost. His unconscious destruction of the flower made a knot in Jim's stomach. He sat there with a ball of it in his belly. He wanted to tell Frank to be quiet, please, be quiet. But Frank's anger persisted; it was high and hurt his ears and made him afraid. It put him back with his father again and the angers and punishments that he could never understand. He looked into Frank's face. The skin was drawn and strained, the eyes slightly crazed, his mouth a downward slit, the flesh red and the eyes bulging, the flesh of his face was as though a fist behind him held it bunched at the base of his skull, some red-fisted demon pulling the skin back from his face.

The red face of Jim's father, the obscene red nakedness of the man in the shower, the blooded faces of the men in his dreams, the man in the pink suit.

Frank raved and the flower was utterly dead, shriveled and hanging forlornly over the side of the paper cup. Frank, spluttering with rage, began tapping the point of his cigarette against the dead blossom, leaving charred stains of gray ash on the wrinkled skin of it. Jim kept glancing at Doctor Sylvan to see if he had known what Frank was doing to the flower, but the doctor had been listening to the discussion and did not seem to have seen any of it.

The Group got very noisy. Everyone was shouting. There was a great deal of feeling in everyone. Paul paced around the room, pompous and aroused, his face cracking as he spoke. John, who still stood at the window, fell to his knees on the floor and wrapped his arms around the steampipe, pressing his head fervently against the cold metal of the pipe. (A pole to grow upon, a father to grow amongst the leaves of.)

"What's he? Play acting again?" Paul said, swinging around to look at him.

"Whatta ham," said another, and turned away, scowling.

Doctor Sylvan got up and went over to John and touched him on the shoulder.

"Come on, John. Get up and go back to your seat."

John got up abruptly and dropped his trousers and shorts and taking his penis he inserted it between his legs and squeezed his thighs together tight and sat down quickly, prissily, hiding it, as though he no longer wanted it there for him to see.

Doctor Sylvan went back to his seat. "Let's go on."

"Whatta we supposed to do, Doc? Ignore him?" said Paul.

"Boy, try and do that!" said another, laughing.

The others joined in, laughing, and then the Group fell into silence again.

John took his belt and tied it tightly around his waist, his skin was pinched and bulging from the pressure. Jim thought he would hurt himself and clasped his hands and sat tense in his seat.

John pulled tighter, tighter on the belt. Cut in half, not there. To be half a thing—6—6—6th floor, 6th month you shall be born, 6 stones along the road, in Jim's dreams always the number 6. To be a bleeding stump, the suffering in knowing one is half a thing and always a yearning backwards toward death. The knowing, the knowing he was 28 going on 17.

He closed his eyes and could not look, he couldn't look any more at John with his wide leather belt wrapped tightly around his middle, choking him. He did not open his eyes until he heard Doctor Sylvan say, "All right, John, let it go now." And when he opened them and looked across he saw that John was loosening his belt and John was crying.

"Let's go on," the doctor said.

Jim began to feel more withdrawn. The talk, of suicide, and marriage, everyone vehement and loud, and what John had done at the pipe and with his belt, closed him off. He put his head in his arms and tears came to his eyes. He wanted to cry out that it need not be if one only has something to live for. Inside, the room was alive with voices, each, it seemed, crying out for love me, care for me, save me, don't lock me out, don't neglect me. In every voice there was a crying and he wanted to quiet everyone, to say that each must live, to touch them and be touched by them, to heal, as hands, touching.

To touch Marvin, fat and gross and breathing heavily, to touch him who was so afraid and lonely, so afraid of being left out of things. To touch Cal who walked with his head held so stiffly back, as though it would snap, holding it that way as though to tell the world, I don't need anyone, I can get along without anyone. He fooled no one, his eyes (even though the brows were held high in arrogance) were wandering, looking —he was searching, searching. To touch him and bend his head, bring it forward and down, make it straight and level, straighten and level his gaze, unbend his neck with his touch. And put life back into the expressionless eyes of Bill, whose hands and voice trembled, whose voice broke, whose eyes stared out cold and unmoving, as though they had seen some terrible thing and were frozen with fear. There was the boy whose name he didn't know, whose head shook from some nervous spasm, whose hands also shook, the fingers blistered and charred from smoking cigarettes down too close. Jim looked at him and tears welled up in him. He seemed to be suffering so, but with what fierce attention his eyes stayed on the face of whoever was speaking, yet he himself did not speak, only listened, hands and head trembling. Jim placed his arm around him and the boy turned his head quickly, as though stung, a look of surprise on his face, the look of a man who's not used to being touched.

Jim smiled and let his arm fall away from the boy's neck and he laid his head in his arms and the tears again welled up in him. He wanted to touch everyone, to heal, to bring what was outside the window, warm sun and the green trees, to touch as with that kind of healing, of warmth and tender growth of new green things out of the broken and lacerated pasts of each of them sitting there at the table.

He felt a hand on his arm and looking up saw it was the doctor who had reached across and touched him. There was a silence in the room. The doctor's fingers were warm and gentle on his arm. How dearly Jim loved him. He cried, with joy, feeling the warmth and gentleness of his touch. How dearly he loved him and he would never let him go from him, he would be with him always, wherever he went he would have him with him, and he would not have to run, he could go and come back, and he would be there for him, and he would love him always.

After Group the table was cleared of the coffee cups and spoons, the ash trays. Only the dead morning glory remained in its paper cup. Jim waited around, hanging near the door, anxious to see what would happen: if it would be thrown away, if Doctor Sylvan would forget that he had given it to him, or, even if he remembered, whether he would want it now that it was shriveled and dead.

No one had touched the flower, it remained alone in the center of the big table. Jim watched as Doctor Sylvan broke away from a group of patients and came over to the table and picked up the flower and took it into the kitchen. Jim followed him and watched him empty the water in the sink and throw the cup in the trash. He came out holding the dead flower in his hand. He paused and smiled at Jim, holding the flower up between his thumb and forefinger.

"I didn't think you'd remember," Jim said, and suddenly snatched the flower out of the doctor's hand and mashed it between his fingers and threw it on the floor. His head drooped and he turned to go but the doctor put his arm on his shoulder and drew him back.

"Jim, I'll always have the morning glory. And so will you. We'll remember it, vividly, the beauty of it. Even though the flower died—I saw it!—the gesture behind the giving of it didn't. That can't be destroyed."

Jim looked into his face and took his hand and held it tightly and then turned and went out the door and up the long hall where he showed the attendant his parole card. The attendant unlocked the door and let him out.

As he walked out of the building he suddenly felt a compulsion to look up and there, looking down at him between the bars of the second floor porch, were those fierce suffering eyes of the boy in the Group. He paused and looked up into those eyes and there was no need to say anything, or to make any sign other than gazing into that grief-stricken face. Because it seemed they did not need to know any more than that, that they had touched, had made contact. He felt less alone, less cut off.

Taking the beat-up tennis ball out of his pocket he bounced it hard on the sidewalk, caught it and bounced it hard again. He walked off bouncing the ball fiercely, feeling the eyes from the second floor porch following him as he went. There were the green leaves lit by the sun; birds, jays of incredible blues, the air was full of the cries of birds swarming amongst the ivy which clung to the walls of the buildings.

◆ THE DOCTOR

JIM SAT WAITING on the big lumpy sofa outside Doctor Sylvan's office door. He had a peach he kept rubbing the fuzz off with his thumb. He didn't like the peach. It was small and hard. A mental state hospital peach, he called it. He didn't know what he was going to do with the peach. He thought he would give it to Doctor Sylvan but he looked at it again, turning it around and around in his hand, and decided it wasn't good enough. He looked up and down the long hall for some place to throw it away but there wasn't any place. The hall was empty of anything except for the couch and potted ferns in the windows at either end of the hall. He stuffed the peach into his pocket and from his other pocket pulled out his beat-up tennis ball. He stood up and started bouncing it against the wall and catching it. He walked along the hall doing this until a nurse came out of one of the offices and told him to cut it out.

"I only do this because I'm nervous," he said.

"Well, it's very annoying," said the nurse.

He shrugged his shoulders, bounced the ball once more off the wall and walked to the other end of the hall and looked out the open window.

The low stucco buildings of the hospital with their harsh green windows and heavy wire screening stretched out in all directions as far as the eye could see. The dark porches on every floor were even more sombre with their grime-streaked walls and heavy bars. Here and there a patient stood, hands gripping the bars and gazing out on the early spring afternoon with a dead unchanging expression on his face. Some even managed to get their heads completely through the bars and looked down at the ground as though not seeing anything. Jim wondered how they got their heads between the bars. He had tried it once and couldn't even get a part of his head through. He wondered how they got them back in again.

One man stood on the railing of a porch, holding the bars with tight fists, his legs wide. He was singing a song Jim did not know—"Green eyes, her green eyes in the fair morning"—the words sounding in the still afternoon air heavy and leaden, sounding neither joyous nor sorrowful, empty words intoned monotonously out over the trees and flowers below.

The sharp scream of a woman in one of the back wards suddenly split the air.

"I am dead! I am dead!" the voice screamed over and over in a piercing shrill note.

Jim shuddered and closed his eyes and turned away from the window. His bright feeling of happiness with the day disappeared and a quick chill and sadness came over him. He began to bounce the ball furiously as though to drown out the screams, and then, over the thud of the ball striking the polished floor, he heard the brisk quick tapping of Doctor Sylvan's footsteps coming in the opposite direction. He stopped bouncing the ball, holding it tight in his hand, watching Doctor Sylvan as he hurried up to him.

Doctor Sylvan with his dark curly hair; his eyes dark too, with a light and warmth in them. He smiled and his teeth were very white, looking even whiter in the darkness of his face. His mouth was soft, the lips dark and sensual.

"Hello, Jim. Sorry I'm late. I had to go home after lunch. The baby has a fever."

Jim scuffed his toe on the floor.

"Is he all right?"

Doctor Sylvan smiled. "I think he'll live. Even though his old man's treating him."

He paused, his countenance changing, and looked into Jim's eyes. "How are you?"

Jim was silent and looked away. Doctor Sylvan took him by the arm and they walked back to the office. Doctor Sylvan opened the door and they went in. He sat behind the desk and Jim sat down on the green leather chaise lounge against the wall. Jim couldn't look at the doctor and when he talked his eyes looked past him or to the side. He felt very tired and only wanted to sleep. He wanted not to be there with him, feeling that way, and not knowing what to say but only feeling tight and withdrawn, everything suddenly flat and hopeless.

Doctor Sylvan leaned forward in his chair. "What is it?" he asked.

Jim couldn't tell him but was only aware of the ashen light of the hot spring afternoon coming in at the window and feeling as though he were buried and without hope. He got up from the couch and walked to the sink in the corner. He picked up a glass on the file cabinet and turning on the tap filled it with water.

"I can't," he said. "I can't tell you."

Doctor Sylvan was standing behind the desk now.

"Yes, that's just like you," he said sarcastically. "So selfish you're never able to tell anyone anything."

He made a quick gesture of disgust with his hand.

Jim felt hot tears rush to his eyes. He threw the glass as hard as he could in the sink and smashed it to pieces. He covered his face with his hands and, beginning to cry, turned rocking from side to side in the middle of the room.

"What can I tell you?" he said in a choked voice. "I want to slap and punch you. I'm afraid to have you close to me and I'm afraid you'll go away and leave me. Sometimes I don't know who you are or what I want you to be to me. Sometimes you're my father, and another time you're my mother, and then my brother, my friend. I get you mixed up and I don't know what you are because you're all of these things to me. And I'm confused now about so many things. Sometimes I don't know whether I'm a boy or a girl or whether I'm a child or a man. I seem to be so many things and can change so swiftly from one to the other. I don't feel that I'm *here,* as though I'm buried, as though there's some wall between me and what's around me."

He stopped and looked at Doctor Sylvan, making a helpless gesture with his hands.

"You know all this."

"Maybe there's no longer any reason for you to go on loving me as you've loved me," Doctor Sylvan said quietly. "Loving me with the love that's been pent up in you over the years, a love that you could never find anyone to give to."

Jim didn't know what to say and let his arms drop at his sides, his face averted.

"Must I take you in my arms?" Doctor Sylvan said, taking a step forward. "Hold you and caress you? Do you want me to do that?"

Doctor Sylvan walked over to the couch. "Come here and sit beside me," he said, sitting down.

Jim's hands reached out to grab, as though to hold on to something, but the fingers recoiled. He couldn't go to him and stood as though rooted in the middle of the room. Doctor Sylvan was watching him, quietly, almost without expression. Jim still couldn't look him in the eyes and hit his fists against his head and closed his eyes and turned away, saying, "If you don't have feelings then you don't get hurt."

"But you have feeling."

"Yes, and I don't want to. I don't want to have feeling. I've wanted to kill it."

"And you can't," Doctor Sylvan said mockingly.

Jim glared at him, then began pacing around the room. He stopped near the window, pressing his knuckles against the glass.

"Well, if you came only to stare out the window," Doctor Sylvan said harshly, "I might as well go about my business."

He began to get up with an air of boredom.

Jim wheeled on him.

"You nasty sonofabitch!" he shouted, his slim face contorted, ugly. "You're a cocksucker!"

"And don't forget to say I'm a nasty little kike," said Doctor Sylvan, going to his desk and beginning to calmly rifle through some papers there.

Jim stalked over and leaning across the desk screamed in his face, "Yeah—a little kike from Brooklyn trying to be a big psychiatrist! A flashy little silver-and-gold-thread kike psychiatrist from Brooklyn."

"I've been called that before," said Doctor Sylvan softly. "And it's the Bronx, Jim, not Brooklyn."

"I'm sure you have," Jim said, and let out a deep breath and walked away from the desk. He was trembling and he jammed his hands in his pockets to hide the fact that they were shaking. Doctor Sylvan continued to thumb through papers and to ignore him and Jim turned his back on the doctor and went over to a shelf near the door where there were books and magazines. He thumbed through a few but his fingers trembled so much he stopped leafing and his hand gripped a hand grenade, a souvenir Doctor Sylvan had brought back with him from the war and had made into a cigarette lighter. Jim fingered it and held it tight in his hand. He plucked at the pin but it was embedded in the cold heavy metal and would not yield. He was suddenly seized with an impulse to throw it at Doctor Sylvan with all his might. Drops of sweat ran down his face. He bit his lower lip until it hurt and his hands began to shake worse than ever. Fear and disgust for the impulse rose up in him and he could not fight back the tears that spilled suddenly down his cheeks. He put down the souvenir lighter and walked away, going to the window and looking out, his shoulders shaking with sobs.

Outside were the green trees and grass bright in the warm afternoon sunlight. When will it be there for me? he asked himself bitterly. When will I be there again in the warm afternoon sunshine?

Doctor Sylvan got up and came over and stood beside him. He put his hand on Jim's shoulder but Jim wrenched away, a terrified look on his face, as though the doctor had struck him. He pulled Jim around to face him, then seized his arm at the wrist and said, "Must I make you slap me, hard?" And with that he swung back Jim's arm and yanked it forward so that Jim's hand struck him square in the face.

"You see! I'm not dead! You haven't killed me," said Doctor Sylvan.

Jim's hand stung from the impact. He gasped, his fingers curled slowly into a loose fist of withdrawal as he tried to pull his arm away from the doctor.

"It wasn't I—I didn't do that!" he cried.

"Or punch me in the belly?" Doctor Sylvan went on, persistent, a hard glint in his eyes, holding Jim's wrist now with both hands. "Would you like to punch me in the belly?"

He snapped Jim's arm forward, aiming for his own stomach, but Jim lurched away and broke the doctor's grip before the fist landed in his stomach.

Jim felt sick and he realized in that instant that it wasn't in his heart to strike and hurt him.

"It wasn't I who did that," he cried softly. "It wasn't I."

Jim reached out hands to him and Doctor Sylvan came to Jim and Jim put his arms about him and held him, close and dear. Doctor Sylvan spoke to him to quiet him and Jim felt awkward and stumbled as he gripped him. His fingers dug into the doctor's back—not rough, but feeling himself to be a justborn vine reaching delicate tendrils to a pole to grow upon. Doctor Sylvan holding him thus, Jim realized how all his life it was the unsaid love that sat as a stone upon his shoulders. He had been carrying it so long, and in the realization it was as though the weight of it had shifted. He had touched another and had been touched. He felt lightened and glimpsed for an instant over the doctor's shoulder the trees outside the window and they were there as they had not been for a long time, and himself; and Doctor Sylvan was there for him, and the afternoon.

But then, just as swiftly, Jim felt himself wandering again, felt himself, inwardly, turning from him.

"Come on. Come with me," said Doctor Sylvan, smiling. "Let's find out what Jim's going to do, what Jim wants to do."

He led Jim to the couch and they sat down, the doctor still holding Jim's hands.

Jim laid his head in the doctor's lap and the doctor stroked his hair and whispered to him quietly. Jim put his arms about him and held him close and the emptiness and flatness dissolved in him. He felt alive and hopeful again. He felt like a child who had been lost and alone and had found his way home again. It was like holding in his arms, and being held by, mother, father, a friend, whose words were warm and brought hope and light into his heart. He placed his head against Doctor Sylvan's chest and heard his heart beating within. He listened to its strong steady beat and heard Doctor Sylvan saying, "Take strength from me, Jim. I have enough strength for both of us. Take strength from me and live."

His voice was soft and warm and Jim looked up into his eyes.

"Then I must go? I must leave the hospital now?"

Doctor Sylvan said, "Yes, Jim. Now it's time to go."

Jim placed his hands about Doctor Sylvan's arms and held on.

"Your arms are like the cables of a bridge," he said. He was suddenly frightened but did not let go the doctor's arms. He was glad that he had finally asked the question and heard his answer. He would go, and Doctor Sylvan's dark arms were like a bridge and his heart was strong.

He knew that and had always known that—so many torn bridges in the past, the gaps he wasn't able to cross over. Perhaps it would be different now.

He threw his arms around the doctor's neck and held him tightly. For a moment all his fears and doubts had evaporated. He had seen the possibility of all his longings—to have a place where he was wanted and loved, no more distances between himself and others, no more estrangements, no more having to run, to hide, to be devious. But up swarmed the old doubts and memories of what the past had been and he placed his head against Doctor Sylvan's chest and told him in a rush, "I will run from you, I will run because I'm afraid, and I don't want to run and I want to stop and I will run from you but I will stop if you care enough for me that you'll come for me wherever I have run to."

"I have a long arm," Doctor Sylvan said. "You can run, but I have a long arm and I'll bring you back."

Jim felt a deep sense of relief—that he had always wanted to hear this. Some old locked door in him opened and that fear that he would always have to run was behind the door and it was not now as big as it had always been.

Doctor Sylvan glanced at his watch.

"You'd better hurry back to your building. It's almost suppertime and the doors'll be locked. I'll see you tomorrow morning."

Jim did not go but stood hesitating.

"I've got this peach," he said, reaching into his pocket. "It's not a good one." He held it in his hand, his fingers lightly touching the shriveled gnarled fruit, his eyes cast down shyly. "I want to give you something and this is all I got."

He extended the peach to Doctor Sylvan. The doctor's eyes shone and he took the peach, smiling.

" 'The small stunted fruit is the sweetest,' " he said.

Jim looked at him.

"Didn't you know that?" Doctor Sylvan asked.

"No. I didn't."

"Remember it. And thank you very much for the gift."

He put out his hand. Jim looked at it a moment, then shuffled forward and gripped it in his own firmly. He flung his arms about Doctor Sylvan and squeezed him tight and turning ran to the door and opened it quickly and ran out and down the hall toward the stairs.

Doctor Sylvan looked at the peach a moment. His face was very still. Then he put the peach in his pocket.

AFTER SUPPER that evening Jim, along with Frank, showed the attendant on duty their parole cards and the attendant unlocked the door and let them out of the building. They stepped out onto the walk and on either side the lusterless eyes of other patients peered down at them from between the bars of the upper porches. There was a heavy smell of honeysuckle in the evening air. Jim lifted his nose and sniffed, trying to find out where the odor was coming from. He thought it was the bushes in front of the porches but the blossoms there had a funky smell. Turning, he spied it, a patch of the honeysuckle growing on the slope across the street from the building.

He touched Frank's arm. "Come on, Frank. Let's go zip honeysuckle."

Frank was silent, a morose expression on his lean face, his mouth sullen, turned down at the corners. He shrugged his shoulders and Jim ran ahead, crossing the street at a run, and Frank followed slowly, his head bowed, an indifferent shuffle in his long thin body as he walked.

Jim had already climbed up the wall and into the flowers by the time Frank got there. He picked several of the blossoms and bit the ends off and sucked the drop of clear sweet juice each flower held. He handed a fistful of the honeysuckle to Frank and Frank took it and with a faraway look on his face mashed the blossoms between his fingers with a swift agitated gesture and threw the pulpy remains over his shoulder into the grass.

"Come on," he said. "Let's walk down to the gate."

Jim scrambled down out of the flowers and leapt off the wall.

"They're not as sweet this year," he said, walking beside Frank. He took his tennis ball out of his hip pocket and began bouncing it on the sidewalk. They passed other patients on the way, some dressed in the gray and shapeless state clothes. Others wore loud pink and green coats, a few, bright yellow pants. Someone had once complained to the Director that the patients' clothes were too drab so the state had got those brilliantly colored coats and pants. They seemed so bizarre and gaudy, out of place on the slack mumbling figures that passed Jim and Frank. Like a cruel joke. Jim always felt like it was the Depression in the hospital, mostly everybody looked so poor and beat down. Like the men in the Bowery who stand in soup lines. He wanted to tell Frank about this, and the clothes, but Frank had that hard angry look on his face so he didn't tell him but kept bouncing the ball so there would not be so much silence between them.

As they walked down toward the gate, a sudden soft rain began to fall. They started to run for the trees near the high barbed wire fence and as they approached the gatehouse on the opposite side of the street the policeman on duty stepped out of the door and stood watching them, hands on hips.

"The bastard probably thinks we're going to escape," Frank snapped, panting as they ran.

They stopped under a tree directly across from the gatehouse, brushing water from their faces and catching their breath.

"It won't last long," Jim said.

The policeman scrutinized them a moment longer, looked up and down the street, then disappeared inside the little house.

Frank was trembling although it wasn't cold. He stood with his arms crossed tightly against his chest. He stared quietly at the ground, breathing easier now—but there was a whiteness at the base of his nostrils as of some inner repressed anger, a holding back.

Jim stood quietly with his hands in his hip pockets and lifted his head up and felt the soft falling rain between the leaves on his face. He breathed deeply, smelling everything. There was the rich heavy smell of pine trees across the road— like in California, he thought, near the sea, the hot smell of pine trees. The forsythia was gone. The way the leaves come out *after* the flowers, he thought. Now there was dogwood, peach and pear, apple blossoms.

He turned to Frank.

"You want to have a catch?"

He flipped his tennis ball up amongst the branches of the tree and caught it.

Frank didn't answer.

"Plenty of room under here," Jim went on, spinning the ball up again.

Frank shuffled his feet a little.

"No," he said.

"Why not, Frank? Come on."

"No. I said I don't want to have a catch."

He scratched around in his shirt pocket, found a cigarette and with shaking hands lit it. He stood smoking silently, not looking at Jim.

Jim gazed at him, his mouth open a little, puzzled. Then he started chucking the ball up and catching it behind his back.

"Let's go climb a tree. You want to climb a tree, Frank?"

"No, not now. Look. It's raining."

"I mean after, Frank. After it stops."

Frank sent a thin stream of smoke out through his tight-pressed lips.

"Frank, I'm going to leave the hospital."

Frank didn't say anything.

"I saw Doctor Sylvan today and I'm going to leave the hospital. I'm going to live here in the county and go on seeing him."

Frank was still silent. Jim caught the ball and held it. He stared at Frank, bewildered.

"Don't you care, Frank? You're the first one I told."

"Huh? Yes. Yes, I care. Congratulations. Why don't you put that goddamn ball away? It gets on my nerves."

Jim looked at the ball and then at Frank. His mouth began to tremble, his face went solemn.

"You want me to leave you alone? I'll leave you alone, Frank."

Jim started to walk off. A look of wild alarm came into Frank's face.

"Please don't do that. Stay with me, Jim."

Jim stopped, his back still to Frank, and peered down, rubbing his toe in the dust at the foot of the tree. Then he swung around slowly and looked up at Frank.

"Okay," he said.

He ran out from beneath the tree and held out his hand, palm upward. "Look. It's stopped raining. Let's go on down to the courts and see if anybody's playing. We still got time before we have to go in."

Frank flipped his cigarette in the dirt and ground it out with his heel. He came out from beneath the tree and joined Jim and together they walked off in the direction of the tennis courts.

Jim kept his eyes averted as they walked past the buildings on either side of the street. He stared at the ground, not liking to see the other patients locked in on the porches. That always made his heart sink, made him get depressed. Some of the patients were pacing rapidly back and forth, while others stood mute and alone, lost in some profound and unknowable silence. They each seemed alone, each cut off from the other and from the life about them. Others clutched the bars and shouted senseless phrases to no one in particular, or screamed obscenities and challenges to some invisible enemy out of the past. A thin colored boy, his lips fluttering drily, clasped the bars lightly with his long fingers as he spoke to "Dear Jesus," his soft voice almost inaudible, his eyes wide and serious as he spoke with warmth and intimacy to the air.

Jim tried not to listen and quickened his footsteps to get past the buildings, but Frank wanted to know was he going to a fire and Jim slowed down reluctantly, still not looking and trying not to hear.

When they got to the tennis courts Jim recognized a few student nurses playing. There were also a couple of internes. They were all wearing gleaming white shirts and shorts and dirty scuffed tennis sneakers. They looked healthy and tanned, like creatures from another, greener world in contrast to the slouched figures of several parole patients who stood here and there around the big court, their fingers hooked in the mesh-wire fence as they watched, almost with apathy, as though they were there only to lean on the fence, to be held up by it, and not to watch the games.

The girls were amateurish, lobbing the ball back and forth and laughing good-naturedly at their incompetence. The young internes were better, smashing at the ball with more agility, almost with ferocity. Jim and Frank found a bench where they could get a good view and sat down, Jim hitching up his heels on the edge of the bench and wrapping his arms around his knees and jutting his chin out and resting it on his kneecaps.

The blonde was there, laughing gaily as she missed a shot; the blonde he had a secret crush on. His heart beat rapidly in his chest. Hearing her bright laugh made him feel alive and warm. Mainly, this was why he wanted to come to the tennis courts, and he did this every evening after supper, hoping to see her playing with her friend. He had even, finally, after much asking around, found out her name. Her name was Linda and she was twenty years old and she was a student nurse working in the Children's Unit. She was a tall, broadly built blonde. She had hair that was always falling down, sort of messy and like she didn't much care about it. She had the kind of face that always looked like it just got up ten minutes ago. Not awful and dopey, but fresh and dreamily sleepy. He would've liked to wake up with her beside him. He would hold her close in his arms. Her body would be very soft and her face very soft and sleepy. She would smell very good and there was that wonderful blonde hair he could bury his face in and she would laugh. He never told Doctor Sylvan this because it might've sounded corny, but when he kissed her her breath would smell like honey. He couldn't get out of his mind those blue eyes of hers that were dreamy, and yet sometimes very merry and quick, as now—

"I could go a coke."

"Huh?" Jim yanked his head up as though he had been sleeping. "What did you say?"

"I said how about going and getting us a coke?"

"Okay. Only I don't have any money, Frank."

"Here. Here's two dimes."

Jim took the money and stood up.

"Back in a minute."

He started to walk off toward the bowling alley where the coke machine was, looking back over his shoulder at the blonde as she dove after a shot and missed, laughing.

"Jim."

He stopped and looked at Frank.

"I'm glad you're going home." He smiled and then winked quickly. "I really am."

Jim swung around and ran over the grass and across the road and into the bowling alley. The place was full of the loud noise of the clash and clatter of falling pins, but most of the commotion came from Negro attendants standing around playing at the pool tables in the rear, black felt hats and zany-shaped hats tipped back on their heads, teasing and egging on the other players. Jim hurried past them, dodging the high-angled pool cues and went directly to the coke machine. He felt happy because Frank had said he was glad he was going home and didn't seem withdrawn and angry any more. He put the dimes in the machine and the bottles clunked down the slot and he opened them and went to the door and outside again.

When he got to the bench Frank was gone. Jim stood holding the two bottles of coke and turned his head in every direction but could see no sign of him. He put the bottles down on the bench and scratched his head and curled his lower lip, wondering what could have become of him. He knew that Frank got nauseous when he was upset, as he was now. Maybe he had gone to the men's room to throw up. Or maybe he just went to take a leak. He waited a minute or so and then picked up the cokes and headed for the bus station. He went into the men's room but Frank wasn't there. He even jumped up at each of the toilet doors and looked over to make sure.

He went outside and looked toward the tennis courts and, not seeing him, put down the bottles on a bench with a sinking feeling in his stomach. He wondered if Frank was going to "do something foolish," as Doctor Sylvan put it. Frank had tried to commit suicide and that was how he had come to the hospital. Once he had even tried it in the hospital and they had locked him away on the maximum security ward for a few weeks. Then Jim remembered that at supper Frank had been talking to Allain, the Frenchman. Allain was flat and despairing. He felt he had nothing to live for. He thought he would be better off dead. He talked of flinging himself under the back double-wheels of one of the big trucks that made deliveries on the grounds. "It will crack my spine, like so!" he would say and would snap his fingers together and there would come a gleam, almost of pleasure, in his dull eyes. Jim did not like to be around him.

Where could Frank have gone? Jim wondered. Maybe it was nothing to be worried about but he decided to walk down to the ball-field. Maybe he would find Frank there. He looked at the clock in the bus terminal. He would have to hurry.

"Hey, chico!" he called to a slightly built boy, a Puerto Rican, who was just coming out of the men's room. "You want these?" Jim said, pointing to the cokes.

The boy paused, cocking his head to one side, looking at Jim suspiciously.

"Whud I gotta do?"

"Nothing. I don't want anything. They're yours," Jim said with an impatient gesture of his hands.

"I don't have to do nothing?"

"No! For Christsake, take them. Good-bye."

Jim ran off down the flagstone path, leaving the cokes with the Puerto Rican boy. The street to the ball-field was lined with voluminous green trees. The branches hung down low and full and the leaves slapped at Jim's face as he hurried under them, so that he was constantly ducking his head. The homes on this street were for the attendants and other workers at the hospital and they had a less grim look than the buildings the patients were in. It was getting late and the patients were wandering back slowly for bedcheck, singly and in pairs.

At the end of the block he came to the ball-field—a vast expanse of broad green grass beyond which was a valley with low hills in the distance. He liked to come here. It was so quiet and open, a world apart from the locks and keys and noise and drugged lifelessness of the hospital. If he did not look at the barbed wire fence he felt that he could be anywhere, not here in the hospital, where everything and everyone seemed dead and unmoving, as though within the confines of the high chain fences the clock had stopped forever.

The field was deserted now, all the benches empty. He knew Frank wasn't there but he decided to walk around anyway. At the far end of the field the ground sloped down and he thought maybe Frank was lying there, out of sight on the incline, watching the sun set as he sometimes did. Jim walked all around the field, his shoes getting damp in the wet grass. Frank was not on the slope and he walked to the fence where the road ran by. There was a double row of pine trees near the fence, growing so close together their branches interlocked forming a sort of corridor of trees. Jim walked beneath them and breathed in the pungent odor of the pines. It was cool and dark beneath the trees. A car went by on the highway and Jim ran to the fence to watch the car move up the long darkening asphalt road which led into town. The flickering tail lights of the car disappeared over a hill and their going left Jim with a brief moment of poignant sadness. Soon he would be on the other side of this fence. Soon he would be as the people in the car; moving away from this place where time did not change, nor faces change—the young unlived faces of the mentally ill. The hospital was like a gray limbo of silence and non-life. But as with the car—to him its red stop lights had twinkled almost merrily—he would be moving again, he would be going back again into life. His heart beat fast with anticipation and fear. He would be going home. It was a thought he was not yet used to.

Tired from his walking he sat down on a bench under the pines to rest before starting back to the building. He gazed out over the hospital farm and to the valley where the low soft hills began. The sun was setting over them. He felt suddenly very lonely. He took his tennis ball out of his pocket and began tossing it from hand to hand. So he would be less lonely he started to think of Doctor Sylvan. From his hands, to take his hands, to pull him up and bring him back to the living. He felt safe with him. Only if his hands were there, hands across a dark abyss. Jim felt a slow welling up of tears. That he cares. How wonderful it is, he thought, to know he cares.

There were hundreds of blackbirds out on the grass. The sun was very low now, moving down the sky behind the wide tree a little distance away, the leaves taking some of the glare out of it. Some boys were yelling in one of the buildings behind Jim. A flock of grackles flew down close to him. He hated grackles. He called them "pigbirds." Because they were eating, eating, always eating, their black heads bobbing up and down over the grass, and never up in the trees singing. Never once had he heard a grackle sing. He picked up a stone near his foot and flung it at the grackles and they flew up, alarmed, and winged farther down the field, alighting in a flock and swiftly going on with their bobbing and picking over the grass.

More and more blackbirds, robins, bluejays flew onto the broad field. There were thousands of dandelions going to fluff, the light seeds floating, like feathers, up into the air. The sun dipped very low, through a haze. The air was pink. The dump was sending up white smoke beyond the fence.

Jim felt the earth was rushing backward, away from the sun. The leaves, I like the leaves like this, he thought. Fine and light spring leaves. Sylvan is leaves, fine and light. And those blood-red leaves. Strange, they were so green last year. Now blood-red leaves on the trees.

Sylvan is leaves, fine and light, and blood-red leaves.

Sylvan is leaves, and the woods, dark; dark his mouth, his

dark Jewish mouth, stain of lilac, an old Sephardic stain, the yellow dust of Andalusia— Oh, but something flashy, gold and silver threads in everything about him— A sort of magician scattering stars from his finger tips.

The sun was gone now. The trees were dark shapes against the sky. Jim rubbed at his eyes with his knuckles, then pulled out his handkerchief and blew his nose. Then he looked about him, as though suddenly aware for the first time of the slow-gathering darkness. He leapt up from the bench. It was very late. He would have to hurry if he wanted to get back before the doors were locked. He didn't want to be put on elopement status with the police out looking for him. He ran over the grass and down the street, heading in the direction of his building. As he ran he remembered Frank—he had forgotten that he had disappeared and now he wondered again what had happened to him. He began to worry once more, but then thought if Frank had been sick to his stomach he most probably had gone back to the building. This thought made him feel better and as he ran he felt a sense of relief. That's probably what Frank had done, he told himself. There had been nothing to worry about in the first place.

When Jim got back to the building he still had a few minutes before the doors were locked for the night so he went over and stood outside the windows of Frank's ward and looked in. He saw Allain playing cards in the dayroom and called to him and asked him if he'd seen Frank. He said, No, he hadn't. Then Jim went around the porch to where the rooms were and counted off six windows and stood on tiptoe and called Frank's name in the window but there was no answer. He stood for a moment leaning his back against the stucco wall of the building, tugging at his lower lip. The old worry rose up in him again. Maybe Frank had run away, "eloped," as they called it in the hospital. Maybe he had done "something foolish" after all. Jim felt sick to his stomach again as he thought about it. But there was nothing he could do now. He walked out of the bushes and around the porch just in time to hurry in the front door before the attendant locked it for the night.

EACH PATIENT STOOD outside the door of his room as the attendant walked down the hall with a list in his hand counting each one and checking him off on his census chart. It seemed to take a long time to Jim. He was impatient to go across the hall to Frank's ward to see if he had gotten back yet. He thought Frank might've gotten mixed up on the time, had wandered off somewhere to be by himself, and was now only late for bedcheck. He watched the attendant going from room to room, counting. Why doesn't he hurry? Jim thought. Why's he taking so much time? Now if only no one's missing.

"Okay, fellas!" the attendant called from the end of the hall. "Bedcheck's over."

Jim gave a sigh of relief and hurried down the hall and out the door and across the hall to Frank's ward. The bed-check there was late and the attendant was still counting the patients. Jim stood outside the door craning his neck to see if he could spot Frank, but the hall was too gloomy and crowded. He thought maybe Frank had come back during his own ward's bedcheck. The attendant was short one patient and Jim knew that it was Frank. The attendant came out in the hall calling Frank's name and asking if anyone had seen him. No one had and Jim was wondering what he should do when there was a loud knock at the front door. The attendant went and un-locked the door and Frank came in, walking very fast, his face wild and strained, his hands jammed deep in his pockets.

"Where you been, buddy?" said the attendant, glancing at his watch. "You're twenty minutes late."

Frank muttered something about not having "heard the bell" and hurried past the attendant.

"Let's get the hell in here on time," the attendant called after him. "I'll have your goddamn parole card lifted you don't watch out."

Frank said nothing but continued on down the hall at a fast pace and went into his room, slamming the door behind him.

Jim felt much better now that Frank had returned. Frank had looked very upset. Jim decided to wait awhile before going to see him, to give him a chance to rest and pull himself together. He went back to his room and ate a sandwich he had saved from supper. It was dry and tasteless and he only took a few bites out of it then wrapped it back in its paper and took it down the hall into the section and flushed it down the toilet. He lit a cigarette and then began making faces at himself in the mirror for awhile. When he got tired of that he flipped out the cigarette and went over to Frank's ward and down the hall to Room 6. The door was closed and the room was dark. Jim looked through the small square of glass, holding his hands up to his eyes to keep out the light, and could barely make out Frank's long thin figure lying on the bed. Jim knocked lightly and through the glass saw Frank sit bolt upright and look out at Jim, an expression of fear and panic in his eyes. Jim opened the door quickly and went in, closing the door behind him.

"It's you," Frank said, and seemed relieved. He sat up, his head bowed and Jim sat down beside him on the bed and put his arm around his shoulders.

"What's the matter, Frank?"

Frank didn't answer but held himself stiff as though holding back.

"You mustn't listen to Allain," Jim said. "I saw you talking to him. Because he's hopeless doesn't mean you're hopeless.

He's flat and stagnant but you're not. You shouldn't listen to him. You shouldn't listen to any of that."

"But you don't know," Frank said. "Tonight at supper Allain was telling me all that, about how he had no desire to live—I wanted to tell him that he must live—and I suddenly realized that I couldn't *give* him a reason, that I'd forgotten why I myself wanted to live."

His voice was high-pitched and tight, as though he were choking, choking back tears of fear and panic.

"But you'll remember," Jim said, holding him close. "You'll remember again even though you forget for awhile. It's hard sometimes to remember why you want to live. You want to stop, to not go on. But something happens, the touch of another, or one kind word. Sometimes just the way the day is, with the sun and all—"

Frank abruptly thrust his arms out straight and blurted, "Yes— When I do this!"

In the dim light coming in from the hall Jim saw deep gashes in his wrists, the blood drying over the ragged wounds. He struck a match and took Frank's hands and looked at the wrists carefully. The cuts were ugly as though he had hacked savagely and quickly. They had stopped bleeding.

Jim blew out the match and held Frank's hands tight. Frank gripped his firmly, holding on until Jim's fingers ached from the pressure. His shoulders began to shake, terrible sobs came from him. He began to speak in a raucous whisper.

"I don't know what I'm doing any more. I don't know what I'm thinking or feeling. They stopped me and that's why it's not as bad as it might've been."

"Who stopped you, Frank? What happened?"

"I'd gone down to the ball-field after I'd run from you on the bench. I didn't want to be with anyone. I felt trapped and wanted to run. I wanted to end it. I went to the greenhouse and hid in some bushes between the fence and the greenhouse. I didn't know what to do and I was shaking like a leaf. Then I saw the fence and I ran over to it and reached up and hooked my arms in the barbed wire and hacked at the barbs, just hacking back and forth senselessly with my arms, gritting my teeth till they ached, sawing my flesh in a kind of fury, at life, at my life, at the pain and emptiness of it. Then some colored boys came along—a couple of those delinquents from Building 'C.' They were poking through the grass with sticks and when I saw them coming I stopped cutting myself on the barbed wire and spun around and crouched down with my back to the fence and hid my arms behind my back. My arms were soaked with blood. They came up to me—you know how they are— tough, and smiling. They asked me where the bottle was. I guess I looked so wild they thought I was drunk and had a bottle. They kept asking me where I'd hidden it and I didn't understand them and thought, in my confusion, they meant my life. They started beating around in the bushes with their sticks, saying, 'Come on, come on— Tell us.' I started to run, I just kept running. When I got to the water fountain near the street I stopped to catch my breath, then I washed off my arms as best I could in the water there. Then I started running again and I ran until I got back to the building."

When he finished he began to cry again, hoarse broken sobs, like the sobs of a man who hasn't cried for a long time. Jim caressed his hands and told him he was glad the colored boys had come and interrupted him, told him he was glad that he hadn't cut himself any deeper, that he had lived.

There was a washcloth hanging at the foot of his bed. Jim got up and took it in his hands.

"I'll moisten this with warm water," he said, "to clear away the dried blood on your arms."

"No," Frank said quickly. "That'll leave stains. I don't want the attendant to see it and have to explain."

"Maybe you better leave your door open a little," Jim said. "He might get suspicious."

"No. Not yet. Wait awhile."

"I'll go wet some paper towels in the night-section," Jim said. "I'll be right back."

He started to leave, then paused.

"You better keep your sleeves rolled all the way down. Button the cuffs. You don't want anybody to see. They'll put you up on maximum security ward again."

"I will. I know."

"If anybody sees the cuts tell them you scraped your arms climbing a tree."

"Or a fence," Frank said and grinned sourly.

Jim went out, looking both ways up and down the hall. There were only a few patients wandering about, some only in their underwear, restless before sleep. None of the attendants were in sight. He went quickly to the night-section at the end of the corridor and dampened paper towels at the sink and brought them back to the room, shutting the door after him. He washed the wounds as best he could and dried them with dry towels he had also brought from the section.

"They sting," Frank gasped through clenched teeth as Jim dabbed lightly at the wounds. "God, they sting."

"I sure wish we had something to put on these," Jim said. "Hope you don't get lockjaw. Now just keep your sleeves rolled down. I'm going to get rid of these."

He went out again, wadding the bloodstained towels into a ball and stuffing them in his pocket. He hurried back down to the section and swiftly flung the wadded towels into a toilet and, kicking at the pedal, flushed them away. He went back to Frank's room.

"You want to come to my room? Mr. Toby's ward-charge over there tonight. Less chance of anybody barging in when he's on duty."

"No. Wait. A minute."

"All right."

Frank was trembling. Jim sat down next to him and tried to talk to him. He didn't know what to say. He wanted to say something reassuring, something to quiet Frank, make him feel less alone. But he didn't want it to sound corny or phony. He wanted to speak his feelings calmly, something that Frank could believe and maybe listen to. He spoke very low and there was a warmth in his heart as though he were speaking to and holding onto the hands of another boy, in another time, a boy out of his own past lacerated by his sorrow and despair. He had been broken and hadn't wanted to live, and sitting now, close to this other boy who was wandering and lost and frightened, Jim spoke of how he must live, spoke of sunlight and the flowering forsythia, spoke of faces and the touch of hands. He asked him did he love someone and Frank said, yes, once—Jim told him not to be afraid, not to be afraid to love, not to be afraid of the love of another. He felt warm and excited, the way he got when he was intensely moved, as though he were lifted out of himself, or rather driven by his feeling to the very core of his being, the real Jim who was clear-eyed and sure of his touch, sure of his gentleness and feeling. The words came up out of this deep and unknown place without effort, words that he had never heard himself speak before. Jim told Frank he was in a panic and afraid, stuttered and stammered and felt so lost and wandering now only because he was beginning to feel again— After so long a time of utter isolation he was reaching out and touching, and being touched in return.

"Remember that dream you told me, Frank? The dream

where you were taking a shabby overcoat out of a closet and brushing it off to wear it? You remember? You didn't understand the dream and you didn't like the coat because it was shabby and patched. I've been thinking about that dream and it seems to be telling you that you've discovered again something you haven't used in a long time. It's grown shabby and dusty with disuse. But a coat's warm and you need to wear it to keep you warm and protect you against the cold. It's like your overcoat is your feelings that you locked away in the closet of yourself so long ago and only now have opened up and taken out again. And they're warm feelings that make you feel alive, and protect you. Things are going to be better, Frank, because you brushed off the overcoat and you're going to wear it again."

Jim stopped talking. He felt suddenly embarrassed. He thought maybe he was talking too much.

Frank was silent, too. Then he nodded his head slowly.

"Yes. I'm glad of that," he said. "Now the dream has meaning for me."

He was still for a moment as though lost in deep thought, then said, "I've had this same dream again and again for years. I've never told anybody about it. And I always wake up from it screaming and in a cold sweat. It's that I'm carrying on my shoulders the bones of my father. He's been dead for some time and his flesh is rotting. The smell of him makes me gag. I ask everyone I meet if they will take my father from me, but they put their hands to their noses and turn away in disgust. I walk on, carrying the dead body of my father on my back and I look for someone to take him from me and I look for some place to put him down. I wonder, How will I bury the bones of my father? I keep wandering, searching, and yet can find no proper place to put him down."

He stopped and bit his lower lip, reflecting.

"Maybe when I find someone and love them very much," he began in a halting voice as though he were asking a question, "and tell them all the unsaid things, all that I had never told my father, then maybe I will have found the place to put him down. Maybe then he'll be buried, and at rest."

There was a silence in the room. Frank suddenly clenched his teeth and swung to the window and smashed the screen with his fist. The impact made a blunt dead sound. The screen was unyielding, as though it had not been touched. Frank put his bruised knuckles to his mouth and licked at the pain.

The door opened swiftly and the attendant stepped in.

"What's the noise in here?"

"Nothing," Jim said. "I backed into the window."

Frank stood in the corner, silent.

"You ain't from this ward, are you?"

"No," Jim said.

"Beat it." The attendant made a brusque movement with his hand. "And you there, leave this door open or I'll write you up in the book."

Frank nodded and the attendant went out, swinging the door wide, leaving it open.

"Come on, Frank," Jim urged gently. "Let's go over to my room. It's brighter there, and larger. It'll be safer, too."

"All right. I feel better now. Let's go."

Some of the blood had stained Frank's shirt. "You better put on a jacket," Jim said, pointing to the bloodied sleeves. "Hide that."

"Yeah. Sure."

Frank slipped on a jacket and they went out and crossed the hallway that separated the two wards and went past the dayroom where the television set blared. Several patients were sitting before it in mute concentration. Jim's ward was a fairly quiet ward, the ward a patient was sent to before leaving the hospital. They slipped quickly past the office door where the ward-charge sat at his desk in his white coat and black bow-tie, his head bent over the tray of small plastic medicine cups, dropping into each one the last pills of the day.

In Jim's room Frank went to the window and bowed his head and pressed his forehead against the heavy screening. Outside the window moonlight filled the broad exercise yard. Behind that, bleak with its dimly lit windows, rose the building containing the back wards where were kept the most disturbed and hopeless patients. Now and then a scream was heard in the quiet night air. There came the sound of a man's voice repeating the same incoherent phrase over and over, meaningless, monotonous. Too much misery in this place, Jim thought. Too much pain. The ground itself must be alive and writhing with the sorrow and pain of so many thousands. Perhaps that was why the grass seemed so much greener here, the trees—living inanimate things feeding so richly off the misery of the dead, feeding so hungrily out of the dying and still-born, the suffering which seemed to permeate the earth and air, of the non-dead and the non-living who wandered, as shades, through the wards and grounds of the hospital.

Frank's shoulders drooped and he turned sideways from the window and began to cry again, softly, making no noise. He had pressed his head so hard against the screen, the imprint of the strong mesh-wire was ridged, deep and red, in the flesh of his brow.

Jim stayed close to him and held him, as one holds a child, and tried to comfort him. He soon quieted down. Then Jim suddenly remembered the crossword puzzle in that day's newspaper which he'd been unable to finish. He pulled it out from under his bed and suggested they work on it together. Frank grabbed the paper out of his hands and stared hard at the puzzle.

"A horse famous—famous—a horse famous," he stuttered, his drawn cheeks twitching, his eyes staring as though they would pierce the page. He pressed his hand to his forehead, crying, "I can't—can't say it."

"Go on," Jim insisted gently. "You can."

He took Frank's arm and they sat down side by side on the bed together. Frank began again.

"A horse famous—in myth."

They began to work the crossword puzzle together and Frank even managed to get involved in it and gradually grew calmer. Jim got pretty involved in it, too, and he felt good doing that puzzle, grateful that it had been able to distract Frank's mind, and his own, at last.

When they were almost down to figuring out the last word they heard the voice of the attendant calling, "Bedtime, gentlemen. Lights out now. All lights out."

Frank looked up quickly from the puzzle. Jim placed his hand on his arm.

"You're better now?"

Frank nodded.

Jim hesitated a moment, then said, "You won't do anything tonight?"

Frank tugged absently at the cuffs of his shirt.

"No. I won't have to."

He stood up.

"I hate to go back to that room."

"If I could stay with you I would stay with you tonight," Jim said. "But—well—that's impossible. You know that, Frank."

"I know."

He started toward the door.

"Wait a minute," Jim said. He reached into his pants pocket and pulled out his tennis ball. "Here," he said, coming over to him. "Take this. You know—sort of keep it close to you in bed. Put it under your pillow. Maybe you won't feel so lonely."

He put the ball in Frank's hand. Frank stared at the ball resting in the middle of his palm. Then his fingers closed over it lightly and he looked into Jim's face. There was the faint trace of a smile on Frank's lips as his arm reached out, awkwardly, his arm stiff, as though the gesture were painful, not from the wound in his wrist but, as though he were embarrassed and suddenly shy, like a man who is not used to touching or being touched. His fingers, almost wooden, touched Jim's face, a soft brief touch, then slid to his shoulder and rested there a moment. He turned and walked quickly out of the room.

Jim gazed at the empty doorway for a moment then turned and went to the window and looked out. Looking out through the dense screening made him feel that he was trying to look out from inside the heavily-spun wall of a cocoon. He strained to see. The screaming from the back ward had ceased, only the dull voice shouting the same inanity went on and on. Then presently it, too, stopped. A heavy silence was settling over the hospital as it prepared for night and sleep. The attendant stopped at Jim's door and, counting, checked him off on his list. He turned off Jim's light with his light key and said, "Okay in there, take off your clothes and hit the sack. I don't want to see you up when I come around again."

Jim left the window and sitting down on his chair began taking off his shoes slowly, letting each drop from his hand with a listless gesture. The room was in darkness now but the moon sent a broad shaft of pale light through the window. Jim hated this moment, the moment of sleep and stillness, which might not be sleep or rest, a silence more profound and empty than that which hovered over the place in the daylight hours. Slowly, the fear of the gathering silence and the night began to gnaw at him.

He stood up and slipped out of his clothes and climbed into the high cast-iron bed. He lay quietly on his back, trying to lie as still as possible, closing his eyes, as the old fear and panic leapt up in him. He felt drained and his own shakiness, his own doubts and fears, had been set off strongly again by Frank's slashing his wrists and what had happened during the night. He wanted Doctor Sylvan to be there to touch him, to be with him in his aloneness and fear. He wanted to be close to him, touching and talking quietly, not alone.

The man in the room across the hall began to mumble incoherently in his sleep, as he always did, even in waking. Up and down the hall came scattered heavy snoring. But the screaming in the back had stopped and Jim was glad of that. He heard the sharp clatter of the big key in the lock as the ward-charge locked up the ward for the night. Then followed the sound of the attendant's heels tapping on the tile floor as he patrolled the hall, pausing now and then to look into a room.

The brilliant beam of the attendant's flashlight played on Jim's face for an instant and Jim's eyes snapped open, startled, and he instinctively turned his face away into the pillow. The attendant moved on, the clack-clacking of his heels growing faint as he moved farther down the corridor. Jim turned to the wall and tried to concentrate on sleep, but instead the image of Doctor Sylvan's face arose in his mind and it was a warm and smiling face. Then came an image of Doctor Sylvan's house. He had never seen his house but in his imagination now it had large, brightly-lit rooms. In the living room he saw a red chair and Jim saw himself sitting in the red chair. It was as though he had found a place where he could sit in a red chair and know that in that house was where he belonged. He was himself and nothing was expected of him except that he be himself. He felt sure and confident and wanted. In that place he could come and go, he could leave it and come back to it.

It would be there for him when he needed it. The image made him feel quiet; the thought of what Frank had done, which made him fearful and nauseous, receded and a warmth of hope and happiness leapt up in his breast and his eyes filled with tears.

"Doctor Sylvan," he said softly to himself and saying it made him feel safe and good. Then abruptly, as through fog lifting, he saw the image of his mother and father. At first he was puzzled why they should appear so suddenly and without warning. He tried to push them aside, tried to push them back into the fog so that he could again see Doctor Sylvan, but the images of them persisted and remained vivid. He had not been home for so long. A new feeling began to stir in him. I'll write them a letter, he thought, I'll write them a letter tomorrow and say, Mother, Father, today I was thinking how long it's been since I've lived at home with you and how little I have been with you and because of that how I have never been able to tell you that I love you both very much, that you have each been in my heart always and will always be. . . .

The pillow felt damp beneath his cheek and he suddenly realized that he was crying. He felt very happy as though some heavy weight had lifted from him. The darkness and fear began to recede in him and a pleasant drowsiness crept over him. Soon he was fast asleep.

Toward morning he had a dream. He dreamed of a great gloomy house. All about the house was the murk and gloom of twilight. All was dark and damp. Jim went out of the house with some others, to the right, and ate some food there in the mud, like pigs. When they returned a nurselike figure appeared out of the shadows.

"It's time to go," she said to Jim. "You are going back to the city now."

He was very frightened but he wanted to go. The nurse

went away and a beautiful woman came up to him. She said he could ask her any questions he liked. He asked her if it was all right to make love and eat good food and drink wine? She said that it was really very good to do this.

Jim started on his journey to the city. The grounds of the great house, the grounds leading from it, were wet black mud. It was like a drained swamp or a swamp at low tide. But in the mud was a vaguely defined path and Jim tried to follow it in the darkness as best he could.

Ahead of him, not on the faint traces of the path, but to the right, in the mud, stood three figures. They were neither men nor boys but there was something of each about them.

"I want to avoid them," Jim said to himself.

One of the figures approached and beckoned to him. But Jim didn't let the figure get close to him. He kept his eyes down to follow the path. He walked on and passed the figures, not looking at them. The path became more distinct, it was easier to follow, and now on either side short sturdy green plants were growing. They were like plants that grow in a cold climate, like plants that bloom in all seasons. Then suddenly ahead the city loomed up, a splendid bright city. In the air was a sense of morning. Near the gate leading into the city was a girl with an incredibly lovely face. She was standing, her hands crossed at her breast, smiling at him, waiting.

THE NEXT MORNING Jim sat on the sofa outside Doctor Sylvan's office. A warm spring breeze blew in from the window at the end of the corridor. Jim sat quietly, delighting in the odors the wind carried of the peppery smell of lilac and fresh-mown grass. The door opened and a patient Jim did not know stepped out of the office and went away down the hall. Doctor Sylvan poked his head out and motioned Jim inside. Jim got up and went in. Doctor Sylvan pointed to the couch and Jim sat down on it. Doctor Sylvan went and sat behind the desk.

"How's your baby?"

"Much better, thank you. When you get married, Jim, learn not to take your first baby's illnesses too seriously. They're really much stronger than we give them credit for."

Jim smiled. "I won't," he said.

"You look pale. You've got rings under your eyes. Didn't get any sleep last night?"

Jim looked away, unsure what to say. He began rubbing his hands together nervously.

"Come on, Jim. Tell me. What is it?"

"Well, I don't know how to tell you. I don't know if I *should* tell you."

"And who am I that you can't tell?" said Doctor Sylvan softly.

"Well, you see," Jim began uneasily, and he told him everything that had happened the night before with Frank. Doctor Sylvan listened attentively and quietly and when Jim finished he was silent for a moment, then asked, "Did you see this boy Frank this morning?"

"I saw him at breakfast. I went up to him and said, 'You didn't die. I'm glad you didn't. You looked so terrible last night. I thought you were going to die. You want to live. I can see it in your eyes. You're going to live.' And it was true," Jim added. "A change seems to have come over him."

"How did those cuts look?"

"I looked at them later, in the section," Jim said. "They're awful looking but they're healing okay. He didn't say anything. I mean, complain about them. I got him some bandages at the Exchange."

He gripped his hands tightly and leaning forward, his face

tense, said, "You're not going to report Frank, are you? I mean —because I told you?"

Doctor Sylvan leaned back in his chair and gazed up at the ceiling.

"No," he said, "I'm not going to do that. I don't remember a word you said to me about it. It'll be a secret between you and me."

A look of relief came into Jim's face. He sat back, more relaxed.

"Frank asked if he could keep my tennis ball a while longer."

"And?"

"Well—I said he could."

Doctor Sylvan smiled. "I'm very proud of you." He paused, then said, "But what's more important is how it has affected you. I mean, all that happened with this boy Frank."

"It made me afraid," Jim blurted out. "It brought back all my fears—all my doubts— It made me remember my own attempt at death— My own failure— It—" He stopped and put his hand to his mouth and looked down at the floor.

"Last night I wanted you so badly to be near me," he began again, in a choked voice. "Sometimes I feel so discouraged. Maybe it's too late. Maybe— Maybe I can't live again. I'm a little different, a little better—"

"You're a whole lot better than the withdrawn silent boy I met a year ago," Doctor Sylvan interrupted.

"Oh, but the same old fatigue and depression," Jim went on, "the same old unnameable fears leap up to choke me and drag me down to the dead again. It's as though nothing is changed and I get so exhausted with the struggle."

"Jim, listen to me. You weren't meant to die. You're meant to live. You must hold on and continue to fight. I know what you are. You aren't any of that that you thought you were. I know in my heart what you will become. You're only the seed now, the promise—what you were in the beginning, intact, but now not yet fully come into being. But you will. I believe this with all my heart, Jim. Sometimes it's a curse to be this thing, a fatal thing, because one has no choice. It's as though the stars of the soul have left immutable traces and although they swing and veer within one, they are the stars of destiny which say: This man shall be this, in spite of everything, and he shall have no choice. And that's why it's like a curse, because one must do that. Some men are doomed to touch the very bottom before they are blessed again to rise up anew. It's a very lonely and painful business. There's no kidding yourself. You are *different*—very much a part of but then, too, apart from others, and aswarm with passions and angers and all the petty irritations and childishnesses that must go with this staked-out thing that is so excruciatingly sensitive. You are that, Jim. And you've spent so much of your life running from it. But it's a very hard thing and it's no wonder anyone would run from such a task and responsibility. Yet, if it's written in the roof of your soul, those stars that are immutable, even though they swing, like a beehive in the self, then a man must do that thing or die. Even if he's frustrated and distracted from it by so many things around him, still he must find a way to overcome all these things, or he will die, and the thing that he must make out of himself dies, stillborn, within him.

"You mustn't lack belief, Jim. Nor question yourself. Not at this time. You must believe and have no doubt."

There was a light and softness in Jim's eyes. He suddenly felt light, like a seed-feather released from its tight-packed pod.

"I'd lost all hope until I came to you," he said at length. "I couldn't believe that it would ever be different, that I might possibly live again. Maybe, when I leave this place I won't be as destructive to myself as in the past. I don't want the hope to die in me. I don't want to see only nothingness again. But I know I will be afraid. For a long while yet. Afraid I'll fall back down again, become buried under the river of my life, buried where no one can touch me, where no one will again offer me hands."

"If you fall, it won't be as far this time. And I'll always be there to catch you. I won't let you fall far."

"But I have such a heaviness in my chest—I'm so afraid—sometimes your hands may not be there for me—"

Doctor Sylvan stood up. "Take my hand," he said.

Jim looked at him, curious, then took his hand.

Doctor Sylvan said, "Now this is how strong a hand can be."

He grasped Jim's hand firmly and pulled him to his feet. It was good to feel that strength and warmth. Doctor Sylvan looked into his eyes with a clear and serious gaze.

"My hand is always here for you," he said.

Jim knelt and wrapped his arms around the doctor's legs and pressed his head against his thighs. He began to cry, not saying anything, as though he were crying out of himself all the terror and loneliness of his past life. It was as though he were holding on to a life stronger than his own, beginning to take from this man's life a strength he had never known, a beginning of the discovery of the hidden and unborn strength and life in himself.

Doctor Sylvan caressed his head and tried to quiet him.

"Everything will be all right," he murmured. "You will succeed, Jim. Believe in me, and in yourself. You will live again."

He took Jim beneath the arms and helped him to stand up. Jim's face was red and streaked with tears.

"Go on," Doctor Sylvan said. "Go to the sink and wash your face. I've got to get your papers ready to send you to staff this week."

He patted him on the back and Jim broke into a smile and went to the sink in the corner. He turned on the tap and cupped his hands under it and splashed cold water on his face. He dried his face with paper towels and then turned to the doctor. He tried to say something but his throat worked noiselessly— Only his hands fluttered the inner intensity of his meaning, his long hands like mute birds flying swiftly about his shoulders.

"Hurry now," the doctor said, glancing at his watch. "You'll miss lunch."

Jim ran to him and threw his arms about him and kissed him on the mouth, then he opened the door and hurried out. Doctor Sylvan went to the door and watched Jim walk down the hall.

"Hold your head up, Jim," he called.

That made Jim smile and he waved back at the doctor, a wide grin on his face, and pushed his shoulders back and held his head erect. The doctor smiled, nodding approval, and waved in return. Then Jim sprinted down the stairs two at a time and was gone.

Doctor Sylvan closed the door.

❧ THE MEETING

JIM SAT on the back steps of Doctor Sylvan's house. He was finishing a bottle of beer and felt pleasantly tired. His clothes were all packed now and after finishing that, he had mowed the lawn—as though trying to show by this one last gesture his appreciation to the doctor and his wife for letting him stay with them after he had left the hospital.

He was going to move into a place of his own at the other end of town. The thought frightened him and he tried not to think of it. Doctor Sylvan had told Jim he was ready to try it on his own a little and they had talked about it and Jim had agreed. They had found the place only the day before and Jim had decided to leave that evening instead of waiting around, worrying about the move. Lately, he had begun to feel uneasy about staying there, as though he were taking advantage of the Sylvans' kindness.

It'll be better to have a place of my own, he thought, and

it's not too far away. I can walk from there to here and go on seeing them.

Doctor Sylvan was taking a shower after a long day of planting trees and weed pulling and rock picking in the backyard. There was a little slope of land out back that he and Jim had cleared a considerable part of, and Jim looked over the yard in the fading light at the job they had done, feeling a sense of satisfaction.

The screen door opened and the doctor's wife Elizabeth came out carrying their son. Ben was about two years old and was dressed in his pajamas. He was clapping his little fat hands and burbled down at Jim.

"Say good night," cooed Elizabeth. "Say good night to Uncle Jim."

She crouched down on the step with the baby and Jim swung around to receive a big wet kiss on his cheek.

"Good night, Ben," he whispered in the child's ear, and squeezed the little hand that reached down for the buttons on his shirt.

"It's such a nice night," said Elizabeth, straightening up and swinging the child to one hip as she gazed out over the yard. "You two did such a fine job."

"My back's broke," smiled Jim, hugging his knees.

Elizabeth laughed.

"To bed now," she said softly to the child. "Wave nightie-night to Uncle Jim."

Ben curled his fingers in a little wave, smiling, and Jim waved back, as Elizabeth opened the door and took the child back into the house.

Jim tilted the bottle to his mouth and drank the rest of the beer. Then he leaned back against the screen door, propping himself on his elbows on the step. There was a chill in the late autumn night. The grass was so soft and pleasant to look at.

In the woods beyond the house the crickets were singing. A dog barked farther down the block.

He had been out of the hospital two months. Sometimes it had gone badly and his mind had been filled with images of death. In town, when he walked down the main street, he felt acutely self-conscious and gangly, as though others could read in his eyes the secret of his lostness and past death. It was as though his time at the hospital had set him apart from others, marked him, made him different from them. He had lived for such a long time behind locked doors, had been told what to do day after day and treated like a helpless invalid, that he felt strange coming out into the world again where there was no one to order him about, no big metal keys and noisy locks, no high wire fences. That he could come and go as he pleased was still very new to him and he sometimes feared that he was dreaming it was so.

To have lost so much, he thought. So much of what I used to take for granted.

It was as though he had to relearn how to live, how to take up his life once more, live it for himself, give it shape and direction. Sometimes he felt overwhelmed with panic— he wanted to run, to run backwards, away from the burden of his new-found life. It seemed so impossible to him that he could ever be as he once was.

Now, to walk into a drugstore and buy a pack of razor blades with his own money, filled him with elation.

Going outside the gates of the hospital had been like going out into ruins. The other world of him was shattered and he would have to begin building, as though these were the ruins in himself. He was so filled with fear and doubt. And yet he must go on. He felt desolate and bleak and hopeless. Telling Doctor Sylvan this, the doctor had told him rubble can be cleared away, stopped drains unstuck and new buildings built, green seeds spring between the pavement cracks—like birds, birds of the soul, each with a seed in its beak, dropping seeds on the broken desolate ground of the self.

The past few months had been a very bad time for Jim since leaving the hospital, and his need for Doctor Sylvan had been greater than ever. He was so tired and had circles under his eyes. But Doctor Sylvan had been there for him, comforting and strong. He had not been alone.

He got up off the step and walked around to the side of the house. There was the wide lawn and a few tall sparse oaks. Farther on, in the next house, warm windows shone in the darkness. He lifted his head and in the clear frosty sky the stars were flung far, sparkling brightly. A strong feeling of hope arose in him. "What will be?" he whispered. He searched the sky as though he would find there, amongst the stars, an answer.

The stars blurred in his eyes and he was choked with his feeling as out of the stillness of the night he felt wrapped around by a presence, invisible and wordless, near to him. It was like a strength standing close to him in the darkness, as though the question in his heart had brought down from the stars an immutable answer. A something in the grass, close by him, near in the air, filling the night and Jim with a quietness of strength—an unseen touching out of the black firmament, touching the tall thin boy standing, head uplifted, in the frost-shining grass.

Looking up at the night sky, he remembered his dreams of hunger, of pink slices of ham, of wine and cheese. He would awake with acute pangs of hunger from sleep, awake out of dreams of his body full of holes. He craved red strawberry preserves and dark red wine. It was as though around him was the unbearable agony of spring which his mind knew but which his body no longer knew.

He had felt locked in, the shine gone from everything. It was as though he had to go back, to where it all began, from where he had taken the wrong turnings. He felt old, old—buried under the sea. He had had to go back and begin again, to break down utterly, completely, without hope, his psyche like rotten meat. Then it was he realized the meaning in what he had once heard an old Jew say: How terrible is that past which awaits us.

Jim thought of it as a mud-hole he carried within him. And yet, for all its stink and vileness, he saw it laden with seeds from which the flowers of the self spring. It was the bed for the seeds of him. Mud begets mud. A bath it seemed to take, a scrubbing away of what was dark and wet and blinding in him—the warm, comfortable mud which made him have life equal only to a slug. He saw his feelings and his imagination like a pock-hole of air in this mud, the hole the seed leaps down into and pushes up from, simultaneously rooting itself in the blackness and mystery of its underself while lifting delicate green fingers to the surface, to get its head up and above that blackness—which can also smother and kill, keep him half a thing.

He saw the sun and the sky to nurture it, and the blackness of itself strong beneath it—a new self like a garden.

"Jim?"

It was Doctor Sylvan's voice in the darkness. He was standing by the corner of the house watching him. Jim turned to him.

"Are you ready?" Doctor Sylvan asked.

"Yes." Jim took a few steps toward him.

"You sure you want to go tonight? Why not wait till the morning?" said the doctor.

"No. I've made up my mind. I want to go now."

He touched Doctor Sylvan's arm lightly and walking past him, headed around the house to the front door. The doctor followed him.

Jim's bags stood near the door in the hallway. As he went in, Elizabeth came down the hall from the baby's room, a finger to her lips.

"Ben's just going to sleep," she whispered.

Doctor Sylvan came in behind Jim. Elizabeth looked at him, questioning.

"He says he wants to go tonight," he said to her over Jim's shoulder.

"Well," Jim said, self-consciously, banging his fists on his thighs. "I just think it's better if I do."

"Tomorrow would do just as well," said Elizabeth, a look of concern in her eyes.

Jim looked uncertainly from one face to the other, then quickly leaned over and picked up two of the bags.

"I'm going now, Elizabeth," he said, feeling a tight lump in his throat. "I want to thank you for everything."

He kissed her briefly on the cheek.

"It's not good-bye, Jim," she said. "We'll be seeing you often."

"Yes, I know." Jim felt suddenly very awkward. "Well, it's time." He turned to the doctor. Doctor Sylvan reached over and picked up the remaining bag.

"Good luck, Jim," said Elizabeth as she opened the door for them.

"I'll be back soon," said the doctor, kissing his wife.

Jim hurried down the steps and along the path to the car. He opened the door, threw the bags in the back seat, then sat down in front, waiting, his hands folded tightly in his lap. Doctor Sylvan got in on the other side, putting the bag he had carried between them on the seat. He turned on the ignition and let the car roll backwards down the drive.

DOCTOR SYLVAN parked the car in the street. It had rained on the drive over and the air had turned cool. As they went up the driveway the leaves of the trees on either side hung down wet and low. It was dark and the house itself was in darkness and could not be seen clearly. Jim, holding his bags in one arm, fumbled in his pocket for the key and unlocked the door. A switch was near the door and he flicked it on. The house smelled damp, unlived in. They walked out to the kitchen and there put down the bags.

"Leave your stuff and come back in the morning," said the doctor, gazing out the rear windows.

"I want to stay here. I want to start on my own now."

There was an edge of defiance in Jim's voice.

Doctor Sylvan rested a hand on his shoulder.

"All right," he said quietly. "Do you have enough blankets?"

"I think so. Yes, I do."

"Shall I stay for awhile, keep you company till you get unpacked?"

"No. I'll be all right. I've got to do this myself."

Jim stared down at the floor. There was a moment of silence, then the doctor said, "It's going to be all right, Jim."

Jim looked into his eyes, feeling his throat constrict. He took Doctor Sylvan's hand and held it for a moment. Then turning away, said, "I better get started unpacking. And tomorrow I'll get up early and start cleaning the place." He looked around the room and laughed. "It sure is a mess."

"I'll get Elizabeth to bring over a mop and broom."

"And plenty of soap," said Jim.

They laughed and Doctor Sylvan turned to go. Jim walked

with him to the door and paused there a moment, his hand on the knob.

"Thanks for everything," he said and cast down his eyes. "I mean, for putting me up and all."

"And thank you, too," said Doctor Sylvan.

Jim looked at him, puzzled.

"Don't you know why?" asked the doctor.

Jim shook his head.

"Someday I'll tell you. Not now. It's only that you give me something back."

He touched Jim's hand on the knob and Jim let his hand fall. The doctor opened the door and went out. Jim stood in the open doorway watching him as he walked down the drive, a slight vivid figure in the darkness, an aliveness in his movement.

It had stopped raining. There was the new moon with a star hanging directly beneath it. There was a feel of frost in the air. Jim waited until he heard the car start and then closed the door. He turned, with hands clasping the knob, his back against the door, facing the empty room. In one of the corners near the ceiling long dusty cobwebs were swaying.

I'll knock them down in the morning, he thought, and moving away from the door walked out to the other room to unpack his bags.

THE ROOM was so silent. Outside the windows, the night was still. Jim turned over on his side, curling his hands under his cheek and tried to concentrate on sleeping. But sleep would not come. He felt fearful and alone. Maybe he should have stayed at Doctor Sylvan's house, he thought. Then thought fiercely, No, it would be difficult now, in the beginning, but soon it would be all right. It would be a matter of time.

The quietness of the house. He wished that there was someone there to talk to, someone in the darkness of the room so he would not feel so lonely. Then, as had happened so often in his last months at the hospital, the image of the boy crept into his mind—the dying boy in the infirmary at the mental hospital. Jim didn't want to think of him, pressed his hands tightly over his eyes to shut out the thought of him, but the more he tried to blot him out, the more stubbornly he arose in his mind. He let his arms fall helplessly at his sides, giving himself up to the insistence of the memory:

. . . The boy had been no more than nine or ten years old. Deaf and dumb, and so thin he barely raised the sheets. Dark close-cropped hair, a boy's summer haircut. His face was very pale, his thin arms lay listless on the sheets. His eyes were sunken, closed, like dark holes. There were feeding tubes stuck in his veins, and the only sign he was alive, the slow rise and fall of the sheets and continual low cries of his pain, moans like an animal, or the moans of some creature who has never learned to speak, who can only cry out that he is in agony and the hurt won't go away.

Jim, who had been transferred from his building to the infirmary for some minor ailment, wondered how the boy had ended up in such a place. One of the nurses told him the parents could no longer take care of the boy and the only place that would take him in was the mental hospital.

All day and all night Jim could hear him crying out and tried not to listen. He would go to the farthest end of the hall or, if it was at night, stuff his pillow over his ears, but there was no escaping those low cries of pain from the mute creature lying so still on the bed.

Jim would pass his room and he wanted to go in. He wanted to lift him, to hold him close to him, to somehow try to comfort him. He wanted to ease his pain. The boy seemed so far beyond reach. Jim wanted to put his hand on his head, caress his brow and cheeks, to touch him with his hands. As though in that way to reach him, to let him know that he wasn't alone, that someone was there to touch him, to be with him.

But he didn't go in. He was frightened. And also repulsed. Frightened of the boy's dying and repulsed because the smell of death was all around him. The boy wouldn't live, that was certain, and Jim was secretly glad. He would wake each morning hoping no longer to hear the boy's cries and, listening, would hear, with disappointment, the low bleating of his misery.

He did not die and the cries would continue all through the day. Jim walked past his room, still wanting to go in and comfort him, but he could only stand at the door and gaze in, his heart filling with sadness at the sight of him, at the tubes stuck in the veins of his arms and more tubes stuffed down his nostrils, and his eyes darker holes, his thin lips dry and flaked, his tongue fluttering out, fluttering drily over the lips, the throat tight and quivering from the low animal groans coming up out of his body.

Jim hoped that all that chalk-white and colorless fluid dripping into him would save the boy, that it might be miraculous fluid to make him live again, for it would take a miracle to do that. But he couldn't believe that such a miracle could happen and he wanted him to die, to end his suffering, to end the cries that constantly reminded him of his own suffering.

Death was hovering all about him and frightened Jim and he would turn and go to the far end of the hall to get away from it.

And on the fourth day, in the early hours of the morning, he died. Jim knew he had died because when he awoke there was no more crying. He listened intently—two—three—four minutes, and still no sound of it. He felt suddenly relieved and thought how wonderful it was that the boy had died, that he was no longer in agony but was freed of it by death.

Now, lying alone in his bed in his new house, once more beginning to live his own life, Jim thought of the boy. It was as though he also wanted to lift the sick and dying boy of himself in his arms. He knew how one is hurt and in pain and needs to be comforted, how one can't speak of his pain, but in the eyes is always the mute crying out for help and tenderness. There is no answer, and the child is always crying. No hand to touch him, to quiet him, to make him feel warm and less alone. Then one day he stops crying altogether, he can't cry any more. Something has died in him, and walls of silence build up slowly around him. He withdraws and becomes remote. Because he has not been touched, he can't touch, he has never known it and can't know it in himself. There has never been any way for him to know it. Transparent walls of silence, like one-sided glass, build up around him. He can see out but no one can see in. No one can ever again enter there. Jim thought of his past. He saw the keys to the walls as warm words and warm hands. The keys were warm words and hands over and over, melting the rock, the warmth of love melting the heart that has gone to stone for lack of it. The power and the heat of love which can melt stones, which can melt the stone of such a heart that has tried to lock out everything. Because no one had ever encircled him with their arms, held his head close. Lonely in his fear, he wanted only to be held close and warm, to be touched. The keys that melt granite walls of silence, that melt walls of silence surrounding those who cried so long and alone and now no longer cry. The damned ones who are neither in nor out of life, who try to hide, who only see out but let no one see in or enter there.

Jim gazed out into the darkness of the room. Who would quiet the child? As Doctor Sylvan had held him, as he, Jim, had wanted to hold the boy, letting him know he wasn't alone. Not in life and yet not out of it, Jim had forgotten how to cry and had stood off, fierce and alone, cold and distant, and yet he held within him, as seeds, an intense and unfulfilled longing, a hunger for life.

He craved to live, imagining now in the silent room that he held the dying boy of him close in his arms. A doll to rock, to whisper over, to caress and hold, to keep close in bed, hold soft in the hollow of his shoulder. No, it was not that. He shut his eyes tight, rubbing his knuckles over his forehead. It was the boy, thin and dying, who cried out and was stuck with needles, had tubes thrust down his nostrils, who was never touched, except by bedpans, urinals, the stick of needles.

Jim had known that himself, awaking after three days, unconscious, in another hospital— Tubes in each arm and down his nose, and a hole in his throat from the tracheotomy. Brought there in a rubber sack, more dead than alive. His hands had been cold. Hungry fingers that wanted always to reach out but could not. There had been the walls of silence as tough and thick as any fortress. His lips cold and blue, lips that wanted to caress, to brush the face.

But he had not died. And on the third day he had awakened to see a dark face bending over him. He was tied to the bed and could not move, did not know where he was. The dark face of the colored nurse was smiling as she said, "Thought we was gonna lose *you*, honey. You had one foot angling off to Saint Peter's Gate and the other sliding on a banana peel." She had laughed, a rich deep laugh that made him feel good, and warm. The nurse had swayed down close to his face with her big smile and he had smelled brandy on her breath. "It's all right now," she had whispered softly. "It's all right, honey." And he had fallen off to sleep again, smiling and feeling warm inside, forgetting to care about not being able to move.

All this he remembered as though he had been behind walls, the warmth of flesh, and words, as things apart from him, as a part only of others. The prison of himself he saw now as walls partly of his own building, guarded by guards of his own making; locks, too, and high forbidding gates. There were signs six feet high—KEEP OUT— Signs 6′ 2″ tall— He had been a walking KEEP OUT sign, a prison. And yearned and almost died for lack of one warm word, a hand.

He let his face fall sideways on the pillow. Father, he whispered, I have wandered. I have left your place. And now I'm in a place where nothing but cold winds blow. I'm alone and need you, Father, to come and touch me— Warmth of your hands, to bring me up and out, back into life.

The child was crying. In endless dreams Jim heard him crying. He was a child sitting in the midst of rubble. The child was hungry and alone and he was crying hot tears of hunger and aloneness. The food of the hands that is warm fingers and the touch of life, the food of the hands that comforts, that keeps the child alive, lets no stone of silence rise. The child was crying in his heart, and at night, in dreams, he was crying and Jim touched him and wondered if he lived. He was very dear to him and yet he wondered if the child could be alive. It seemed as though he had cried so long. And no one heard, and no one had come. The child had been crying so long alone, he was getting weak and only whimpered, he no longer cried. Was the child alive? Jim had come, in his dreams, and yet he was not certain that the child lived.

Outside, again, soft rain began to fall. Jim listened to its pattering on the roof. The gentle beat of the rain was lulling and his limbs relaxed. He lay less tense in the bed. He thought of the river which he knew was close by, the river moving darkly in the night. He began to nod off, thinking, I will find the child. Soon, he was fast asleep.

THE NEXT MORNING when Jim awoke the room was full of sunlight. He didn't know what time it was but by the sun in the sky he knew that it was late. He kicked off the blankets and got out of bed and dressed hurriedly. Going into the bathroom he splashed water on his face and ran a comb through his hair. Then, coming out into the front room, he rolled up his sleeves and started to clean the place and put it in order.

First, he swept the rooms with a worn-down broom he found in the hall. Then he dusted the furniture with some old rags that were piled in a corner. That done, he wadded some newspapers together and, filling a bucket with warm water, began to wash the windows.

The sun was high in the sky when he finished. He stepped back, looking at the last sparkling window in the kitchen, and wiped the sweat from his forehead. The rooms seemed lighter now. Having cleaned them and set things right made him feel a part of the place, made him feel that he lived there. He suddenly felt a little weak and realized that he hadn't had any breakfast. He was very hungry. He emptied the pail of dirty water in the bathroom and threw the soggy used newspapers in the trash basket in the kitchen. Then he put on his jacket and went out.

The day was crisp and clear. The last leaves were hanging on the trees and as he went down the drive and started along the pavement leading to the center of town, he walked under trees whose leaves were a soft yellow. As he went beneath them he looked at his hands and they were yellow from the light of the leaves— It was as though he were walking through pure yellowness.

The town was not very big. There was the main street on which he was walking now. On either side there was a church, several grocery stores and bars, a shoe repair shop. He came to a luncheonette and went in and had a big breakfast of ham and eggs and coffee. After eating, he felt better and decided to take a hike out through the town and into the country beyond.

As he walked along the shoulder of the highway an occasional car passed by. He looked at the countryside, watched all the trees going bare now with the approach of winter. There was brown brush up the slopes of the fields along the road. The smell of the air was sweet to him.

He had been walking for close to an hour and was getting tired and about to turn back when, turning a bend in the road, he saw up ahead two women near a stalled car. The one woman, tall and bony, had the hood of the car up and was leaning far in under it, looking around the motor, while the other, a small dark girl, was crouched by the side of the road picking the last of the late wild flowers which grew in the brush.

As he approached, the woman straightened up from beneath the hood and putting her hands on her hips gazed at Jim through her thick horn-rimmed glasses. As Jim got closer, he saw that the girl picking flowers was oriental. She was so busy snipping the delicate stems with her fingernails that she did not see him.

"What's the trouble?" Jim said to the tall woman with the glasses.

"Oh Lord, I don't know," she answered with a perplexed smile as she ran the greasy back of her hand over her brow, leaving a dark smudge. "It just *won't* start."

"I don't know much about cars," Jim said, "but let me take a look."

"I'd appreciate it," she said, flinging out her arms gratefully.

As Jim walked up to the engine he was aware that the girl, whom he now saw to be Japanese, was squatting perfectly still and staring at him, solemn-faced, over her shoulder. He gave her an awkward little smile as he passed her, but she did not smile back. Jim stuck his head under the hood and looked around.

"It just conked out," the tall woman was saying. "We drove along fine for several hours, then it just stalled and I couldn't get it going again."

She was wiping her hands on some tissues from her pocketbook.

Jim jiggled all the wires, making sure there were no loose connections.

"How old's your battery?" he asked.

"I don't know. I think it's pretty new. About a year old."

"I'm not a mechanic," Jim said, "so I don't know what to tell you. Everything *looks* okay."

He ducked out from beneath the hood and rubbed his hands on the thighs of his trousers. The Japanese girl, a fat little bouquet of flowers in one hand, was staring at him over the front fender.

"Is there a town near here?" said the tall woman.

"About two miles farther on," Jim said.

"Excuse me," said the Japanese girl, stepping forward. "But now that this kind gentleman is here, perhaps he and I can push the car, while you steer, Miss Brewster. Perhaps then it will go."

"Yes," Jim said. "Maybe all it needs is a push."

He looked at the girl's face and it was very lovely. He found himself blushing and turned away, afraid she might see. His heart was beating fast. To hide his confusion, he reached up and slammed down the hood.

"You get behind the wheel," he said to Miss Brewster. "Maybe the two of us can get it started. Look," he said, pointing. "The road slopes down a little there. It'll make it easy."

Miss Brewster got into the car. The Japanese girl carefully laid her bunch of flowers in the grass by the side of the road, then walked around to the rear of the car with Jim and leaned her hands against the trunk. Jim saw how tiny her hands were.

"Okay," he called up front. "Got it out of gear?"

"Yes," answered Miss Brewster.

"Now," he said, turning to the girl, "when I count three, push. All right?"

The girl nodded her head once, still with that solemn expression on her face.

Jim turned around, put his two hands under the bumper, getting a firm grip on it, and leaning his back against the car, dug his heels into the gravel.

"One—two—*three!*" he counted, through clenched teeth, and gave a shove.

As he pushed, out of the corner of his eye, he saw that the little Japanese girl was shoving with all her might and his heart gave a lurch of happiness as he saw her stick the tip of her tongue out one corner of her mouth from the effort.

The car began to roll down the grade and as it rolled faster, Jim turned, trotting after it, and heaved the front of his body against it. The car got up a good speed but would not start. Miss Brewster braked it a little farther on, sitting at the wheel with a look of dismay on her face. Jim came up and leaned one elbow in the window, breathing heavily.

"You sure you got enough gas?" he asked.

"Gas?" The woman looked at him with a blank expression on her face. "Gas," she repeated in a flat voice.

Jim let his arms drop at his sides and going around to the rear of the car, unscrewed the gas lid and squinting an eye, peeped in.

The Japanese girl followed him. "That very well might be the difficulty," she said.

"Huh?" Jim suddenly grinned at her, she looked so serious.

"Gasoline," she answered, nodding ominously toward the tank. Then in a whisper, "Miss Brewster is what is called an absent-minded professor."

"Oh?" said Jim, smiling more broadly.

He found a small branch and peeling off the tiny limbs, stuck it down into the gas tank. He pulled it out and held it up to the sunlight.

"Bone dry," he said.

The Japanese girl held her hand to her mouth and giggled. Jim looked at her.

"After all our efforts," she said, and giggled again. Jim began to laugh, too.

Miss Brewster had gotten out of the car and had come around and was standing beside them.

"No gas," Jim said, wagging the dry branch in front of her.

"How really stupid of me!" she said. "I'm so forgetful of these things," and taking off her glasses she began to polish them on the hem of her skirt. "I'm dreadfully sorry."

Jim screwed the lid back on. "I'll walk back to the gas station in town and get you a couple of gallons."

"I really mustn't put you to any more trouble," said Miss Brewster, adjusting her glasses on her nose. "You've been kind enough already."

"It's no trouble. It'll only take a minute. I don't suppose you—er—have a gas can?"

"As a matter of fact," said Miss Brewster with an apologetic smile, "I don't."

"Well, I can get one at the station." He started to walk off. "Hold tight until I get back," he called over his shoulder.

As he walked along the gravel strip toward town, he heard soft footsteps behind him. Turning, he saw the Japanese girl running to catch up with him. He stopped and waited for her, filled with a sudden feeling of lightness.

"May I join you?" she asked, out of breath and brushing a strand of her long hair back over her shoulder as she came up to him.

"Sure. Come on."

"You see," she explained, "I might see some more lovely flowers on the way."

They walked together down the road, the girl looking to either side, her eyes alive and bright, like a small bird's, Jim thought. He was silent, feeling a sudden lump of bashfulness in his throat, not knowing what to say.

Finally, after a few moments of painful silence, he screwed up his courage enough to ask, "Where are you and your friend coming from?"

"Oh," she answered vaguely as she gazed up the slopes along the way, "I was invited by a college in upstate to give several lectures on Japanese poetry. I went there on the train and when my talks were over, this lady, who is an instructor at the college and who is going to visit friends in New York City, was kind enough to give me a ride back. So, you see, we are going there until we got stuck."

"You live in the city, too, huh?"

"Yes. Downtown."

He wanted to ask her where, but didn't know how to ask it, afraid that he might say it wrong and frighten her off.

Now and then, the girl would hop off into the brush at the side of the road and return carrying a blossom she had spied. As they walked along her bouquet got bigger and bigger, so that by the time they reached the gas station near the edge of town, she held a sizable bunch of flowers in her small fist.

At the service station she turned to Jim and said quietly,

"Excuse me, please," and walked off to the rear where the rest-rooms were. Jim got the attendant to pump two gallons of gas for him into a can, paid him, then kept looking toward the corner of the building the girl had gone around. In a moment she reappeared. She had washed her face, it was less dusty. Her hair was freshly combed. She still held the flowers in her hand.

"All set?" Jim asked, smiling at her.

"Yes. Thank you very much for waiting."

They started off again, the station attendant eyeing them curiously as they went, back down the road toward the car, Jim carrying the gas. He hated the silence between them, yet it seemed as though she expected him to speak first. And he didn't know what to say. He was furious at himself for being so tongue-tied and secretly wished he knew something about Japanese poetry—to be able at least to talk to her about that.

"Excuse me, but must you walk so fast?" he heard her say, and turning realized that he was walking several paces ahead of her. Her face was flushed and even though the air was slightly cold, a band of sweat was on her brow.

"I'm sorry," he said, and waited for her to catch up.

"Look here," he said, gulping nervously as she drew up to him, "My name's Jim."

He plonked down the fuel can, wiped his hand on his trousers and stuck it out to her. She looked at his hand, then smiled and cast down her eyes.

"My name is Eiko," she said and, taking his hand in hers, held it briefly for a moment, then let it go.

How soft her fingers are, Jim thought, as he gulped again, relieved to have gotten that over with. He picked up the can and they walked on.

Their hands sometimes touched in the swing of their walk and Jim felt his face and eyes become open and alive. Overhead the sky was a cold clear blue. Even the short sere grasses growing at the roadside filled his heart with happiness.

"Are you a teacher?" he asked timidly. "I mean, you mentioned something about poetry. I don't know much about poetry," he confessed.

"I know mostly about Japanese work," she said. "Would you like to hear my favorite verse?"

He nodded his head. She stopped and faced him, laying her hand lightly on his arm.

"The blossom fallen in the grass
flies back to the tree—
No, it is a butterfly."

She smiled shyly and, turning, walked ahead with quick small steps. Jim came hurrying after her, the gas can banging against his legs.

"I liked that," he said. He felt light-headed.

"It is very lovely," she said quietly, then scurried off into the bushes again, having seen another flower.

Then, before Jim knew it, they were rounding the bend, and the car, with Miss Brewster slumped against the front fender, came into view. His spirits sank. The walk back had been too quick. There were so many things he had wanted to say to her, so much he wanted to find out about her. He wanted so badly to see her again, and now it was too late. But perhaps she wouldn't want to see him. He couldn't bear to think of that. Already, Miss Brewster was coming toward them in stiff long strides, one hand shading her eyes from the sun, smiling.

"That was fast," she said.

"It's not far," Jim said, and leaving Eiko's side went to the rear of the automobile. "I'll have you started in a jiffy."

He unscrewed the lid and tipping the can up began emptying the gasoline into the fuel tank. He looked about for Eiko as the gas spilled in, sending up poignant fumes to his nostrils. She was nowhere in sight. Then he saw her in the front seat of the car, her head bent over the flowers, arranging them in her lap. She's probably anxious to get started, he thought sadly. I'll never see her again.

He watched her through the half open window as the last of the gasoline trickled out. When the can was empty he turned to Miss Brewster and said, "Okay. Give it a try."

She got behind the wheel and turned on the ignition. The engine turned over immediately and she gunned it a few times. Jim went to the window on the driver's side and leaned in.

"You're all right now," he said. "Better stop soon and put more gas in. That's only a couple of gallons in there now."

Miss Brewster nodded. Jim glanced across at Eiko but she was staring down at the blossoms in her lap.

"I won't ever forget your kindness," Miss Brewster said. "Can we give you a lift back to town?"

For a brief instant he was tempted to say yes, so that he could be with Eiko that much longer. But he decided it would be futile.

"No," he said. "It would take you out of your way. It's such a nice day," he continued, glancing up at the sky. "I don't mind walking."

"Here," said Miss Brewster, reaching into her purse with an air of embarrassment. "At least let me pay you for the gasoline." She timidly pressed a bill into his hand.

"No. Please," Jim said, waving off the money and taking a step back from the car. "Let it be on me. It wasn't that much. Really."

"Well, I don't know how to thank you."

"Perhaps," Eiko spoke up quietly—and Jim's ears pricked up—"we can repay him by giving him a flower."

"Yes! Will you take one of Eiko's flowers?" laughed Miss Brewster. "She's simply crazy about flowers."

"Well, okay." Jim smiled sheepishly, and stared down at the dust at his feet.

"You will have to come around here to receive it," said Eiko.

Jim walked around the front of the car, feeling a catch and tremor in his throat. When he got to her window he rested the tips of his fingers lightly on the window edge.

"Here," said Eiko, pulling a blossom from the bouquet. "The loveliest one."

Jim took the flower. His hand was trembling. He looked a moment into her smiling eyes. The thought raced through his mind that he should ask, on the spot, if he could see her again, but Miss Brewster had the car in gear and it was slowly rolling away.

"Good-bye," she called, leaning over the wheel and waving to him.

Eiko simply bowed her head to him, smiling. Jim ran a little after the car, then stood still, a stiff smile on his face, clenching the flower, feeling foolish, and angry, too, at his timidity.

The car gathered speed and headed down the highway. Jim watched it go. His throat felt dry. He had the sudden urge to run after it, call out to Eiko, ask if he could see her, beg her to see him again. He bit his lip and kicking at a stone in the road, turned and walked back to town, his shoulders slumping.

The brightness seemed to have gone out of the day. Even though the sun was shining a leadenness seemed to have come over everything. In his disappointment and anger, he had forgotten the flower. Now he looked at it. It was a big yellow blossom with thick fleshy petals. At least I have this, he thought bitterly. He lifted the flower to his nose and sniffed at it, closing his eyes. It had a deep musky odor. He stopped in the road and sank his nose deeper into the heart of the flower. Something delicate scratched his nostrils. Puzzled, he held the flower out and stared at it. Was it a bee? he thought. Carefully, with his fingers, he rooted among the petals. Stuck deep amongst them was a tiny folded slip of paper. His heart beat fast and his hand shook as he gently removed the paper from the flower. Tucking the flower in his shirt front, he opened the slip of paper, his heart leaping in his breast as he read in a neat careful script:

> Eiko
> AB 3–6012

He took the flower from his shirt and kissed it. Then, repeating the telephone number to himself several times, he carefully folded the delicate tissuelike paper and put it into his pocket. With a broad grin on his face, he looked back down the road, in the direction the car had gone, then, doing a little skip, leap and a jump on the shoulder of the highway, he started walking quickly back to town. The sun seemed again to shine over everything. He heard the birds singing. A buoyancy filled his body and there was a jauntiness in his walk as he hurried home, trying to figure out in his mind how long it would take the car to get from where he had left them, back to the city.

✑ E I K O

EIKO LIVED in a loft on the top floor of an old building far down on the Lower East Side. The stairs went straight up from the narrow hallway and sagged to one side so that Jim felt lopsided walking up them. They creaked very much and he wished they didn't creak because he was afraid one of the big brown metal-lined doors on the landings would open and someone would come out and ask him what he was doing there. At the top the stairs turned and became narrower and there was still another flight of stairs and he started up these but suddenly realized they led to the roof. He came down and knocked at one of the two big doors, not believing that she lived there, that she could be inside at that moment waiting for him. He felt he was at the wrong address, that he had made a mistake. There was no answer and he listened hard, over his quick breathing from his fear and the climb, and his heart beating fast with happiness and anticipation. There was no sound within. Surely now he had made a mistake. But he went to the other door at the end

77

of the hall and knocked again, louder this time. There was the quick sound of scurrying feet inside and he let out a soft sigh of relief as the big door scratched open and Eiko stood before him, small and smiling, not quite as he remembered her, she seemed so much darker.

"You are early," she said, and stood aside to let him in.

"I thought we might catch the nine o'clock show."

"Oh, because you must get your bus back. I see."

"You don't mind?"

"Oh, no. Certainly not."

She had small hands and small feet and a bush of black hair, like dark smoke, sweeping to one side of her face and falling over her shoulders. She had a smoky beauty, her face pale, and her eyes dark, the lashes and brows dark as her hair. A strong Japanese face. She was dressed completely in black: a wool sweater and ski pants, on her feet small pointed chukka boots with silver buckles.

She led him into a bare stark room which ran the entire length and width of the building. She took his coat, apologizing that she wasn't ready, she hadn't expected him so early, but she would be ready in a moment.

"You see, I found a skirt," she said, laughing, and holding up for him to see a skirt made of rough wool the color of dark wine. "I told you I had no skirt, but now I have one. I will be back."

She seemed nervous and didn't look him in the eye, but always off to one side, her eyes cast down, a kind of shyness he did not know. He watched her as she hurried off and went into a smaller room at the far end of the loft. He sat down on the low bed, expecting it to be soft, but he sat down abruptly, surprised, his hands feeling a hard material under the white coverlet. He lifted the cloth a little and saw that her mattress was a large flat wooden board. He scratched his head, smiling to himself, and looked around the place. The only furniture in the room, besides the bed, were two old dining-room chairs, placed neatly side by side at the rear of the loft, each covered in plum-colored fabric, faded and splotched. In the center of the room stood a big grand piano, dark and somber, its lid propped open. The bench had sheets of music stacked neatly to one side of the seat. There was a round wire spool near his foot which was turned on end and made to serve as a little table. In the precise center of the spool was a clay ash tray with the image of a fish scratched in its bottom.

He lit a cigarette and leaned back, gripping his knees with his hands, the cigarette dangling loosely between his lips. The walls hadn't been painted for years and were grimy and streaked with soot. The windows, front and back, were frosted so that you couldn't see out. Directly above the piano was a large sky-light and the glass in it, too, was frosted, but he could see the pale light of the moon glowing through the panes.

He thought, Maybe she is very poor.

She came back, wearing the skirt. She had combed her hair and arranged it differently. He helped her on with her coat.

"Do you play?" he said, nodding toward the piano.

"Very badly."

"How did you get a big place like this?"

"Oh, someone died," she laughed. "Now I am worried because my friends all say, 'Oh, Eiko, what a fine big place you have!' and there is this light comes into their eyes—a sort of gleam—you know, of envy—and I become alarmed because I am afraid one of them might poison my cup of coffee—so that they can inherit this place."

He laughed, an open, delighted laugh. A flicker of joy danced in his heart.

She turned out the lights and they went out the door. She had a combination lock on the outside which she set. They went down the stairs, and this time he was less afraid. At the foot of the stairs was a ladder built against the wall and she started to climb it to put out the hall lights but he reached over her head and flicked the switch and helped her down.

"You're a sort of a janitor, too, huh?"

"Yes, a bit," she laughed. "It takes a few dollars off the rent."

Out in the street it was cold and he put on his gloves and pulled up the collar of his jacket as they stood in the middle of the sidewalk, hesitating about which way to go. He was keenly aware of his tallness as he tilted his head to look down at her. She was like a child, so small.

"Where would you like to eat?"

"Oh, I don't know. It does not matter."

"You like Spanish food?"

"Oh yes."

"Come on."

They went down into the subway at the corner and rode uptown. He felt more at ease sitting down with her on the wicker seat. Now she didn't seem so tiny and he didn't feel so gangly and long. He could look into her eyes without craning down. In the car the other passengers were looking at them. He felt a secret pride. She was really very beautiful.

THE WAITER was a typical New York waiter: almost psychotic. He was middle-aged, balding, and was dressed in a red jacket and black trousers. His whole manner was insolent and rough and he threw the knives, forks and plates down on the table with a clatter of vengeance. It seemed he wished the napery were made of metal and crockery as well so he could bang that down, too. Jim watched him with delight, and a little fear. The waiter's face was seamed with spite. It appeared to say: Although I wait on you, don't think you can look down on me or get away with anything. It was as though waitering would be a fine thing if only there were no customers. What a nuisance they seemed to him! But it was as if he put up with them because he knew without them he would have nothing to fight against and he did so need something to fight against. It was as though each of his customers was a personal enemy who was out to get the better of him at every turn. But he always got his in first, just in case they tried to pull anything fast.

Jim watched Eiko's face, but she seemed quite contented, as though the waiter did not exist; the flailing red arms and clash and noise of utensils hitting the table could be, from the serenity of her features, no more than leaves of an aspen stirred by the wind. After the waiter had gone he asked her about it.

"Oh no, he did not bother me," she said, looking surprised. "You see, in Japan all the waiters are so polite and whispering. They are false. This is a relief. I mean, it is more in the open. That's honest. It does not bother me."

She smiled, seeing the look of dismay on his face.

"I guess it's different," he said. "It's just that in America nobody likes to serve. You know, to be a servant, serve anybody, is an awful thing. I guess that's what this waiter's always stewing about. But they get licked all the time and they know it— Well, they're so slavish, finally, so abject, because all they want is the damned tip. But they're gonna make *you* pay, too, to give it to them."

"Yes," she said. "That is very interesting."

Another waiter, tall and slender, stopped at their table. "Would you like to order now, or have a drink?" he asked, smiling and bowing slightly.

Eiko grinned as Jim raised his eyebrows, surprised at the change in manner of this new waiter. Jim ordered two drinks and the young man nodded and went off toward the bar.

Not a moment later, the middle-aged waiter appeared, petulantly flapping open his orderbook and, pencil poised in mid-air, gazed down at them condescendingly through the half-moons of his bifocals.

"Oh, another waiter came and took an order for drinks," Jim said, almost apologetically, and suddenly fearful.

The mouth of the old waiter dropped open and his eyes burned down at Jim in disbelief at this latest betrayal. Well, it was to be expected. He had been caught napping but he would fix these turncoats and also that young go-getter cutting in on his territory. His face went the color of a very ripe tomato. His eyes seemed to swim in a dark fury. His fatty cheeks trembled and Jim distinctly heard him say, through clenched teeth, before he stormed off to the bar, "That spic bastard!"

Eiko put her hand to her mouth and giggled, and Jim laughed, too.

"I hope they make them check their guns before they start work," he said.

The old waiter returned, visibly less red in the face, some of the fury drained from his eyes, but staunchly on his guard and ready for anything. He wasn't going to let Jim and Eiko off so easily and to show his displeasure at their betrayal of him he slopped the drinks down on the table, spilling most of the liquor on the cloth. He stood back, hunching his shoulders grandly, his nose twitching with revengeful pleasure.

"You wish to order now," he barked.

"Yes, yes," Jim said, burying his face in the enormous menu. "Uh—we'll have paella. For two."

"Paella? What kind of paella?" he snapped, slapping his orderbook sharply in the flat of his palm.

Jim buried his nose in the menu again and putting his finger on the words, said, very slowly and carefully, "Paella—a—la—Valenciana."

He peered cautiously over the edge of the menu to see if

the order and his pronunciation met with the approval of the waiter.

"Paella a la Valenciana!" crowed the waiter, in flawless accent, and briskly snapping shut his book, snatched the menus out of their hands and strode off to the kitchen.

Jim gazed at Eiko, his eyes wide in mock fear and awe. "He's sure a terror, isn't he?"

"Oh, but so much nicer than pussyfoot falseness," laughed Eiko.

They both smiled and touched glasses and drank what was left of the drinks.

"I'll tell you something you might not believe," Jim said. "I still can't believe it, it was so crazy. One of my first times in New York—well, I was very green, and wanted to see the Village and all and I got a cab at the train station and said, 'Take me to Greenwich Village.' Well, we start down there, my eyes bugging all the way—I was just a kid—eager to get my first look at the place. All those long-haired girls waiting for me and no beating around the bush. You know. Well, we're tooling along for awhile and I lean over and say to the driver, 'Hey, let me know when we get to the Village, huh?' and he says, 'Buddy, dis *is* Green-which Villitch.' And I say, 'Oh?'—disappointed, you see, because it doesn't look much different from anything else so far. So I say, 'Leave me off at this corner,' and I give him a bill and jump out of the cab and have to wait there at the corner for the light. Suddenly I feel a hot breath down my neck and then a finger poking me on the shoulder and I turn around and see it's the cab driver— He's left his cab parked right smack in the middle of the street—the door flung open and all— He leans close in my face and says, 'Hey, buddy, what about me tip?' I says, 'Huh?' He says, 'Come on, come on. You dint gimme no tip.' I didn't know what he was talking about because I thought there was enough for a tip in the bill I gave him, but he said, No, that was just enough for the fare. I thought it was a pretty weird thing for him to park his cab just like that anyhow, so I told him, 'How come you leave your cab, block traffic this way?'— There were all these horns blowing by this time, you see, and traffic backed up for a couple blocks. I said, 'How come you do all that for a lousy tip?' By this time a little crowd'd gathered and I felt like a fool. The guy turns to me and says, you know, hardboiled and out the side of his mouth, 'Look, buddy, we gotta make a livin', too, ya know.' Somebody in the crowd says, 'Whatta cheapskate.' It was all pretty awful—I mean, with the traffic tied up and all, and all these people pushing around, listening and butting in, and on top of it I see this cop out of the corner of my eye sidling over. I fished in my pocket and gave the guy what change I had and took off as fast as I could in the crowd. I just couldn't believe that. I didn't get over it for days. I thought maybe that's just the way things were in New York."

"And it turns out that they are just that way," laughed Eiko. "But, oh, that must have been humiliating!"

"Well, I was only 18. Now maybe I would just tell him to go to hell."

The waiter plonked a silver bucket on the table and snatching off the lid roughly spooned steaming yellow heaps of paella on each plate. Eiko began to eat immediately, pausing only now and then to shove her hair back from her face and smile across at him and murmur it was good. He ordered wine but she said she didn't want wine, that one drink would be enough. He watched her eat, smiling inwardly, surprised that so small and delicate a creature could have such a good appetite. It was as though, rather, she should pick at her food, daintily, eat little, like a sparrow. When the waiter came to take the empty plates away she looked at the bones regretfully as though she were sorry she could not eat them, too. And suddenly he realized,

with a sharp pain in his heart, that she had been hungry, that
she had eaten like someone who had not eaten for several
days. She looked up at him, grinning, a delightful happiness in
her eyes as she wiped her small mouth busily and carefully
with her napkin.

"That was so good," she said. "So very good."

She was so innocently content, as though some wonderful
thing had happened. The tiny flicker of pain eased in his heart.
Something stirred within him, a feeling of warmth he had not
felt for so long. It crept along his limbs, warm and sure, a strong
and quiet strength of love. He wanted to put his arms around
her, to protect her. The sunniness of her small pleasure made
him feel warm and happy. He laughed suddenly and propped
his elbows on the table, and, chin in hands, said, "Think you
have room for a cup of coffee?"

"Oh yes," she said. "But no dessert. That would make me
fat."

They both laughed and he lifted his arm, signaling the
waiter.

THEY HAD COME IN in the middle of the picture
and as the film ended he got up, excusing himself, saying he was
going to have a cigarette. He slid past her and went up the
aisle and to the water cooler for a drink. Then he pushed open
the men's room door and went in and lit a cigarette. He looked
at himself in the mirror. He was young, and yet how different
he looked this evening. There seemed to be a lightness and
youthfulness in his face. He was reminded of the dream and
told it back to himself:

. . . He had come to a weather-beaten clapboard house
and stopped before the door. Two tiny oriental girls came
running around the corner of the house and stopped and
smiled up at him. The one, older, about 4 years old, was able

to get up the high step by herself and run into the house. The other, much smaller, with black button eyes and black glossy hair cut in a bob with bangs across her forehead tried to climb up but was too small to make it. She turned with a shy smile which asked him to help her up. The smile melted him, made him feel warm and joyful. He put his hand on her little round bottom and gave her a boost up the step and in the door and she toddled away down the hall after her sister. He followed and came into a large room which was subdued and quietly furnished. Sitting on a long low sofa before a low table was an oriental woman. She was handsome and held herself erect with a quiet poise. All about her, and in the room, was a quietness, a sense of calm and delicacy. The children went to her and each laid her head on her lap. The mother smiled at them, warmly, lovingly. Before her was a large flat circular tray on which were arranged various porcelain objects containing food or preparations for food. She was kneading some bright red stuff in a thin white bowl, a meat or paste. She smiled at the stranger and beckoned him to sit down. He did so, on a chair close by, and the children left their mother and sat down on the carpet close to them. A strong peace and happiness filled his heart. . . .

Still before the mirror, he looked closely at his eyes and behind their lightness and innocence was a deadness that startled him and made him look away with a feeling of sadness and shame. Perhaps— And so he would not think of that, he thought of the dream and he thought of the earth outside buried in winter and, as it was with earth, believed there could be such flowerings in himself again.

He took a long drag on the cigarette and turned away from the mirror, the feeling of happiness which had started earlier in the evening returning. Then, abruptly, with a pang that made his knees weak, the fear flashed through his mind that she might not be there when he got back, that she would be gone, that she would leave him. He crunched out the cigarette quickly and ran out of the men's room.

The theatre was in darkness and the picture already begun as he hurried down the aisle, his heart beating fast. At first, in the darkness, he couldn't find her, and his head turned this way and that, desperately, trying to find her amongst all the dark and faceless heads in the audience. "She's gone!" raced through his brain, and then, suddenly, the dark scene on the screen changed to a bright one of a forest of slender white birch trees filmed from a passing train window. In his confusion he had wandered too many rows down and, looking back in the screen's glow, with a rush of relief, he saw her, sitting alone, just as he had left her.

How lovely her face in the reflection of light from the screen. Absorbed, and at rest, her face revealing nothing, but watching the movie with a quietness, an almost imperceptible intensity in the pale features. He paused, for the fraction of an instant, seeing it all, and in that instant was proud that she was with him, that he would sit down beside her, glad that at times her fingers would touch his arm lightly as she was moved by some particular scene in the movie; and sometimes, watching from the corner of his eye, he saw her hand lift to her mouth at some poignant moment, or saw her delicately slanted eyes look down and knew that there were tears shimmering in them. He wanted everyone in the theatre to know they were together, that she belonged to him. All this was in his heart in that moment as he slid into the seat beside her, a feeling of peace and pride and warm love filled him. She looked up, slightly alarmed. She had been so absorbed in the screen she had not been aware it was him returning. He put his hand on her arm and she smiled and together they continued looking at the movie.

AFTER THE MOVIE they took the subway back to her place.

"Would you care for a drink?" she said, once inside. "All I have is Chinese whiskey."

"The Chinese make whiskey?"

"Well, it is rather dreadful stuff. It is like raw alcohol they have put some perfume into."

She went into the other room and came back carrying a bottle and handed it to him. He uncorked it and put it to his lips and drank. The Chinese whiskey was a cross between bad brandy and worse tequila. It *hurt* to drink it.

"Foo!" he said, passing the bottle to her. "That really cuts the phlegm."

But she seemed to enjoy it (he thought maybe she was just pretending to) and he passed the bottle back and forth between them. She took delicate little nips and would coo and ah and run the tip of her tongue over her lips in pleasure.

"We are deceived," she said, indicating the whiskey. "I like to be. Don't you like to be deceived?"

He didn't know what to say and put his fingers to his mouth and stammered. He wasn't sure he understood what she meant. He was embarrassed, for the moment, to answer, but he answered anyway.

"No—I don't like that."

"Oh, you don't?" She seemed very surprised, then giggled and turned her face aside. He felt suddenly foolish, like a stiff-necked puritan, and wanted, at that instant, more than anything, to enjoy being deceived as much as she did.

To cover his confusion he picked up a package lying near the foot of the bed. "What's this? Betel nut, it says."

"Some friend gave it to me. It is a kind of joke."

The small package was rose-colored. There was a picture

of a woman on it, a sort of gypsy with a bandana. She was smiling. "The Greatest Delight" was printed across her body. He opened the package. Inside, the betel nuts were wrapped in tiny packets of neatly wrapped tissue. He took one out, "Looks like bubble gum," he said, and opened the tissue carefully so as not to spill the nuts. They were small and black and he put several in his mouth and began to chew. The flavor at first was aromatic and then bitter.

"It turns your teeth black," she said.

He turned to her, offering a packet of the nuts.

"Have you ever tried it?"

"Oh, no," she said, and took the packet and began to open it. "Thank you so much." She put the nuts in her mouth and began to chew, smiling.

"How do you like them?"

"Oh, they are quite good. Thank you very much." And she began to laugh, putting her hand to her face, chomping away on the hard little pellets.

"Will you make me something with the paper?" he said.

"What do you want me to make?"

"A butterfly."

"A butterfly? Is that your soul?"

"Yes, it's my soul."

"Then I will make you one."

She took the tiny square of paper the nuts had been wrapped in and began creasing and folding it, working small and deftly, her head bent to the work with a quiet absorption. He watched her hands move, they were so small, the fingers gentle and sure with the paper, as they flickered over it, bending it this way and that. And, strangely, her hands were slightly dirty and he wondered what she could have done with them that they could be so soiled—for it was like grit which had gotten into the skin and discolored it, as though she had worked for a long time with some earthen substance that had stained her hands forever.

Her hands suddenly stopped working and she held, pinched between her fingers for him to see, a white paper butterfly, the wings of it stained red from the printing on the underside of the tissue, neatly, delicately made. He reached out to take it from her, touching it gingerly as though the slightest tremor of his hand would crush it. He took it and held it up and looked at it. He turned to her, smiling, and laid his hand on hers, quickly, then withdrawing it again.

"It's very beautiful," he said.

"It's your soul, no?" she said, giggling, hiding her face again behind her hand. He looked at her, wondering, not knowing whether she was laughing at him or not.

"Now I will make your butterfly a little bed, like a flower leaf, so you won't lose him."

There was an old brown paper bag on the piano and taking it up, she tore a piece from it and swiftly fashioned a small square shape, its bottom raised and with two paper ears hanging over the edges to turn up and serve as a kind of lid.

Smilingly, she gave it to him and he tried the butterfly in it for size. It fitted neatly, easily. Perfect.

"Now your soul has a place to rest and you will not lose it so easily."

Hot tears sprang to his eyes, his throat tightened and he felt choked, as he looked quickly into her face.

She dropped her gaze and began playing with her thumb in her lap.

"But the butterfly is not meant to be kept in a cage," she said. "I've left the flaps open. You see? Now it can fly in and out. It will be happier that way."

She looked up and tears were shimmering in her dark eyes.

Her hand reached out, hesitant, and his own hand slid from his thigh and met her fingers and he took her hand and held it warm and loose in his own.

He said, "Thank you very much."

She looked down again. She smiled. "It is your soul. Remember?"

She got up and began walking up and down the room, rubbing her hands together slowly.

"I could not see the moon for so long. I will tell you. My mother is very beautiful. She is very cultivated. People would say they thought she was my sister. But as a child I always tried to please her." She stopped and stared at him. "Can I tell you this?"

He was silent, watching her.

She continued pacing and went on talking without waiting for his answer.

"I seemed to exist only for her, for her pleasure or displeasure. I would make her tea myself and serve her. As a child, when we went out walking, I would watch her steps so I could put my own in time with hers. I was always close to her and doing things for her. At times, when there were visitors in the house, she would point to me and say, 'Eiko is such a good daughter. She anticipates my every want. I never have to lift a finger.' I was so pleased. She was so beautiful, you know. And I wanted so badly that she should love me. But I did not understand what was happening to me. My father was always away on business, in Europe or America. This does not make much sense."

She stopped pacing and stood in front of him, her arms folded tightly across her breast.

"You see, sometimes my mother would say to me, 'Eh, Eiko, which of these two fabrics do you like?' I would be very flattered that she would ask me. Yet, I was afraid to choose for fear of picking the one she did not like. So I would say, 'Ah, Mother, let me see—ah—Mother, which is the one that you prefer?' And she would say, 'There is no question. It is perfectly obvious that this is the better and lovelier of the two. The other is impossible. Wouldn't you say that, Eiko?' 'Oh yes, Mother,' I would say. 'That is the one I was going to select all the time.' And my mother would say, 'I am glad to see you have taste.'

"Letters from a boy I brought to my mother to read first. That is tradition. Sometimes she would simply tear them up in disgust without my seeing them. She said they were foolish and disgusting.

"Then sometimes she would say, 'You know, Eiko, if you had to go to someone's home, if something happened to your father or me, your brother Kazo would find a home. But you would not find a home. You are intelligent, yes, and quick, but your jaws hang too much to one side and your eyes are not right, not right at all. No, it would be hard to find a home for you.' And I would cry, I would cry all night and couldn't sleep."

"That was cruel."

"Oh please," she protested. "I do not tell you this to pity me, but only that you may know me better. That I am as you see me and do the things that I sometimes do."

She looked away as though embarrassed. "But I have not talked about myself for so long. You make me remember things I had forgotten and you somehow make me talk about myself. It is immodest."

She sat down beside him on the bed, her face averted.

"My brother Kazo is so beautiful. All the faces of the boys at my school were beautiful, slender and sensitive faces. They took their faces from the mother. The girls from the father and, so, not as lovely.

"The school I went to it was—well—snobbish. There was a boy's school and a girl's school. Other men did not exist. On a bus others did not exist for us. But if a school uniform got on, if a boy with a uniform, we girls would smile and put our heads together and say, Yes, he is one of us. But we did not speak to him. That was absurd. Out of the question. No, that is not what I want to tell you. I want to tell you about coming back from the hills, after the war. We were piled on top of a truck, too many of us in one place so I could hardly breathe. I was with my mother. It was bad because the road went through the mountains. It was night, too. And it was a dangerous old truck, it groaned and rattled as though it would fall apart at any moment. Its headlights were so poor and the curves so dangerous, a twisting mountain road, you see. My mother pressed close to me. She was frightened. Seeing that, in that moment, she became my daughter. In the face of her fear it was as though in that instant I had given birth to myself." She crossed her hands at her breast. "And I—well—I prayed. Because, you see, I did not think that we would make it. I thought that we would crash down into a ravine and that would be the end of it. But then, you know, we did make it and came into the city at dawn. And there was Tokyo which I had not seen for so long, completely leveled and still smoking in its ruins. But I was happy because I had seen my mother and myself as someone new and this somehow released me. And I was happy because of the dawn making everything alive, and rose, in all that death. We had lived through the night and there was the sun—I began to cry—I was too happy to be alive."

She was silent, her hands resting quietly in her lap. He watched her. Her face was so strange to him. Now it became a man's face, a soldier, peering out amongst palm leaves, the bayonet held loosely, ready, at his thigh. There was this other face, behind her own, of incredible cunning and stealth, of violence and murder, of livid fear.

At moments she seemed quite homely. Something seemed to drain out of her face and her face became tired, almost old, as though her mother had suddenly appeared, witch-like and invisible, to again cast her spell of ugliness upon her. At these times he was aware of her slightly buck teeth. She seemed common and house-worn, like a woman who has had too many children, who has always worked too hard and has slowly had her life drained away serving others. He wished at such moments she would wear lipstick to help take away from her this somberness and darkness which fell upon her so abruptly and without warning: a touch of red, like a flower at her mouth, to keep that dark and deathlike presence at bay. And just as abruptly, the spell would be broken, as though some protecting spirit leapt up in her to drive off the heavy sullen mood—her face would suddenly glow with a warm smile and she would become childlike and delighted again with everything.

He couldn't take his eyes from her and yet, bashful, was afraid to look at her. And yet he wanted her to see him. He wanted to be vivid for her.

Now she became luminous, a light and softness about her.

"I could not see the moon for so long," she said. "But the other night I saw it through my skylight. You see, when I left them—*her*—it was a moon. After that I could not see the moon for a long time."

She got up quickly, pressing her hands together, prayer-like, beneath her chin. "I have a gift for you," she said.

He protested. "But I don't have a gift for you. I don't like to get presents. I don't know how to take them."

She turned away, hiding her face from him. "It's such a

small gift—it's almost nothing—and you have been so kind to me."

He got up and laid his hand lightly on her shoulder.

She smiled around at him, suddenly very bright, and then got down on her hands and knees and reached under the bed. She brought out a fragile bundle of red tissue and handed it to him.

He opened the tissue carefully. Inside was a small Japanese bell made of clay, and from the clapper, which was also made of clay, hung a long paper tail covered in gold foil for the wind to catch and make the bell ring.

He held the bell high over his head and swayed it back and forth. It made a bright tinkling sound.

She was smiling at him and he laughed, he was so delighted with the gift, and he put his arms around her, the bell tinkling in the embrace.

Seeing the face of his watch which had slipped out from beneath his cuff, he said, "It's late. I've got to go."

She waited near the door as he got his coat on, stood with her hands clasped before her and her head bowed—that certain shyness in the way she stood—and a broad strand of her rich black hair tumbling over her breast. He went to her and took her hand and she looked up and smiled at him. He pressed her hand warmly, wanting to take her in his arms again, hold her close, kiss her lips—but he was suddenly awkward and shy, his tongue clumsy and not able to say what was in his heart: that he would like to see her again—soon, soon.

He put his hands upon her, as though to touch her, but his hands couldn't touch her and fumbled nervously about her shoulders, trying desperately for some gesture of tenderness. But their feel was more that they would rend and tear—awkward, the fingers stiff, wooden, the hands of a man not knowing, yet, how to touch or be touched.

He smiled, a broken foolish smile and drew his hands from her quickly, with a torn movement, and hurried out of the room.

But halfway down the stairs he turned. She had come out into the hall and was watching him from the landing, her small hands resting lightly on the railing.

"I'll see you again," he said.

"Yes." She smiled.

"I'll call you."

He swung around and bounded down the stairs two at a time.

Outside, above the buildings, the stars hung fat and sparkling on the low horizon. The moon lit up hard ruts of snow and, in the park across the street, the stark bare trees. The sky was a smoke of stars and everything about him was a keen wild vividness and in his heart was a poignant singing, pain, and joy. He strode over to the park and down a path, oblivious to the cold and the slippery ice underfoot, and, ringing the bell, began to sing, loud and clear, some absurd and tuneless song, the warmth of it, and the tinkling, shattering the iciness of the still night. He sang in his heart to the moon and the sleeping birds and the night and the buildings and the image of her, pale and lovely, which smiled and beckoned before him as he walked, singing down the path, his face a blade.

EIKO AND JIM

RIDING DOWNTOWN on the subway Jim was filled with elation. He was going to see her again. Her face swam before him, as it had the past few days, haunting—the gracefully slanted eyes, the fine-boned Japanese features, her face smiling, now pensive, now her eyes filling with tears, or her face breaking into its quick bright laughter. Her face moved and changed in his imagination and he delighted in watching it, just as, when a boy, he delighted in lying on his back in a field and watching the clouds change shape in the sky. It was as though she had come to live in him, that she would be with him always, as her presence had been with him, intensely, vividly, since he had seen her last.

He looked about the gray car with its grimy newspaper-strewn floor, looked at the tired dreamless faces of the other passengers, their faces masked, as though nothing could ever come into them again and what they now had to look out on was emptiness, nothing. He was so filled with happiness he

97

wanted to share it with them, tell them of his good fortune. He wished that by looking into his face, the other passengers, sunk behind tabloids, might be touched by the light that stirred in him.

He settled himself back in the seat, throwing one leg up over his knee, getting more comfortable. It would be a long ride. He wanted the train to go faster, it did not go fast enough through the dark tunnel. He glanced at his watch. Plenty of time, he told himself. Relax. What if she's not there? Nonsense. Forget it. He slumped down and rested his head against the back of the wicker seat. He closed his eyes, wanting to see her face again, but this time he did not see her face. Instead, the dream of the night before began to unfold itself once again. He tried to push it away, tried to let her face come through, but the dream was too strong, too insistent. As the dream retold itself to him, his face became troubled as though a dark cloud had passed over the small sun of his happiness:

. . . Doctor Sylvan told him he would have to have his penis cut off. The doctor performed the operation himself. Jim was worried about how he was going to get along without a penis. The doctor told him he was going to keep the penis for a while to fix it and then he would put it back on Jim. Jim wondered how he was going to do this but he believed Doctor Sylvan could do this. He looked down and where his penis was there was nothing.

Then, there was to be a sort of play, or festival. A big eunuch was to be in charge of it. A porch was to serve as a stage, and spread out on the grass in an orderly pattern in front of the porch were pine cones and boughs of pine. Jim wasn't sure what the festival was celebrating. The pine boughs made him think it might be Christmas but it wasn't made certain in the dream.

He went inside the porch where the eunuch was directing

a play to be performed. It was to take place in a small enclosure made of three walls and painted bright yellow, like a
child's room. In the enclosure were two beds and in one of
the beds (very snugly and tightly made) a little girl was lying
and the eunuch told her she was to sleep. There was a child in
the other bed but Jim couldn't tell whether it was a boy or a
girl, the child wasn't very clear. The eunuch decided the walls
of the enclosure were too far apart and shoved them together
a little. Then he prepared to rehearse the two children in the
play, a play of sleeping.

At this point Jim looked down and with amazement saw
that a new penis had grown between his legs. He thought, How
can this be? If a finger's cut off it can't grow back and yet my
penis was cut off and has grown back. How wonderful that is!
He looked at it closely and it didn't look so much different from
the old one—it was almost exactly like it and yet there was
something new and different about it.

Then, Doctor Sylvan appeared. He handed Jim the old
penis that he'd cut from him and told him that he'd been unable to fix it. Jim turned the old penis over in his hand and
saw that the bottom of it was black and eroded, as though something had eaten it away. Then he told the doctor that it didn't
matter, he had a new penis which had grown miraculously in
place of the other, like a starfish grows new parts of itself, he told
him, and threw the old penis away. . . .

The train gave a sharp lurch and he opened his eyes as
the bright lights of a station flickered past the windows. He
looked at his watch. He settled himself back again and closed
his eyes, let himself go, gave himself up again to dreaming,
remembering the dream.

The pine cones and the pine boughs—the black blood of
Attis streaming down the rough bark of the pine tree and soak-
ing into the dark earth about the roots. Blood of himself giving

life to the tree, a self-maiming, and dying, so as to give birth to himself, a new life, in him and the tree. To be born again, as in the dream, he, Jim, had grown out of himself a new phallus, as though he had grown, symbolically and actually, a whole new concept of himself as a man. It was as though the dream was saying that the doctor could point out the sickness, even try to cure it, but that the real cure lay within himself, that the regenerative and restorative powers were within him, that he must not look outside himself or to others for a cure but must discover in himself the healing in the seeds of regeneration within him—the child of him which was yet to come into being—the unborn and new Jim with the regenerative force that could bring it to life—bring him to life.

Jim thought of the time he had let himself go in the water and found that he could swim, simply letting himself go and trusting to the water and himself in the water. He knew what it meant and he knew in his heart that this was what he wanted, and needed to do, more than anything.

Now, it was as though he could sink no further and could only cry out for all that he had ever wanted and needed.

The pine trees stayed vivid in his mind. The pine trees, forever green, as was he, springs out of season, and the possibility of green flowerings in the winter of himself—as the pine, tough and substantial, green in winter and green in the intense heat of summer, with incredibly delicate needles, and sweet warm smell of sap and tar. He was this tree, without season, indifferent to frost and heat, and realized with a sudden pang of loneliness this difference which made him, as a man, a part of and yet apart from other life.

Perhaps now he would no longer be a warm, blind and comfortable slug which never gets itself fully born, which lies buried and half asleep in the black mystery of its half-life and never awakens to the life which lies within and beyond it.

He saw himself as flowerings which are forever coming into being, and dying, and new flowerings arising in the wake of the dead ones—as forsythia bursts forth first in early spring like a glad yellow fire announcing to all the death of winter. And in its brief life it is very beautiful and tender, but with its death spring doesn't die—as in the blossomings of himself he would not die with the death of the old Jim but new flowerings would leap up in him—as in the outside spring of the world, when the forsythia dies, then there is lilac and apple blossom, the rose and morning glory.

Then, as though waking, he sat up with a start. The train was pulling into the station where he must get off. The doors slid open and he ran out along the platform and sprinted up the steps to the street. He ran the few blocks to where she lived. Once there, he paused a brief moment at the door of her building and looked up. Seeing lights glowing through the top floor windows of her loft gave him a curious feeling of relief. He pulled open the door and hurried up the long flights of stairs, not afraid this time. When he got to the top landing he knocked at her door, short quick raps. The door opened instantly and Eiko stood there gazing up at him, a faint smile on her face.

"I am ready this time," she said, shyly and, like a little girl, lifted her arms slightly, looking down at her dress. It was a loose-fitting dress, oriental in cut, the color of old gold, a pattern of pale-rose flowers running through the heavy rich fabric. She had her long hair pinned up, Japanese-fashion, pulled back tight from her forehead and sweeping behind in a thick soft wave. There was a faint touch of rouge on her lips.

He felt awkward and self-conscious, aware of his long arms hanging at his sides. His throat was dry. He stuck his hand out impulsively. She looked at it a moment, surprised, the action had been so abrupt, and then, seeing his embarrassment, smiled up at him and took his hand in hers and shook it. He laughed, wishing he had a basketball, anything to do something with his hands, but instead stuck his head in the door and looked around the place.

"It's still the same."

"Oh yes," she said, following his gaze and stepping inside. He followed her. "I want nothing more in it. And I want nothing taken out."

"Well, are you ready?" He thought he might start ripping the buttons off his coat in sheer nervousness if they didn't get a move on, get the evening started, so that he could put an end to his apprehension.

"Yes, we will go now," she said. She reached for her coat and he helped her on with it. She turned out the lights, then set the combination lock on the door and they went downstairs, Jim switching off the hall lights before they went out into the street.

"You remembered," she said, laughing over her shoulder.

"No use having the landlord on your back," he said.

"Look," he continued, "It's too late for a movie. I thought we might just go some place and have a drink or two and talk."

"That sounds fine."

"Then there's this party I've been invited to. But I don't know about that. Maybe you won't want to go to that."

"A party?"

"Yes. Some friends of mine. Down near the bridge."

"Well, let us do this," she said, touching his sleeve with her finger. "There is a pleasant little bar around the corner. We will have a drink and talk and then decide later how we feel about the party. All right?"

"All right."

She took his arm and they walked down the street, turning at the corner. She led him into a dimly lit bar with red neon beer signs burning in the window. The place was not crowded and there was a pleasant feeling of warmth and quiet conversation.

"You see?" she said, as they sat down in a booth near the window. "It's nice, no?"

"Yes," he said, looking around. "Very nice."

The bartender came out from behind the bar and took their order. Jim folded his hands on the table and looked across at her.

"How have you been?"

"Oh, I have been fine, thank you. And you?"

"All right, I guess." He laughed. "Now that we've got the preliminaries over with, let's really talk."

"All right. Let's."

The bartender set the drinks down on the table and Jim paid him. He lifted his glass, "Here's to Eiko." He touched her glass with his.

"Thank you very much," she said.

She took a small sip, looking at him over the rim of her glass. "Well, tell me what you have been thinking," she said.

He looked away, embarrassed. How could he tell her he had been thinking of nothing but her?

"What, nothing? Well, if you have been thinking of nothing we have nothing to talk about," she said, teasingly.

"I had a dream," he blurted.

"Oh? I have dreamed too. Do you dream in color?"

"Yes."

"So do I. That is supposed to be unique. But how can they tell that? Will you tell me your dream?"

"Well—no—I can't really," he said, stammering.

"Then I will tell you mine. May I?"

"Yes, please."

"I have had two dreams. In one my mother comes into a

room where I am and she is carrying a bright red hat. She offers it to me but I am offended, I do not like the hat. It is too loud, too garish, and I turn away, refusing to take it.

"In the other dream my mother again comes into the room. This time she is carrying a purple dress. She holds it out, extending it to me. But I do not like the color and, as with the hat, I refuse to take the dress. I turn my back on my mother and she leaves the dress on a chair and goes quietly out of the room. I go up to the chair and look at the dress. Then I touch it. I want it to be black. I think, if it is black then I will wear it."

Jim was suddenly aware of her clothes. She was dressed in a black coat and black stockings—her tiny pointed slippers were black too. There was in her a darkness and buriedness.

She saw that he was studying her. "I know," she said, staring down into her drink. "I am afraid. And I know that I am afraid."

It was as though, in her refusal to take the purple dress from her mother, she was saying no to life—to the red, the bright sensual and joyful heights; and to the black, the deep darkness and sleep, place of despair and dreaming. She was loneliness of the seed without light and pressed about by the weight of its own buriedness. It was as though she was a half a thing, and it was as though the life in her asked that she be neither one nor the other, strictly, but that she be both, yield to the red in her, and the darkness as well, that each have their play in her, their coming and going, doors opening and closing in herself to the power and sustenance of each. Red and black, the colors which make purple, the dress of life which the mother of herself extends to her, offers her, freely, to wear it, wear the purple dress of life, to be in life and alive. But the darkness of herself said no and she turned her back, turned her back on life—wanting the dress to be black, to submerge herself again in blackness, in the darkness of herself, where the color of the dress did not matter for there was no light to shine upon it. She wore black as though she was in mourning, as though she was in perpetual sorrow for her lost girl, the girl of herself, buried long ago, the life in herself she stifled and smothered, the red girl, the girl of the red hat.

Jim leaned back against the booth. "Take off your coat," he said, softly.

"What?"

"Take off your coat."

She looked at him, puzzled, faintly amused. She slid out of her coat, letting it fall behind her, revealing the soft gold dress beneath.

"Now unpin your hair."

She looked at him, not understanding.

"But I will look a mess. Why do you want me to do that?"

"Just unpin it."

She stared, bewildered, her lower lip began to tremble, a perplexed smile on her face. But she reached up and pulled out the long pins which held her hair in place and the heavy black hair tumbled loosely about her shoulders.

She pushed one side of her hair over her shoulder and let the other hang softly, carelessly, to one side of her face. She eased herself back in the corner of the booth and gazed at him, suddenly langorous, a smile on her face, a slightly saucy smile that he had never seen before. Her eyes, regarding him, were cool yet subtly flirtatious. Her face, in the red light of the neon from the window, was illuminated a soft and lovely rose. She was strangely beautiful. His heart quickened as he watched her. It was as though she had become a different woman, another Eiko.

"Now are you satisfied?" she asked, softly, a certain archness in her voice, her eyebrows lifted ever so slightly.

He could do nothing but gaze at her, silently, in her love-liness. He wished they were alone so he could take her in his arms, hold her close. He reached over the table and covered her hand with his and she dropped her eyes, modest, pleased with the answer in the gesture of his hand.

"Tokyo—Tokyo," he whispered.

She cocked her head to one side, smiling, questioning.

"What was it like? What was it like where you lived?"

She gazed past him, dreamily, with an inwardness of see-ing, as though seeing the faraway vividness of her past.

"We lived in a big house. It was once an embassy. What I liked best was the garden. There was a tree out back I liked to climb and sit in and read. I had the gardener prune the branches just so, so it would be easier for me to climb up. Oh, there was a pond, too. With a rock jutting up in the middle of it. There were two tiny bridges over the pond leading to the rock. I liked to sit on the rock in the middle of the pond and read books and dream. On summer days I would take off my shoes and stockings and splash my feet in the water. That was such a long time ago. I had almost forgotten. It is as though that was another me."

She looked into his eyes, the corners of her mouth crin-kling with a smile.

"That was something of Tokyo. Something I remember."

He gripped her hand.

"Tell me more."

But she drew her hand away and reached for her purse.

"No, I don't want to think of that now. That's past, and I do not want to cry—not here. Come, we'll go to the party—" and here the flirtatious gleam came into her eyes again "—we'll dance and drink vodka, sing old songs. Wouldn't you like to do that?"

"Yes. Yes, very much."

She slipped out of the booth and he got to his feet and held her coat out for her. She put her arms in it and he got his own and put it on. Out on the street they started around the corner toward the subway. A wind had sprung up and she nestled close to him, slipping her hand in his pocket, and he took it, holding it warm and close in his own, as they hurried down the street.

THE PARTY was in an old loft building far downtown, near the river. The streets were deserted as they walked to the place. They passed under the bridge and could hear the traffic rumbling overhead. They entered a narrow street with darkened buildings pressed close on either side. At the far end lights glowed in the upper windows of a building, the only lights on the block. As they got closer they could hear the sound of jazz coming from up above, breaking the stillness of the quiet street.

Jim pushed open the door and they entered a low gloomy hallway, weak bulbs in brackets on the walls. The hall was cold and Eiko shivered and moved close to Jim as they started up the dilapidated stairs, the boards loose and groaning beneath their weight. There were rusting fire gongs on each landing. At the top they paused to catch their breath, smiling at each other, then Jim pushed open the big door and they found themselves in a large room filled with noise—people laughing and dancing or sitting around a big table near the windows, drinking liquor out of paper cups.

A swarm of people so that Jim was tempted to grab Eiko and leave quickly before anyone saw them. But it was too late, already the host, a small man with dark curly hair, staggered toward them, a drink in his hand, his eyes half closed, a loose grin on his face, his body bent forward as though he would pitch forward on his face.

"Ah, Jim, good ole Jim," he said, coming up and laying a hand on Jim's shoulder, more for support Jim thought than anything else.

"Hello, Greg. You look like you got a head start on us."

Greg laughed, loosely, pitching forward clumsily. "Yes. Well, you know how scared I am at my own parties."

Blearily, his eyes made out Eiko for the first time. He tried to focus his gaze on her but his eyes kept sliding away, the foolish grin continued to play about the corners of his mouth.

Jim introduced them.

"A lovely lady. She's a very lovely lady, Jim."

He leaned close to Eiko, weaving, almost falling on her. She pressed closer to Jim.

"Look," Jim said. "Where's the drink? We're thirsty."

"On the table. Help yourself."

Jim took Eiko's arm and started to move away.

"Gonna get us a drink, Greg," he tossed over his shoulder.

"Come back. Bring back the lovely lady," called Greg; his knees buckled and he gripped the edge of a bookcase as he watched them go.

They moved through the crowd, dodging the flying arms and legs of the dancers, Jim meeting friends, shouting hellos, back-slappings, and introducing them to Eiko, briefly, and pushing on again. He found a corner and backed her into it.

"You stay put. I'll go get us a drink."

"Hurry back," she said.

He brushed her lips and started off toward the table where the drinks were. He didn't want to share her with anyone. He even resented having to get the drinks because he would have to leave her, even for those few moments. He wanted to turn back. But instead he wormed his way through the crowd and got the drinks quickly, spilling the liquor impatiently into paper cups, and hurried back to her. He found her in quiet conversation with another woman, and he was jealous of this woman having such intimacy with her and wanted to know, right away, what they had been talking about. But Eiko laughed, saying, "Nothing that would interest you," and he drew her to him, away, in a corner, leaving the other woman to go off somewhere else.

They stood in the corner, sipping their drinks quietly. Jim gazed about the room. There seemed in each one there a desperateness and lostness. They laughed too hard and talked too loudly. There was a self-consciousness in their movements and voices, a certain hardness and lack of innocence. They drank too much, and their pleasure seemed forced, as though they were working hard, working hard at having a good time, as though they wanted to believe, desperately, in the party and in themselves, believe again in an innocence they no longer had, in a deep sense of pleasure in themselves and others, in the life around them, a life which had shrunk, gone out slowly, like some bright warm glow guttering into darkness and disenchantment. The party made Jim feel cold, cut off, a bleak feeling of barrenness filled him. That he could touch no one there, or be touched, that he had no words to speak to them, that if he spoke to them they would not understand, and if they spoke to him he could only listen to them dumbly, uncomprehending. No words to silence the fear and bitterness which filled the room. No words.

The voices each had a hard edge of cynicism in them which was neither youth nor age—a light seemed to have gone out, there was only this desperateness, a seriousness, to play, to have a good time, which frightened him and made him turn away with a feeling of sadness, of hopelessness.

The pine trees! He put his arm about Eiko and drew her to him. She moved to him willingly, with a softness and yielding he had never known in a woman before. He walked her into the other room where now slow music played on the phonograph. The room was high-ceilinged, barren and stark. Huge canvases were stacked against one wall. The room was empty. They danced, she looking up into his face, not speaking. He kissed her and they danced slowly, without much movement. The bleak feeling left him, holding her brought him back to himself. He felt he was again inside his own life. She brought him back with the simple touch of her small hands, her warmth, and the feeling she gave him that she was there for him alone. The music stopped. He didn't want it to stop, he wanted it to go on, didn't want the feeling between them to be broken. But the clamor in the next room leapt up, breaking in his ears with a harshness that brought him back to where they were.

"We'll go," he said.

"Yes. They are all falling over. My ears hurt from the shouting."

"Come on. We'll go away. Just the two of us."

They slipped out and went into the room where they had left their coats. They got into them quickly and went to the door.

The last thing Jim saw before he closed the big metal door behind them was Greg attempting to climb up a high unsupported ladder in the middle of the big room, drunken, and the ladder veering wildly to and fro, sweat pouring down his face, his tense fists gripping rung over rung, the ladder swaying dangerously toward the crowd below, Greg's teeth clenched in a smile that was not a smile but a fierce grimace of rage and determination.

They went down the sagging steps, their arms about each other. On the subway back to her place they sat close, as though they could not get close enough, her head was resting on his shoulder. In his heart there was a calmness and sureness he had not known for a long time.

THE WIND BLEW IN at the window as they lay in bed, a gentle wind bringing with it early odors of lilac—lilacs burning in a flame of green fire. There was the softness of the breeze on their bare arms and shoulders. Below, the street was hushed. He watched her wan face in the shadows. Her hair fell back over the pillow.

She stared up at the ceiling and said, "There was a time I thought people were looking at me. I walked down the street and there were the people all looking. They were not, but I felt they were. That they were seeing into my heart, all my guilt and shame. And I fell down in the street, I could not stand up any more. I fell down in the curb, in the gutter, the weight of my shame pushing me down."

He tried to silence her. "You mustn't. Please. Please, Eiko."

"But I must tell you. I must be honest. I want to tell you."

He put his hand gently to her mouth, but she pulled her face away and began to speak again.

"I can contain myself no longer. I love you—very much. I trust you. You will not hurt me. They have hurt me. They have taken me and used me and made me nothing. And the worst is that I let them. So I am as much to blame. I was beat up. I am so afraid, but with you I am not afraid. Your eyes are so gentle. There is a kindness in you I trust. Your face is so slender and sensitive. But I do not want you to think me prostitute. I would want more than anything that you would not think me that. I do this because I want to do it, I want to be with you. I love you very much. I love you for all this that you are and I can keep silent no longer but must tell you so—because I do not want you to go from me—I do not want to lose you. Now I have said it. I am glad."

She clenched her fists at her sides and turned her head away quickly, her voice catching with a sob.

"Eiko, Eiko," he whispered, laying his hand on her arm.

"Oh, why do you get mixed up with someone as troubled as I?" she cried, wrenching away from him. "I will not hurt you. I would want that I not hurt you." She reached out and put her hands on his face. "You are a slender tree to put my arms around, and in the leaves of you the unseen birds sing. And in you is the smell of bark and leaf—a cleanness I have not known for so long. Let me rest in you, put my arms about you. You are so delicate, yet, strong. You are bird-song, and branch and leaf, as overhead, to reach out, enfold and protect me. Let me be under your shade, and under the sun of you that shines down through your branches—smell the rain of you and my feet pressed against the strength of your roots, my arms clasping you, my tree, my bird—"

He buried his face in her hair. Her face, crushed against the pillow in pain, "I am afraid, afraid," so that he paused, asking her if it was all right, if he was hurting her. She shook her head quickly once, no, her eyes shut tight, her mouth parted slightly. He bent to her, a little clumsy but slowly, with infinite tenderness. Her cries continued sharp, painful, her small hands smoothed his back—Jim, Jim—soft murmurs; hearing his name whispered so, a warmth rushed into his heart and filled him with joy—his name from her mouth soft and murmurous as the wind in at the window carrying with it odor of lilac—green fire in the burning tree—soft buds redolent in the quiet spring rain. Her face was pale and lovely in the shadows. He put his head in the hollow of her breast and held her close, her fingers stroked his hair, and in his heart he vowed to love her forever and ever.

He offered her, gently, darkly, the bright red of his youth and manliness—and she accepted him gladly, with a quiet, a joyful smile.

HE RAN HIS HANDS over her, delighting in the softness, the touch of her. She lay back amongst the pillows, a bemused smile on her face at his delight and fascination. There was a scar on her belly—a tough ridge of purple flesh. His fingers touched it for the first time and a chill trembled up his arms and into his heart. He had the fear that she would not be able to have children, that she was barren. He had the sudden sick realization that this was a great part of her sorrow and doom.

She went rigid and he drew his hand away, quickly, deftly, sensing that she knew he had discovered the scar, fearing that she might know his thoughts.

She withdrew from him, suddenly forlorn, biting her lower lip. Her face was closed to him. He propped himself on one elbow and stared at her.

"Eiko? Eiko, what is it?"

But she said nothing and got out of bed and went to the window and turned, crouching, half sitting on the low sill. She peered down into the street.

"Eiko," he begged, getting up on his knees. "Please."

But she was quiet. Her face became viperlike; her eyes narrowed and became cold and unseeing. The skin of her face went bloodless and pallid, the color drained from it. The skin itself became drawn and tight, stretched over the fine bones of her face so that he was aware of her high broad cheekbones and wide angular jaws. Her nose diminished, became more sharp, razor-fine. Her mouth became a tight slit so that he almost expected a forked tongue to dart out between her thin drawn lips.

The soft peach light of her skin vanished. She became a darkness. Her flesh looked clayey and cold. A subterranean chill gripped his heart, he could not take his eyes from her. There was a cold dry underworldliness about her, as though her very bones were pressed inward, as though she had shrunk into another being. Even the delicate bones of her arms seemed sharp, her fingers like knives. Her abundant hair in the breeze swirled about her face like black water. It was as though some witch had come to cast a spell upon her. Her face took on a blade-keenness, her face honed, as though to touch it would slice. He did not want to look at her, he tried to look away, but she was hypnotic and he was held by the powerful change in her. Remote and austere, she was like someone he had not known before, there was this under-self of her that fascinated and repelled him. He was frightened seeing her like this. He wanted to say some soft word, touch her with the quietness of his love, to bring her up into the world of warm sunlight again, have her be with him as she had always been.

He got up and went to her. He felt awkward and did not know what to do. Hesitantly, he reached out a hand and laid it on her shoulder.

"Oh, Eiko," he breathed, and tears started to his eyes. There was a pain in his heart as though a knife had been plunged there. "Eiko, I would not have wanted to hurt you for the world."

She stirred, as though aware, for the first time, that he was standing beside her. She stared at his hand on her shoulder, then her eyes went to his face and rested there. Her hand reached up and touched his fingers. She began to cry, softly, without noise, her shoulders shaking. He knelt down and put his arms about her, pressed his face against hers, feeling on his cheek the hot tears of her weeping.

"Don't, Eiko, please don't. I love you very much. I don't want you to cry. You see? I'm beginning to cry too."

And she lifted her head, biting her mouth hard, her face contorted with sobbing. She looked at him and threw her arms about his neck.

"Oh, don't do that!" she cried. "I don't want you to do that."

She stopped, trying to catch her breath, and pulled herself up, her hands resting lightly on his shoulders.

"The scar—you see—well, it is not certain," she said, trying to fight back the sobs. "I'm foolish. I'm upset. But it is not certain. So it may not be too bad. It may not. Oh, my Jim, my dearest Jim." And she pressed her lips to his face and he kissed her, her cheek warm and tasting of the salt of her tears.

"Eiko, it's cold here. You feel? There's a wind blowing. You'll catch cold. Come back to bed and I'll tuck you in. We'll sleep and soon it'll be morning—and the sun shining, and the birds in the trees. We'll have a big breakfast—scrambled eggs—"

She gave a quick rich little laugh and took his hand, like a child, delighted and happy, and let him lead her back to bed. He put her under the covers and pulled the sheet up under her chin, but, with a childlike frown, she pushed the blankets away.

"You be close to me," she said. "You are warm."

He climbed in and lay close beside her, taking her hand. They lay silent for awhile.

Then, "I'm so glad I found you," she whispered close to his ear, her voice drowsy. "I feel so lucky."

He smiled in the darkness, feeling the dead weight of his fear for her drift away. He felt buoyant and turned to her, saying, "And I—I'm lucky, too."

But she did not hear for she was already fast asleep.

He could not sleep for a long time he was so filled with happiness. He wanted to crow, to stand in the open window and sing his happiness to the sleeping world. He watched her as she slept, softly breathing, her small breasts rising and falling with a barely perceptible movement. He could not take his eyes from the dark shadows in the curves of her belly and thighs. She was so small and vulnerable, her face pale and at rest in the darkness, sleeping with a child's face, mindless and untroubled. Tangled strands of her rich black hair fell back over the pillow. He would watch over her through the night, let no harm come to her. It was as though he loved, again, the woman in himself, and so he could love her, completely, without resistance, without pretense. Because now he loved the woman in himself he could love this woman, take his life again in his hands, humbly and with awe. Watching her sleeping filled him with wonder and a deep peace. Drowsing, the peppery smell of lilac in an early April morning filled his nostrils.

Soon he himself slowly drifted into sleep and he had a vivid dream. He dreamed he was dancing over brilliant green hills.

✑ EIKO VISITS JIM

JIM LIVED in a small white clapboard house set back behind the big white one, nearer the road, that his landlady lived in. He had come to love the place with its high ceilings and old-style farmhouse walls made of lathing, the lathing put in slanted, practical, and stained the deep warm color of oak. With the old light brackets on the wall giving off a soft yellow light he sometimes dreamed he was in the saloon of an old riverboat—the dark and wandering Mississippi surrounding him in the night.

Out back, in the kitchen where he slept (it was warmer there), were four large windows where sometimes the moonlight shone in so brightly it awakened him and he could not go back to sleep and would sit up in bed and look out at the snow-covered field running down to the pond, frozen now in winter. Here and there over the field were pine trees, their boughs heavy with clumps of snow. Beyond the pond sparse

117

woods began and beyond that, more fields, so that he felt closed in, private, a sense of country and space.

Out front was the busy main street with its shops and houses. It was a small town. He liked living there.

He was very happy tonight. Eiko was going to spend the weekend with him at his place (she liked to ride buses, she said). It was wonderful, knowing she would be with him that night. It was really very wonderful to have someone, to have a girl again. It was like the end of a seven-year drought for him. It was like coming home. After wandering and being mistaken and lost for so long, she made him feel fresh and alive again. He said her name aloud. "Eiko." He liked to say it, liked the sound of it. Her image moved in his imagination, moved in him, as though she had become a part of him. She was so very small, like a child, with her handsome Japanese face. She was quiet and dark, strangely gentle. Now she was coming to be with him tonight. He wanted them to be together as much as they could.

Lately he was dreaming of green, of trees and hills. He knew that he still had a long way to go but at last he was back again on the right path. Sometimes he smelled such a pungent odor of lilac, as though there was in him a bright and wonderful spring. He was embarrassed to be so happy, and fearful too, afraid that it would not last.

But he babbled to anyone who would listen, like someone possessed, about everything and anything. A new light had come into his eyes and a brightness to his face. It was as though she had come to nest in him, as a bright bird sings in the branches of a tree, so he was filled and animated with the joy and gladness of her presence in him.

He did a sort of dance around the room, hopping from one long leg to the other, turning around and around, swinging his arms wide and laughing. He danced out to the kitchen and stood gazing up at the Japanese clay bell Eiko had given him and which he had hung suspended from the ceiling. He reached up and tapped the gold paper tail hanging from the clapper and the bell rang with a bright' and gentle tinkling. Soon she would be here. Soon.

He heard a scratching at the front door and stood still, listening intently. The scratching came again. He went into the other room and looked out through the glass but could see nothing in the darkness. He opened the door and the land-lady's dog burst in, its tail wagging furiously, and leapt about him, shivering and licking Jim's hands, low whines coming from deep in its throat. Jim realized with a sudden sharp pang that the dog was showing its gratefulness, and relief, for being let in out of the freezing night. As the dog jumped about him, eager, its mouth open wide in a kind of grin, its tongue hang-ing out, Jim went to the window and looked out across the yard. The big house was in darkness. His landlady had gone out for the evening, leaving the dog in the cold.

The animal continued to shiver and groan, as though its blood had begun to congeal in the frosty night and it would never get warm again. It lay down on the rug and began lick-ing at its frozen paws, licking feverishly between the toes with its long tongue, lapping at the tough leathery pads be-neath, the thick black claws. After the dog had licked both its front and hind paws thoroughly it got up and began to tug at Jim's trousers. He looked down at the animal, puzzled.

"What is it? What do you want?"

Its brow wrinkled, the dog looked up at him, still pulling at his pants. There was such intelligence in its eyes he almost expected it to speak, to tell him what it wanted. The dog sud-denly bolted away from him and stood in the middle of the room, its head lifted, its nose sniffing the air. Then it ran out into the kitchen as though looking for something and Jim followed it and found that it had gone into the bathroom. He discovered it looking into the toilet, its paws propped on the seat, its tongue hanging to one side and that grinning eagerness on its face, its head turned to him and one paw all but pointing down at the water in the bowl.

"You're thirsty, huh? Come on then."

The dog pranced beside him and Jim went into the kitchen and filled a soup dish with water at the tap. He set it on the floor, the dog nudging and kissing his elbows as he laid it down, and it immediately stuck its nose in the water and began to lap loudly and thirstily. The dog finished the bowl of water quickly and Jim poured it another. Then he went into the front room to look out the window to see if Eiko was coming yet. He glanced at his watch. It was getting late. Her bus should've been there by now.

The dog came in and lay down on the rug with a grunt. Jim turned and smiled at it and it looked back at him, as much as to say, Thank you. It made Jim feel good. He liked having the dog in the house. It made him feel less lonely. He was glad the animal was in out of the cold.

He looked again at his watch. She was twenty minutes late.

He put on his cap and gloves and jacket and opened the door and went out. The blast of cold air stung his ears. He shivered and stuffed his hands deep in his pockets and trudged through the snow down the drive and out to the street. He stood up on a snowbank left by the plows and looked first in the direction the bus would come, then down the street to the corner where she would get off. There was nothing in sight and he waited a few minutes more, turning down the earflaps of his cap and swinging his arms together briskly. The red neon signs of the bars glowed in the night toward the center of town. A few cars passed.

He walked back to the house, pausing at the door to kick the snow off his shoes. He opened the door and went in, his cheeks burning from the cold. The warm air felt good. He threw his jacket and cap on a chair. The dog was sleeping peacefully now, its heavy sides rising and falling slowly, raucous snores coming from down within its chest.

He stood watching the dog. She was the color of rich cream and very fat, so that she waddled when she walked on her short stumpy legs. Jim called her Pigdog, she looked so much like one. The landlady heard him call the dog this one day and she was offended.

"Her name is Cindy," she had said, stiffly. "She's heavy because she's been spayed."

Jim thought the dog's fatness was due to her tipping over the garbage cans and eating what she found there.

He sat down and tried to read but could not concentrate and threw down the book. He listened intently for the low diesel whine of the bus passing in the street. He went to the door again and again and looked out and came back, disappointed, not seeing Eiko running up the yard. "Maybe she's not coming" ran through his mind, and he tried to push the thought away. He kept glancing at his watch and, jamming his hands in his pockets, paced restlessly up and down the room.

The dog had awakened and lay on the rug with its head lifted, watching him, as though sensing in him his worry and impatience. Its dark eyes regarded him with a sadness and its ears stood erect, alert, as though the animal was trying to tell him that it understood, that it was ready to do anything he ordered it to do to help him.

Jim saw the dog watching him with its wide-eyed sadness and he squatted down, resting on his heels, and took the dog's big head in his hands and rolled it affectionately from side to side. Then he nestled his cheek against the dog's jowls and the dog licked at his face, its tail thumping the floor in happiness.

He played with the dog to break the anxiety of his waiting, but he soon tired of that and went to the door again and looked out. There was a small moon glowing through the tall pines in the front yard and the stars stood out crisp and sparkling in the clear night sky. His heart quickened at the sight of it and then he caught his breath, sharp, as he saw Eiko's small dark figure scampering toward him up the drive. He threw open the door and ran out to meet her, taking long ungainly steps over the snow in his haste. She saw him running to her and she let out a little cry and quickened her pace, her arms outstretched to him.

She flung herself into his arms and he held her tight, pressing his face to hers. He lifted her off her feet and burying his face in her hair, swung her around and around in the middle of the yard.

"You're here, you're here," he whispered happily.

"The bus—it took me past the town," she gasped. "I had asked the driver twice—but he had forgotten—I had to walk back—"

She was trembling and in tears, her body shaking convulsively.

"Eiko, my poor Eiko."

He lifted her into his arms and carried her into the house, kicking the door shut with his foot. The dog leapt up, watchful, its head cocked to one side. Jim laid Eiko on the couch and unbuttoned her coat. Her fingers snatched at his hands as he worked and she was biting her lower lip to fight back the tears.

"I was so frightened," she cried, "so frightened of the cars on the highway."

"Be still now," he whispered. "Be still. You'll be all right in a minute."

He took her hands and rubbed them briskly for a few minutes, then he slipped off her boots and rubbed her ankles and feet. He put his hands over her ears and massaged them gently, her cheeks as well.

"Oh, that is so good," she said, closing her eyes. "I'm beginning to come alive." She smiled up at him. He dried her tears with his handkerchief, and she began to shiver less now, to grow quiet.

"I'll get you something to drink and run some hot water in the tub so you can take a bath. Then you can tell me about it."

"Yes. A bath. A bath would be wonderful."

He wrapped a blanket around her and went out into the bathroom and turned the hot tap on full in the tub, then went to the cabinet in the kitchen and taking down a bottle of brandy poured some in a glass and brought it to her. He knelt beside her and gave her the glass and she took it, with a quick grateful smile, her hands fluttering nervously. She took a swallow and lay back, letting out a long sigh of relief.

"I am better. Much better. Thank you."

"I've got water going in the tub."

She took another drink of brandy and clasped his hand. Smiling, she said, "Now I am here. I am glad."

"Eiko, what happened?"

"Well, you see, I had followed your instructions very carefully. And when I got on the bus I made sure to tell the driver to leave me off as you told me. We drove for a long time and I began to get worried. I did not want to go up and bother the driver again, but I was so worried we had passed the place, I went up to him and asked him if we were near there yet.

He said, No, it was some distance away. We rode and rode. And again I began to worry, thinking he had forgotten me. I was so embarrassed to do it, so afraid, and yet I went up a second time and asked him if we were coming to the town. He put on the brakes, saying, Oh my God, we passed it a few miles back."

"What a stupid bus driver!" cried Jim.

"Well, he was apologetic—and he said I could do one of two things. I could come back with him on his return trip or he could let me off at a motel a little farther on and I could call a taxi from there. Since I already felt bad about being late to see you I said I would get off at the motel. He left me off there and I telephoned but could not get a taxi. So I walked back to the road and kept on walking and it was so cold—" she shuddered and her eyes went wide "—but the worst thing was the cars on the highway, they came at me so fast—I was so frightened—"

She began to tremble and cry again and she put her arms around him and he held her close, kissing her ears, her cheeks. "It's all over now. Be still, be still. You're all right now."

He could see her, leaping, in the headlights of the cars, like a startled doe, into the snowbanks at the side of the road, her mouth trembling and her heart beating fast. And climbing out into the road again, looking fearfully behind her, and hurrying along in the dark, trying to keep as far over as possible, squeezing herself small, so that the cars wouldn't hit her.

"I think my ear is frostbitten," she said, feeling one of her ears gingerly. "It burns so."

He looked at the ear carefully. It was red. He touched it.

"It looks all right," he said, and then a teasing light came into his eyes. "But if it's frostbitten it'll fall off in the night and we'll have to look for it under the pillow in the morning."

She giggled, putting her hand to her mouth, and he pulled

her to her feet and put his arms about her waist and drew her
to him.

"Hey, the tub must be full!" and he swung her off her feet
and into his arms and carried her, laughing and kicking, out
to the bathroom. Once inside, he set her down, still holding
her. She was so small he could rest his chin on the top of her
head, smell her soft dark hair.

"Everything's here," he said. "If you need anything, hol-
ler."

He clutched the doorknob but did not leave. The bathroom was warm and steamy and Eiko stood, her cheeks
flushed, with her hands clasped loosely at her stomach, gazing
shyly up at him, a softness in her face.

"Wait a minute," he said, and ran into the other room and
poked around in the closet and brought back a big flannel
bathrobe and handed it to her.

"You can wear this."

She took the robe and held the soft warm fabric to her
cheek.

"I was afraid to come," she murmured, not looking at him.
"I don't know why. But now I'm not afraid."

He took her face between his hands. "You see? It's nice
here, Eiko. You'll like it. And in the morning you can see the
pond and the pine trees out back. Everything's covered in snow
but you'll see how nice it is."

"Yes. I want to see it."

"When we wake up we'll have a big breakfast. Wait'll you
taste the coffee I make."

"Yes," she laughed. "I can't wait."

He felt suddenly shy and turned to go, then swung around
again and kissed her, still with a shyness, an awkwardness in
his gestures. There was that softness in her face—she seemed
less dark, less remote than the last time he had seen her.

"Take your time. No, don't take your time. Oh—well, do what you want."

She laughed gaily at his confusion and he went out, closing the door quietly behind him.

He went into the other room, stooping to scruff the dog's neck, and went over to the radio and turned it on. He listened a moment and soon soft music filled the room. He went about dimming a few of the lights, then he looked about the room and, satisfied, went to the window and peered out.

The light of the moon sparkled blindingly on the snow. The pines were black columns pressed against the cold light sky. Wind murmured through the branches with a gentle lifting and falling of the boughs, amongst them the soft low droning, wavering, quiet. He listened to the wind through the pines and then turned his head, hearing the splashings of Eiko in her bath. He pressed his cheek against the cold pane. The dog stretched, shutting its eyes tight, its jaws snapped wide and its tongue curled as it yawned with a shrill whine. It lay back and went to sleep again.

Jim's breath made a cloud against the glass. He moved his face away and with his finger traced the image of a flower on the steamy part of the window. He looked at what he had done, then continued to gaze out into the night, suddenly lost in deep thought.

Wind shook the branches of the pines.

Two years. Two years in a mental hospital. How could he possibly tell her about that? How could he possibly tell anyone about it? He didn't want to alarm her, to confuse or mislead her about it. "Eiko, I have something I want to tell you. Please understand. I wasn't violent—all my violence was turned in upon myself. . . ." She would find out. Perhaps he should tell her. "Eiko, I was alone . . . I was cut off . . . I wanted to die . . . But now, you see, it's all different. . . ."

He saw again a thin figure sitting quietly on a caged porch, staring through the bars, his eyes vacant and unseeing, his eyes looking through the bars at the green trees and not seeing the green trees, not believing they were there. Not the sky, not himself there, as though an invisible wall had come between him and the life around him, cutting him off from life, isolating him.

Two years. Two years of sitting on benches, constructed like crude heavy church pews, on the porches, on the wards, in dark hallways. Dead eyes and in his heart a deadness, not wanting to live, as though the quick of him had flown out of him and gone away, lost forever. He could not be touched and he could not touch. Yet, he was lonely for hands and the touch of hands, warm hands to break down the walls of silence.

Doctor Sylvan talking to him, talking for months. And Jim could not hear him. A voice breaking on dumbness—his heart a stone and his ears stopped up to all sound. Until his hands reached out one day and for the first time touched him, touched Doctor Sylvan on the arm—a reaching out from his isolation and loneliness, touching another living being, feeling the warmth of the flesh. He had burst into tears and he was held, sure and strong in the arms of the doctor, the doctor cradling him again in life. For an instant he was there as he had not been for so long; the doctor there. The trees were there outside the window, the sky. It was a beginning. Only for a few seconds were they real to him—but it was a first step, like seeing for the first time a small opening of light far ahead in the darkness that engulfed him.

He had been dead for so long and now he was coming alive again. He had been buried under the river of his life, sunk deep in himself where no life could touch him, where he could no longer reach out hands to touch another. He had been beyond hope and beyond dreaming. The light of his world had gradually shrunk. He had been falling, falling slowly down into darkness, into his despair of ever reaching out again, to take life in his hands once more. Failure upon failure drove him down, remorselessly, steadily, with a purposiveness he did not see or understand. At first he fought, he did desperate things, thrashing against the eclipse of his life. Once—twice—a third time he burst to the surface. There were no hands to grasp—nothing to keep him up. He began the slow descent, down into the nether regions of himself—floating down into despair and aloneness, the dark reaches of himself sending up, like flares in a fearful and slow-gathering darkness, flashes of warning—images of destructedness he did not, could not, understand. He had been utterly alone now, beyond understanding, beyond help, beneath, now, the warmth and comfort of hands, of sure words that would bring him back, keep him in life. Where would he go? Where was he going? He did not know and less and less was able to care. There was only the descent and a light going out of the world, a light going out in him, taking with it his desire to live, taking with it the sense and sureness of himself, that firm and central place in him.

He had lost everything. Will it end now? Surely it must end now, he had told himself, a voice screaming echoes in an empty room. He was sunk, beyond bottom, buried deeper than he had ever dreamed, and feared, to go. He had lost so much and could not believe that he had lost it. It would come back tomorrow, the next day. This would not last, could not last. He must die. Certainly he would die. There would be some mercy in it. He would not be made to suffer so. Darkness and the darkness beyond darkness—settling down beyond bottom—he had lost so much, he had been emptied, an empty thing, a rag bag flung down—

Now, gazing out into the clear night, he could see the purpose in the emptiness, the destructedness which dredged him out, sent him down into the deeps of himself to become a shell, a hollow thing, suffering in blackness and blind to the purpose of his despair and suffering. It was as though he must first be emptied, as though he must, painfully and in anguish, be cleansed of all that which had been in him, so that a new thing, a seed, might grow in him. A tiny greenness, as now, sensing in himself the first tender stirrings—odors of a distant spring— As now, he began to feel a new growth and life in him. But trying not to think of it, trying not to hope too much— As though it would be too much luck to have his life back again, to dream of having salvaged from the subterranean vaults of his being some tiny slender shoot of his life, a stirring, a small green stirring, the inexorable seed in the cleansed emptiness of his body and spirit. As though to hope and dream too much for it would be to ask too much, would be the risk of having dreamed to live again only to once more lose the chance of life.

He was like a man brought back from the dead. The drama in the inner deeps of his being had been silent. It was as though no one had seen, noticed. They could not understand when he tried to speak of it. He gave up trying and grew silent. He listened to the stirrings of new life within and dared not hope too much. But at times a wild elation filled him—that it could be so, that life could again move in him, that he would walk out again, as onto broad green hills and stand in sunlight and be at peace and at one with the life in himself and the life around him.

He had been brought back from the dead, and at times there was something in his eyes. It was as though he had seen an ineffable darkness, as though he had been to a far place few men have ever seen, that few men have ever returned from. He had made the long and perilous journey there and had returned. He had suffered, he had known anguish, he had wanted, even begged for, death. But he had come back, and he was intact. His eyes had seen something—an emptiness and darkness, a secret in the black core of existence.

He had come back and he was not the same. The journey had emptied him, had taken all that out of him which had once been him, had made of him a clean place for the coming in of new life—a small green thing to grow in that emptiness— As though in the descent, in the tortuous going down, he had lost his life only to find, in the black depths of himself, the stirrings of a new life, a new man.

She had come into the room so silently he did not hear her he had been so lost in thought. She stood in the doorway watching him, her small body bundled up in his big robe and held bunched about her middle. She was in her barefeet. He became aware of her presence and turned and gazed at her quietly. A lump came to his throat and his fingers tensed on the edges of the sill seeing her fresh and rosy from her bath, a ridiculous bundle of a small girl with only the tips of her fingers showing at the edges of the long sleeves, an uncertain smile on her face as though she were intruding, and her black hair—almost as long as she was—falling in loose long waves over her shoulders.

He sat down on the couch and motioned to her and she came to him and settled herself in his lap, putting her arms about his neck. She smelled so fragrant and cleanly warm. He put his face in the hollow of her neck and breathed deeply the clean warmth of her. His hands slipped in at the throat of the robe and touched her small breasts gently.

"Eiko, Eiko," he whispered.

He carried her to the bed and laid her down and kissed her. Then he went about the room turning out the lights, leaving only a small blue night light burning in the corner. He returned to her and lay down beside her. She moved over on her side to face him and part of the robe fell away, revealing in the soft blue illumination the sloping curve of hip and thigh.

His hand moved over her, moved down the sleek roundness of her belly, a melon, a ripeness, that thrilled him.

He stood up and slipped out of his clothes quickly, letting them drop in a heap about his feet. Then he lay close to her, delighting in the fragrant warm smell of her body.

The room was silent, except for the soft breathing of the sleeping dog in the far corner and the music on the radio which played muted, as though far away. The walls were deep with shadows and the night light cast a blurred bluish glow upon her face and shoulders.

Alive to her, he moved close and kissed her throat, his hands stroking the smoothness of her skin. Her lips parted and her eyes closed, her breath caught and her face looked as though she were dreaming as he moved to her, quietly and easily, without haste, whispering, "Eiko, Eiko," again and again.

Outside the windows the moon had sunk low in the sky. It was now a big tangerine moon sloping down behind the pine trees which were slender and dark against the star-filled horizon.

HE LIFTED HIS HEAD from beneath the sheet, still not fully awake, and with pleasant surprise saw her lying beside him and took keen pleasure in the morning-warm smell of her body. He broke into a grin and nestled his nose in her hair, remembering the night with a rush of happiness. She sighed in her sleep and moved away from him.

The morning sun shone in at the windows. The dog, Cindy, lay sleeping in the doorway to the kitchen, its head between its paws. Jim reached for his cigarettes and lighting one, lay back amongst the pillows, lazily blowing smoke-rings and watching them grow large and fade away.

She stirred.

"Hello."

She raised her head and, lifting the sheet a little, peered out like a heavy-lidded turtle. She pushed her thick hair back from her eyes and smiled up at him.

"I want to take a bath," she said.

"Not me. I'm not going to take a bath."

She looked surprised. "You're not?"

"I want to keep on me anything of you that might've rubbed off."

She laughed sleepily. "You are silly." She rumpled his hair with her fingers. He gripped her hands at the wrists, holding them firmly.

"Hey, what do you want to take another bath for?" he exclaimed in mock incredulity. "You had a perfectly good bath last night. What do you want another one for?"

"Well, as you remember, I have no tub. I have to take— ah—what would you say? *Dishpan* baths. So you see," she said brightly, "whenever I go to a place where there is a tub I take as many baths as I can."

He laughed and let go her wrists.

"Go take your bath then," he said, sliding out of the bed. "I'll get us some breakfast."

She knelt up and flung her arms about him and kissed him before hopping out of the bed ahead of him. "I am the first one up!" she cried, running off to the bathroom, skipping lightly over the dog in the doorway as she ran.

The dog heaved itself up and yawned, blinking stupidly in the light. She went over to Jim, her tail wagging, and Jim leaned down and petted her.

"Morning, Pigdog."

The dog ran over to the door and scratched at it.

"Okay, okay. A minute."

He pulled on his shorts and trousers and, slipping a T-shirt over his head, went to the door and opened it. Cindy shot out like a bullet, emitting short sharp barks, her breath steaming in the cold morning air, her body on its short legs sawing up and down, like a rocking horse, as she frisked about the yard.

Jim, snorting through his nostrils, shivered and closed the door.

THERE WAS a yellowness over all the world it seemed to Jim. The sun burst over the snow-buried fields outside the kitchen windows and with it there seemed to have risen in him a small sun of happiness that warmed his limbs and made him feel lightheaded. Softly humming to himself, he broke eggs into a big white bowl and beat them rapidly with a fork, then dropped the mixture into the sizzling frying pan. A strong aroma of freshly-made coffee filled the room.

"How can an American man understand an oriental woman?" came Eiko's voice from behind the closed bathroom door.

"What?"

"I said, how can an American man understand an oriental woman?"

"I don't understand *any* woman!" Jim shouted. "Oriental or not. Hurry up out of there. These eggs are almost done."

A moment later she came out of the bath, her cheeks pink, her hair freshly combed. She was dressed in her dark sweater and ski pants.

She paused and sniffed the air. "Mmm, it smells so good."

"I can fry eggs and make coffee and that's about the end

of my cooking ability." He smiled, leaning down to receive
her kiss. "Oh, and toast rolls!" he said, stooping quickly and
pulling open the oven door. "Just in time." He took out a pan
of crisp brown rolls and put them on a plate on the table.

"You sit down there and I'll dish it out."

She sat down at the table by the windows and Jim spooned
out the scrambled eggs onto plates, then poured the coffee.

He sat down opposite her and they ate in silence. There
seemed no need to speak. He felt at rest in himself, and satisfied, curiously emptied, yet, filled. He felt more sure of himself, and sure of her. And Eiko, too, seemed blissfully content.
He watched her as she ate, taking small bites from the hot yellow roll in her hands. She seemed to take pleasure in these
small things, a breakfast, being content to sit quiet with him,
turning her gaze now and then out the windows.

"It is very beautiful here," she said.

"Yes. Maybe the kids'll come this morning and go skat-
ing on the pond. Sometimes there're fifteen or twenty of them
and they get a big fire going in that old cement trough," he
said, pointing with his fork.

"I would like to see that. Do you skate?"

"Not since I was 16. I'd like to try it again."

"I used to skate a lot—in Japan."

"I didn't know they ice skated there."

"Oh, yes."

They lapsed into silence, which was not silence. There
seemed a something in the room, like a benign presence, im-
buing the four walls, and Eiko and Jim, with a warmth and
light, a yellowness that seemed to suffuse everything. They
were each quiet and there was a softness in her face; they
seemed filled with the pleasure and acceptance of each other.

The snow was so bright it hurt the eyes to look out the windows for very long. There was a wind and clumps of snow were blowing from the pine trees. Jim watched the loose snow blow in long sparkling trails over the fields. Suddenly a trio of bluejays flew into view, alighting in the snow with a brilliant blue beating of their wings. Jim watched Eiko as she sat, holding her breath, her mouth a small o, her eyes wide at the sight of them. Now, watching her, he knew that he did not have to be always *at* her—that he had to be always touching her. They had touched, in the night, deeply and irrevocably; they had met in darkness and had recognized each other. An unspoken wedding. And, yet, each remained a stranger to the other. They knew and they did not know—they had met, in a deep and mindless place—and now their bodies and spirits were satisfied, complete and fulfilled. Now he could care and not care, touch her or not touch her. She would be with him always, no matter where she would go, no matter where he would go, she would be with him. Apart, they would be together, for they had touched, deeply and wordlessly in a dark and unknown place, each in the other.

He wanted to bring her back to him, tried to distract her from the jays.

"I've had two dreams," he said.

"Oh!" she laughed, clapping her hands, turning from the birds. "Now you are paying me back for my telling you my dreams of the purple dress and red hat."

"No," he grinned. "These just seemed such wonderful dreams—I—well—I want to tell you."

"Yes. Let me hear them."

"It's the first dream made me want to tell you them," he began. "It had a—well, I'll tell you. I was to meet my mother in a certain building—she was coming to visit me. I was already late. I went to meet her, going up a long corridor.

Coming down in the opposite direction was a handsome well-dressed woman. She carried herself very well. There was a pleasant calmness in her face. The thing was that she was wearing a lovely dark blue hat—that kind of simple square-fronted hat that women wear in Japan when they get married."

"Oh yes!" interrupted Eiko, giggling and clapping her hands again. "Was she Japanese?"

"Well, no— The woman seemed to resemble my mother and as she approached me I looked at her but I thought, That's certainly not my mother, and I hurried on. I got only a few steps when I heard the woman speak to me. I turned and the woman was smiling at me and I saw, with surprise, that she was my mother and that I'd walked right past her and hadn't recognized her. She came up to me, embracing and kissing me. I was very glad to see her and as we walked down the hall a friend of mine came up to us. I wanted them to meet and I stopped and introduced them. 'Mother, I want you to meet my friend, Joe. Joe, this is my mother.' They both smiled and shook hands, they were very warm toward each other. 'Jamie is a wonderful son,' my mother said to him, calling me 'Jamie' which she hasn't done for so long. And my friend said, 'I like Jim very much.' I felt warm and good hearing this, I was so glad they liked each other.

"Now, you see," he said, smiling sheepishly, "it was mainly that Japanese wedding hat I wanted to tell you about."

"The hat is made that way to hide the horns—did you know that?" She laughed, holding an erect finger up on either side of her brow. "To hide during the ceremony the fact that the bride can be a devil as well."

He laughed.

"Well, it is an old Japanese superstition." She paused, as though pondering the dream he had just told her. "That's very interesting," she said slowly. "But you said there was a second dream. Tell me that, too."

"In that dream I was in my brother's house. It was the house he and his wife lived in just after they were married. They spent their honeymoon there. It had a red couch in the living room."

"Always red!" she laughed.

"I was standing in the kitchen and my brother and his wife came in. She was wearing—now you can laugh again," he smiled, "she was wearing a bright red dress. I went over to her to kiss her as I always do, but she backed away and looking out of the corners of her eyes, nodded toward the door. My father came in, followed by my mother. My mother stood in the doorway, in the background, and my father came to me and I was amazed, I'd never seen him looking so well. His face was a marvelous color and there was such life in his eyes. He came up to me with a warm wonderful smile on his face and said, 'It's so good to see you, son.' Then he put his arms around me and held me close. And I—well, I didn't know what to do. I was confused because my father had never touched me before, had never embraced me. He had never called me 'son.' But he was so open and warm, I put my arms around him, too, and kissed him on the mouth and pressed my head against his chest. I just held onto him because I knew, as though for the first time in my life, that he was my father and that I was his son."

He looked away, out over the fields, a tightness in his throat and sudden hot tears springing to his eyes.

"Well, you know," he said, quietly, not looking at her, "just the way he said it—'It's so good to see you.' It was wonderful to be called son—because—you see—I had never known—had never heard him call me that."

He broke off and stared down at his hands in his lap.

She was silent a moment, and then spoke.

"They are beautiful dreams. Strange," she said, gazing out the window, "that one must marry first the mother— whether one is a man or a woman—before he or she can marry another. And the father, too, as though one must wed him as well before one can wed another. Perhaps this, before you can love yourself, deeply, or can then love another. Otherwise, there seems always to be a yearning, a yearning back to them, like a child who is lost and frightened. His life is never satisfied. It is like drinking the salty ocean water and one's thirst is never quenched. One drinks more and more and gets thirstier and thirstier. I think that's what is meant, what is the meaning of it—a wedding of the two in you and not a looking back to the mother and father of one's childhood—a longing to remain a child, forever hungry and forever unfulfilled."

She looked at him directly.

"I have learned this in myself from knowing you. I have learned to understand this."

She paused a moment, casting her eyes down, as though uncertain how to go on.

"Jim, I have something I want to tell you."

He looked at her, puzzled, waiting.

"I woke up in the night. I could not sleep. I was thinking —I don't know how to tell you what I was thinking. I wanted to go away. I wanted to leave you. I thought that I would get up quietly and dress and slip out. I was going to leave you a note. I would not have wanted to hurt you. I lay there, writing the note in my head. Then I realized I would have to take the bus and I listened for the sound of one passing in the street, but there was no sound. I listened for what seemed hours. Everything was still and dark. And I knew the buses were not running. That it was freezing outside and there was no way to get away."

"Eiko," he said, with a catch in his voice. "Why? Why?"

"But I'm so glad I didn't go," she said, smiling brightly. "I'm so very glad. The night is over now and it's morning. Everything is all right. See? The sun is shining!"

And she laughed gaily and got up from her chair and ran around the table to kiss him.

"Why would you have wanted to do that, Eiko?" he asked, putting his arms about her. "I don't know why you would want to do that."

Her face grew serious, wistful.

"Because I was running again. Because I wanted to run from you. I wanted to run from all that you are and all that you have given me. All that you are offering me, all that I have ever wanted. It's so strange to run from the very thing you want and need most. Can you understand that?"

He nodded his head slowly and pressed her to him, laying his face against her stomach.

"But you mustn't run away. I don't want you to." He looked up at her, his face serious and troubled. "You promise?"

She nodded her head solemnly, like a child, and leaned down and kissed the top of his head.

"Now I will pour you some coffee," she said. "I want to wait on you."

She went to the stove and brought back the pot and poured fresh coffee into his cup.

She gazed at him quietly, holding the pot aloft.

"Please—understand—" she breathed, her lower lip quivering, her voice a soft and tearful pleading. She could not speak.

"Eiko—are you ashamed?"

She looked away, tears filling her eyes and falling down her cheeks.

"I am ashamed—sometimes. Sometimes I think it is not right."

He got up and took the coffee pot from her and set it down on the table. Then he gripped her by the shoulders and pulled her around to face him. Her face was haunted, frightened.

"Eiko, look at me. Why must there be that guilt? It's like a dark thing between us. It's like a worm at the core of an apple, and the worm crawls and gnaws away from within until the apple begins to shrivel and rot. I don't want that to happen to us. I don't want this dark thing between us, cutting us away from each other, making us ashamed, so we can't look each other in the eye. Look at me, Eiko," and here her tear-filled eyes looked up to meet his, "I don't want that worm of guilt eating away at what's between us. Do you see what it can do? What can happen to us?"

Sniffling, she nodded her head yes and rested her head against his shoulder. He pulled out his handkerchief and put it in her hand and she drew away from him and blew her nose hard and dabbed at her eyes.

"Now we will not talk about that any more," she said, twisting the handkerchief around and around her thumb. She forced a timid little smile and said, "May I take this?"—indicating the handkerchief.

"What for?" he laughed.

"I want to wash it for you and iron it for you. May I?"

"All right."

"Good. Now we will sit down and finish our coffee."

The chill which had seemed to come over everything had vanished and Jim sensed the joyous yellowness come into the room again. He felt good now and, smiling across at her, picked up the cup of coffee she had poured for him.

He rode with her to the edge of town. The big powerful bus moved too fast along the highway it seemed to him. Soon he would have to get off and leave her. If only the bus would slow down, or pick up more passengers—anything to delay his departure from her. The thought of this made him silent because he did not want to see her go. He sat beside her on the plush high-backed seat and held her hand, not knowing what to say. So poignant was the thought of her leaving that he could not bring himself to look at her, as though he had, to protect himself from the pain of it, already taken leave of her.

She sat quietly beside him, near the window, as though lost in thought, watching the snow-covered fields and the thin bare woods flash by.

"Look. I want to see you again. Soon."

She turned her head from the window, but he did not look at her. She leaned over and kissed his cheek.

"I'll call you. I'll call you tonight to see if you got home okay."

He squeezed her hand.

"I've got to go now. That's my stop just ahead."

He started to get up but she did not release his hand, and continued to hold it tightly.

"I have had a beautiful time," she said, and there were tears glistening in her eyes. "I wanted to tell you that."

He bent down and kissed her mouth, quickly, and started to go.

"Jim."

He swung around to look at her. There was a stark loveliness in her face. Her mouth trembled.

"Don't think too badly of me."

His mouth opened. A look of surprise came over his face.

"No— Oh, Eiko, no."

She looked away.

"Hurry now. You'll miss your stop."

He hastened back to her, kissed her hard. "I love you," he murmured, and ran to the front of the bus to be let off. The bus driver put on the brakes and the bus came to a halt. The folding doors slapped open and Jim leapt down and stood off on the shoulder of the road as the bus started up again. He watched each dark-tinted window as it passed and then saw her—her face pale and smiling, waving at him, looking, to Jim, at that instant through the smoked green glass of the window, as though she were some remote and lovely undersea creature. He waved back, grinning, and the bus moved on. He watched it go as it gathered speed down the highway. It turned a curve farther on and disappeared from sight.

He started walking back into town, his hands stuffed deep in his pockets and kicking with the toe of his boot loose stones along the asphalt shoulder. Perhaps he should have ridden with her back to the city. Just to see that she got there all right. Just to be with her that much longer. But she had protested it was unnecessary and hadn't wanted him to do that. He would see her again soon. Very soon. And this thought comforted him.

A cold wind began to blow and he pulled his muffler up around his chin and leaned into the wind, hunching his shoulders. A flock of blackbirds flew up from several trees near the road, the bare branches shining and thrashing in the wind and sun. Soon it will be spring, he thought. Suddenly he realized that he was headed home, alone, that she would not be there. He had gone home to the empty house many times but this was the first time the thought struck him as distasteful. But maybe it wouldn't be so bad, he thought—perhaps her presence had served as a kind of blessing to the house; perhaps this spirit of her lingered in the rooms like a benign and comforting warmth. He thought of the yellowness of the morning hours they had spent together and quickened his footsteps, eager to see if this were so, if some part of her had imbued the place with her quietness and loveliness. The thought of the big rooms being cold and ashen left him and he broke into a trot, hurrying homeward down the road with a silent happiness in his heart. It would be so, he thought joyfully, because he and the house would be lonely for her.

◦§ GREEN BEER

JIM SAT DOWN wearily on the bottom step of the brownstone house. He wasn't sure where he was and tried to make out the street signs on the corner, but they were too far away. He leaned back on his elbows and rested his head on a higher step, closing his eyes. He had been in the city since the day before, walking the streets aimlessly, looking for Eiko. He had been to her loft a dozen times that day and knocked at her door but there had been no answer. And he had called her, for the past week, so many times he had lost count and had let the phone ring longer and longer, hoping with all his heart that she would pick it up and he would hear her voice. He kept his eyes closed now, wondering what he should do and where he should search for her next. His feet hurt from so much walking and he felt hot and tired. He couldn't understand Eiko's sudden disappearance and was worried that perhaps she was ill or that something terrible had happened to her. As he lay back on the step he imagined, with a heart-sickening pang, that she had

144

been run over by a car. He saw her lying unconscious in a hospital bed, her lovely Japanese face the color of ashes. With a sharper pang, he imagined her small body stretched lifeless on a slab in the morgue, unidentified, her body pale and cold.

He sat up with a shudder and opened his eyes. He would not think of that. It was too unbearable. He looked up and down the street. What shall I do? he thought. I don't know any of her friends. Maybe I should call the police.

At the corner was a drugstore and Jim pulled himself up off the steps and walked down towards it. I'll call her again, he thought, daring not to hope too much. And after that I don't know what I will do.

When he got to the drugstore he went in and walked to the telephone booths in the rear. He stepped into one and closing the door after him, dropped a dime in the slot and, with a heavy feeling of futility, dialed Eiko's number. He sat tense, apprehensive, as the phone on the other end rang. He did not expect anything, he knew that her phone would ring and ring, that she would not answer and that he would hang up, frustrated, angry, just as it had been for the past week. It was ridiculous to go on trying, he thought bitterly, and as he lifted the receiver from his ear to put it back on the cradle, his heart almost stopped beating and the receiver trembled in his hand as the phone at the other end clicked up and he heard Eiko's voice say, "Hello?"

"Eiko! This is Jim," he blurted into the mouthpiece.

"Yes. You are talking too loud. You hurt my ear."

"I'm just nervous I'm so happy. Excuse me. For Godsakes, where have you been? I've been worried sick."

He felt so relieved to hear her voice it was as though a heavy stone had been lifted from his shoulders.

There was a pause.

"Eiko?"

"You may come to see me," she said finally.

"Eiko, is there anything the matter?" he asked, an uncontrollable tremor in his words.

She ignored the question. "It is now three forty-five. You may come at four-thirty."

"I can't wait to see you," Jim said, smiling eagerly into the receiver. "It's been so long, Eiko."

"Has it?"

There was a crispness in her voice. "Four-thirty then. Good-bye." She hung up.

The smile left Jim's face and a look of bewilderment came into it. He stared into the earpiece, puzzled, then set the receiver slowly back on the hook. He slid open the door and as he crossed the store and went out into the street a jauntiness came back into his step, the tiredness he had felt earlier left him and he began to feel happy again. He was going to see her.

He hurried off in the direction of the subway. On the ride downtown he worried about his meeting with Eiko. She had sounded so different, so unlike the Eiko he had known. He suddenly wondered if there could be something wrong between them, but just as quickly pushed the thought from his mind. He didn't want to think of that. "You may come at four-thirty," she had told him on the telephone, as though, like a queen to a devoted servant, she was granting him a brief audience to plead his case. A feeling of dark apprehension came over him.

Once out of the subway Jim stopped in at a nearby liquor store on the way and bought a bottle of red wine. Maybe this will help to ease things a little, he thought to himself hopefully as he went out of the store, clutching in one arm the brown paper bag with the wine and walked down the street to the building where she lived. The first surge of lightheaded joy at hearing her voice was slowly vanishing, his happiness was dissolving and in its place uneasy doubts crowded in.

He climbed the stairs to Eiko's loft with a heavy heart. He paused at the first landing and gripped the railing. The long flights of stairs went straight up to the top floor and he stood for a moment as though he wanted to turn around and go back down, as though he were not able to climb so high. Instead, he sighed and taking a firmer grip on the brown paper bag, he plodded up the steps again with great effort, his head bowed and his shoulders stooped. Perhaps it won't be as bad as I think, he thought. I'll try to make everything all right.

When he got to the top, he walked down the dark hallway to her door and waited a moment, listening. There was no sound within. He knocked loudly, impatiently.

In a moment the door opened and Eiko stood before him, her face very pale, her delicate oriental features drawn, the small slanted eyes cold and lifeless, her long black hair almost without lustre. She was not as he remembered her. The once soft glossy hair was swept back severely over her forehead. She did not smile but with a brief curt gesture of her hand motioned him inside. He saw that she was not wearing lipstick. As he stepped past her, he gazed at her, questioning, feeling awkward and tongue-tied, a sinking feeling in his stomach at the change in her. Her lips were thin and drawn, as though she no longer had a mouth.

He stood in the middle of the room and gazed about him self-consciously. He stared at Eiko and then stared away as she closed the door with a smart snap. She came into the room, standing well away from him, her hands stiff at her sides, her face set, revealing nothing.

The loft was as he remembered it—an enormous stark room with tall frosted-over windows at either end, a skylight, all darkened now with early evening. The grand piano, its top closed, stood in the middle of the floor—the floor with its heavy planking scarred and grease-caked as though a factory with its machines had been there before Eiko had moved in. There was the wide low bed near the wall. There were the gray bricks exposed through the broken plaster, and the two stiff-backed chairs against the wall. There was only one new touch: a rough canvas was stretched over the bricks and it was smeared with thick black strokes of paint forming, in a gray background, abstract shapes which were almost indistinguishable from the drabness and brokenness of the wall on which it hung.

Eiko, just as when Jim had first visited her, was dressed completely in black—black sweater and black close-fitting trousers. Even her stockings and pointed shoes were black. She was like some dark nether-creature with her swarm of jet hair tumbling over her shoulders, and only her hands and face, like white paper, revealed out of the animate darkness she seemed to him.

"Aren't you going to say hello?" Jim said timidly, and laughed, a nervous laugh that quickly died away. He turned from her, not able to bear the cold determination in her eyes.

"We will have tea," said Eiko, and turning curtly walked off in a tiny stiff gait toward the kitchen at the rear.

"I brought some wine," Jim called to her, holding up the paper bag. "Red wine," he added hopefully. "You like it so well. Remember, Eiko?"

She turned halfway around. "I do not care for any wine," she said, nodding her head briefly, then marched into the kitchen.

"Eiko?" And he felt his voice sounded too loud in the emptiness of the huge loft. He took a step forward and stopped, looking about him fearfully, as though he expected echoes of her name to come crashing down around his ears.

There was silence. She stood in the doorway, her fingers clutching the jamb, gazing at him coolly. He took a few steps to her, his arms extended, a pleading, almost tearful look on his face.

"Eiko, what's the matter?" he asked softly.

She glanced at him a moment, her eyes glinting, a chill and darkness in them he had not seen before. Then, as though for the fraction of an instant touched by the genuine bewilderment in his face, she dropped her gaze, staring at the floor, her lower lip trembling.

"I will make tea," she said and spun around, disappearing into the kitchen.

Jim dropped his arms and turned back to the center of the room. He put the bag down on the small round table by the bed. Slowly, he began taking off his coat and bunching it up threw it on the bed. He put his hands in his pockets and strode over to the windows. He rubbed his fingers against a sooty pane as though to try to see out, then rapped his knuckles hard against the glass and swung around, chewing pensively at his knuckles, and leaned heavily against the sill.

Eiko came out of the kitchen carrying a tray with two earthen cups and a small pot of tea. She seemed unaware of him standing in the dark corner and he watched her as she walked down the length of the long room, her eyes lowered steadfastly on the tray. She set it down on the table near the bed and stood up straight, clasping her hands at her breast, her head, darting here and there about the room, like a small eager bird, Jim thought, as he stepped out of the shadows near the darkening windows and into the lighted area of the room.

She looked at him, then, with a look of indifference, knelt down to pour the tea.

"Did you think I'd gone?"

"Your coat is still here," she said, nodding toward the bed. In her two slender hands she held up to him a cup of steaming tea. He took it and sat down on the edge of the bed, carefully, so as not to spill the tea and glanced at her. Eiko remained kneeling on the floor and held her cup to her mouth and took a small sip. She did not look at him or speak.

He put down his cup on the table and held out his hand to her.

"Come on, Eiko. Sit beside me here." And he smoothed out a part of the coverlet next to him on the bed.

She did not stir or take notice of his hand. Jim let it fall lifeless in his lap.

"Eiko. You're so different. I don't understand. Please tell me."

She looked at him, a quiet defiance in her eyes.

"We will drink our tea. We will speak of simple things."

She buried her tiny nose in her cup and drank again.

Jim slid off the bed and crouched down beside her. Tentatively he reached out, as though fearful that to touch her would burn him. He rested his fingers lightly on her shoulders.

"What's the matter?" he asked, his voice dry and cracked. "Have I done something to hurt you?"

She shrank away, a surly twist to her mouth, as if something unclean had touched her. She put down her teacup and stood up, folding her thin arms tightly over her breast. She moved away from him, her back turned.

He arose too quickly and awkwardly bumped the table with his knee, sloshing tea out of the pot. He leaned down abruptly to steady it. Eiko had gone to the shadowy front of the room, to the windows, and was looking out, staring out on nothingness. He moved to her with slow heavy steps, his fingers uncoiling, reaching out to her.

"Please—tell me," he breathed. "You make me very unhappy not to tell me. I've been walking the streets since yester-day looking for you."

"There is nothing to tell. That is all over," she said flatly.

"Over?" And he said it so quietly it was almost a whisper. He went to the window and stood before her. "But why, Eiko?"

"Because," she said, glaring up into his face, her mouth twisted, her eyes squinted, ugly. "Because it is over. I want no more of that."

She was an Eiko he no longer knew. His face looked stunned, unbelieving. A dull ache began to throb in his heart.

He moved to put his arms about her but she hurried away from him and stalked out of the shadows and into the light of the room. Going to the table, she squatted and poured more tea into the cups, her hand trembling slightly.

"I don't want to talk about it," she said. "We will drink our tea and not talk about that."

"I've brought wine," Jim said, as he stepped out of the darkness of the corner and stood near her, his hands clenching and unclenching at his sides. "It's good wine, Eiko. You'll like it. It's red wine. The kind you like."

She clasped her face slowly in her hands, her face which had become suddenly tormented, as though she were about to cry.

"I do terrible things when I drink," she said with a catch in her throat. "I do not want to drink."

"Let me open it. Just taste a little of it," he coaxed.

"Do as you like."

Regaining her composure, she sipped at her tea. With long eager steps, Jim strode out to the kitchen. He rattled around in several drawers.

"Where's your corkscrew?" he called.

There was no answer.

He came to the doorway and called again. "Do you have a corkscrew?"

"I haven't any," she answered quietly, still kneeling by the table.

"I'll use a knife then," and he plunged back into the kitchen where he fumbled around in the drawers once more. He pulled out a long bread knife, closed the drawer, and came back into the room, running his thumb over the edge of the blade.

"You keep sharp knives," he said, and leaning over took the wine from the bag. He stood over her, his legs spread wide, the bottle clutched in one hand, the knife resting loosely in the palm of the other. He hefted the knife lightly in his hand and stared down at her.

She was silent, her dark head bowed on her slender neck, the flesh of her neck the color of cream in the warm light of the lamp suspended from the ceiling. Her tiny hands were folded in her lap, her legs tucked demurely under her as she knelt.

He stood over her, tall and erect, as though waiting for her to speak.

I could plunge the knife into her neck, he thought. Into the soft white skin and see the dark blood spurt.

"A dull knife is a nuisance," she murmured, unmoving. Jim's hands began to shake. Beads of sweat formed on his upper lip. He set the bottle firmly on the table and taking the knife plunged it deep into the cork of the bottle and pulled out the stopper with a sucking noise. There was a quiet pop. He held the knife aloft, over Eiko's head, the cork impaled on the tip of the blade. Drops of the red wine spilled down on her thighs. She started up, feeling the wetness on her legs. Jim leaned down quickly, apologetically, to brush at the wine stains.

"I'm sorry," he said, his hands moving too quickly over her, his hands drained of color and trembling.

"It's all right!" she answered petulantly, pushing his hands away. She rubbed at the spots on her trousers. "The cloth is black and the wine doesn't show."

He seemed not to know what to do, as though anything he might do would be wrong. He knelt beside her, held the bottle to her.

"Are you sure you won't have a glass? Try it, Eiko."

She closed her eyes and did not answer. He stood up, jerkily, and not knowing what else to do tilted the bottle to his mouth and drank. He wiped his mouth with the back of his hand and stood quietly gazing down at her.

"Where have you been? For a whole week, Eiko, you haven't answered your phone."

"I have been here," she said with sudden direct honesty, looking straight into his eyes. "I have been hiding."

"Hiding?"

"From you. From everything. I do not know how to explain."

"Oh, Eiko," he breathed, squatting down close to her on his heels. "Why didn't you tell me? Why didn't you let me know? What can I possibly be to you that you can't tell me?"

"I am afraid of you," she said quietly.

He stared at her, not understanding.

"Oh, you will not hurt me," she said quickly. "I do not fear that. Except that you are like a door opening and you bring with you a life I cannot take or bear. I have been happy these past two weeks, not answering the telephone, keeping the door locked to everyone and everything. I have not gone out. I even managed to find myself singing in the mornings. I have written dozens of poems. See?" And she fluttered her fingers toward the piano on top of which a sheaf of papers lay neatly stacked. "I have painted a picture." And here, again, her hand motioned to the far wall where the dark unrecognizable shapes of the painting hung. "I have been happy in my way, like a little cricket singing in its cage."

She smiled wryly and twisted her fingers in her lap.

"But I must tell you," she said, looking up into his eyes once more. "It is over between us."

He started up, protesting, but she waved him back.

"I know what I am and what I must do," she said. "I will wear black and keep the door locked and not answer the telephone. Sometimes I will sing in the mornings and know that the sunlight is outside the windows. It will be pleasant to know the sunlight is there, but I do not wish to be out in it. Now you know why I have not called you or wanted to see you. I see you now to tell you this. It is nothing you have done. It is nothing either of us have done. It was all there—far back in some instant we had no control over. A pattern, a shape, with pieces falling neatly into place. Like numbers, immutable. There is no way out. It is as it is."

"Oh no, Eiko, you're wrong," he breathed softly and gripped her by the arms and with serious eyes looked into her face. But she closed her eyes and shivered, turning her face into her shoulder and with a sharp cry of anguish leapt up and like a small frightened animal scurried to a far corner of the room, pressing herself into the corner, seeming to want to make herself small, to hide in some way from him. It was as though she tried to become one with the wall.

"Eiko, don't run from me," Jim said, advancing toward her. "I don't know why you should want to run from me."

She leaned back tighter against the wall, her hands hidden behind her, her shoulders hunched, a look on her face as though she would spring at him if he came nearer.

"Eiko. Don't look so scared," he said, a few steps from her now. "I'm not going to hurt you."

Her eyes darted from side to side as he approached and, to keep her from escaping, Jim stretched out his arms wide and leaned his hands against either wall, hemming her in.

"We've had such fine times together, Eiko," he said, bending close to her. "Walking here to see you I was thinking of them. Remember when you came to visit me? The pine trees —and the pond in the back yard? You wore my bathrobe."

"That was another me!" she cried, a look of desperation in her face. "That was not I! That was another Eiko."

With her hands she shoved out at him, to drive him away, but he held fast and she ducked under his elbow and scampered back to the middle of the room.

Jim swung around and stared after her, perplexed, a troubled expression on his face.

She was breathing rapidly, rubbing fiercely at her arms as though they were cold.

"I don't want to go," Jim said quietly, walking to the table. "I don't want to leave, seeing you like this. So unhappy. It frightens me and makes me sad."

"I cannot tell you more than I have. I have no words," she said in an almost inaudible whisper. "Perhaps it is better that you go."

"I know what," Jim said, coming toward her. "Let's go have some dinner. Have you been eating, Eiko? You'll feel better after you eat, and we can talk. Oh, Eiko, I'll hold you in my arms and you can tell me everything."

And he really did believe that the strength of his love could change everything between them, make everything right again. His eyes brightened and, encouraged by his feeling, he smiled more broadly and put his arms about her. For the briefest moment the soft light he loved came into her dark eyes. Her face drained of its clayey-ness and took on the warm peach hue he had remembered. A rush of hope flickered in his heart only to die down as quickly, for in an instant the bright change in her vanished and her features became once more empty, grim and set, set against him.

His face collapsed, seeing her so. His hands felt suddenly numb on her shoulders, the fingers cold, as though the life had bled out of them. His arms dropped like dead sticks at his sides and, dejected, his head bowed, he walked away from her and stood staring down at the scarred greasy planking of the floor.

I've tried, he thought bitterly. And I don't understand. I don't know what more I can do.

"I want you to leave me now," he heard her say, her voice in his ears like dead flowers rattling in the wind. A coldness congealed his heart and he felt dizzy. He thought that he was going to fall and moved toward the wall as though to brace himself, a heaviness in his chest like weights of lead. He could barely breathe. The image of his mother and father rose vividly in his mind. The father who had never touched him, the mother whom he had tried to touch, he tried desperately to touch them all his life, to reach them, to be held, strong and upright in their arms—a stripling green thing dreaming of poles to grow upon.

He had been so closed and fearful of touching because he did not know how to touch. He saw that his hands fluttered now, sweating and nervous, like birds. But they didn't know how to do it. There was only his strong desire to touch, to touch this girl again without embarrassment and shame. Birds of the hands, crippled things flapping in a deep nest, a cage of the hands.

There was the same suffocating heaviness in his chest— He had sought, always, to reach out, but it was as though his hands were not made to touch or to hold for long, or he himself be touched or held. To hold what he loved dearly. Broken hands, the fingers cracked, leapt into his mind—trembling butterfly wings in the grass—birds of the hands, the fingers like broken wings, his hands fluttering now against the grimy brick wall like maimed things, the fingers trying to dig in, to hold on, to find something permanent, solid, to cling to, to grow straight and strong upon. With his nails it seemed he was trying to scratch out the cold blackness of the grime to get to the warm familiar red of the brick beneath. He pressed his head against the wall, crying, his fingers clawing at the loose bricks.

Eiko made a swift gesture to his shuddering back, her brow wrinkled in sudden anguish and sympathy, but as swiftly dropped her hand and biting her lower lip, turned away from him.

"Of course, we can see each other now and then," she said. "We can go to a museum. Or talk of simple things over a cup of tea."

Her words were like dry paper, blank and meaningless to him. He turned about to face her, took a step toward her. She shrank back. There was terror in her eyes, seeing the look of hurt and rage on his face. He gripped her wrist tightly and she winced.

"Please let me go," she said, a quaver in her voice, her fingers toying dumbly at her throat. "You are hurting me."

He made a quick movement with his arm as though he were going to strike her and she leapt back, alarmed, but instead he swooped over to the table and seizing the bottle of wine in his hand, clutched it tightly about the neck, his knuckles going white, and swinging around heaved the bottle at the wall with all his strength. The glass smashed and exploded in a burst of green splinters about him. The wall was splashed with the dark wine and trickles of it ran down the blackened brick.

Tears sprang to his eyes and his throat worked noiselessly.

He put his hands to his mouth and closed his eyes, tears spilling out over his cheeks. Going to the bed he picked up his coat and silently walked toward the door.

Eiko stood stiff, cold, her lips dry and thin, and yet she seemed so forlorn as, with his last glimpse of her before he slammed the door shut behind him, he saw her standing, a small dark creature, utterly alone in the middle of the empty room.

Jim ran down the steep flights of stairs—running, running again, he thought in sudden panic. Out in the street he stood for a moment undecided, looking both ways. He did not know where to go. He could get the bus and go home. The loneliness of the house. The thought of the house depressed him. Again, he looked up and down the street. His heart was beating fast and he felt feverish. People hurried home in the early spring dusk. The street lights were coming on. He wiped his face with his handkerchief, then jammed his fists in his pockets and began to walk, aimlessly, not watching where he was going, his eyes down on the pavement. He wanted to get out of the neighborhood as quickly as possible, get away from where she lived, away from her. He had a bad taste in his mouth, acrid. He coughed phlegm from his throat and spit into the gutter.

Ahead, he saw a green neon sign burning in the darkening deserted street. He headed toward it, his head bunched between his shoulders, looking as though he were fearful someone might strike him from behind.

The heaviness grew in his chest—a dull ache of suppressed rage and hopelessness. There was a sudden sliver of pain in his heart, like a needle had been jabbed there. He tried hard not to think of Eiko, to block out the thought of her. The heaviness mounted, and the dull persistent ache. He would *not* think about her, he told himself angrily. He would *will* not to think of her. But he knew it was no good. Kidding himself. He felt sud-

denly bone-weary, drained. To lift each foot up and put it
down seemed to take a tremendous effort. When he got to the
swaying neon sign of the bar he decided he would have a shot.
Perhaps that would lift his spirits. He pushed open the door
and went in.

The bar was empty. He paused a moment at the door, disappointed. He had wanted it to be warm and glowing, filled
with the quiet talk of workmen having a beer before going
home to supper, to lose himself in the quiet talk and laughter
of men. The place seemed to be just opening. Only half the
lights were on. The other half of the room, where there were
fat leatherette booths, was in shadow. A slightly pretentious
place, as though its owners had tried to make it a kind of fancy
cocktail lounge.

"Good evening." It was the bartender coming around behind the big curving bar.

"Hello." Jim took off his coat and hung it on a rack near the
door, then went and sat down on one of the high overstuffed
stools at the bar.

"Cool enough for you?" asked the bartender, wiping the
space in front of Jim. "Doesn't seem like spring."

"No."

"What'll you have?"

"A shot. And a beer chaser."

The bartender reached for a bottle. He was young and
plump, about Jim's age. He set the beer and whiskey in front
of Jim.

"Here's to spring," Jim said, lifting the shot glass.

"The sooner the better," smiled the barman.

Jim swallowed the whiskey in one gulp and ordered another.

"Could you turn those lights on?"

"What?"

"Aren't you going to turn your lights on?" Jim repeated, nodding toward the darkened part of the room.

"I always leave them off. When there's not much business."

"It'd be cheerier. If they were on, I mean."

The bartender stooped beneath the bar and flicked a switch. The other side of the room was instantly bathed in a soft chrome-yellow light.

"How's that?"

"Much better," Jim said. "Thanks."

The bartender looked at him and smiled. Jim held the shot glass up again, tilting it toward the bartender. "To the end of darkness," he said, and drank the whiskey neat.

The bartender moved on to the other end of the counter and Jim sat slumped and heavy on the stool, waiting for the whiskey to warm him. He felt stunned and as he sat waiting for the calming warmth of the drink, he remembered the inertness of his past illness. It was like that now, he thought, like being buried in mud, unable to lift or sink deeper. In the mire. Like pigs. Dreams of sties. The not caring, not wanting to live. To stay buried in mud, where life couldn't touch him. To be safe and protected—dead and not yet dead.

He ordered another drink and sipped it slowly. He gazed about the empty room, wishing there were others there, someone he could talk to, or listen to. But the bar was silent. The bartender, his leg propped on a beer case, was figuring up something on a piece of paper at the far end of the bar.

The face of Doctor Sylvan came into Jim's mind—Doctor Sylvan who had brought him back to life, whose warm hands had reached out and touched him, hands that had helped lift him from the darkness of his buried life when he had lost all hope of ever living again. He wanted to talk to him. He would tell him everything and Doctor Sylvan would listen and his face would be dark and quiet and he would understand. Then Jim knew he would not feel so much alone.

He looked around the place. There were telephone booths in the rear. He could call him, long-distance, tell him what had happened with Eiko. He started to get off the stool but then sat back down again, burying his head in his hands, mute, lost in the coldness and bitterness of his failure, his hurt. He realized that he was ashamed to tell Doctor Sylvan that he had failed. He saw the darkness again, the deadness and being cut off, without hope that anything would be different. Failure upon failure crushing him and a gnawing fear began in him that he would fall down again, sprawled and lost in emptiness.

The mental hospital and his years there arose before him — And the day he had first touched Doctor Sylvan. He had never done that before. He had gone around choked with anger, his heart locked in stone because he didn't know what to do with it, with his anger and fear. It was like a light had gone out in him. There had been no more light in the day, only an aching, like a stone in his throat. He had taken pleasure in nothing. It was as though the ground had shrunk beneath his feet. Because he had no ground to stand on, he felt dizzy and faint and never knew whether he could make it from this place to that place. He had nothing to stand on, to hold onto, because he had shrunk all into himself. It was like he had been in a high place, perilous, because he didn't have any more ground under him.

In the night, dreams of flowers had darted up from his unconscious. Flowers don't have to go devious ways, he thought. But he had dreamed of a yellow chrysanthemum in black earth and he was loosening the soil around the roots with his fingers. Doctor Sylvan had told him he was that flower and this his own hands, uncaged, could do.

He wanted to believe that it would be so because Doctor

Sylvan believed, had wanted them to believe together. Yet, that afternoon seeing Eiko was like something had died in his heart and he was afraid that now would be no different from any other dark and hopeless time, the days a dreary sameness, hopeless and beyond help.

The door opened and two young soldiers came in, each carrying a heavy duffle bag on his shoulder. They dumped them down near the coat rack and stepped up to the bar and seated themselves. Jim lifted his head, as though he had been drowsing, and stared at them.

"Phew!" gasped one, lifting his stiff-crowned cap and rubbing at his forehead. "Good to get that load of dirty skivvies off my back."

They ordered beer.

"Where you off to?" asked the barman, opening the beer and nodding toward the duffle bags.

"San Francisco. Train leaves in—" The second soldier checked his watch. "Hour and thirty-five minutes."

"Then off to Korea," said the other, his face flushed from carrying the bag.

The bartender put the beers in front of them. They lifted their glasses to him and drank thirstily.

"Good luck," said the bartender. "You'll need it. I hear Korea's a dead place." And he swiped at the bar with his rag.

"We'll be in a little one-by-two-mile valley," said the second soldier. "Be stuck there fourteen months."

"And *no* women," said the first, and blushing suddenly, grinned down shyly into his beer.

"Sure, they'll let you go out on the town."

"Not from what they told us. There *ain't* no town to go out *on.*"

Good-looking kids, thought Jim, listening. No more than nineteen apiece. Eyes warm and light and looking out on everything in innocence. No fear there yet. The ignorance of the young. Would they end up in the gorse, he wondered, their young pink entrails strewn amongst the tough waxen leaves? He shuddered. Not to think of that. Not to think of any of it.

". . . Fourteen months without women. . . ." he heard the second soldier repeating. Jim caught at the words, pulling himself back. He gazed at the trio at the other end of the bar, caught the eye of the bartender and ordered another beer and shot.

"Have to watch ourselves bending over for the soap in the shower," laughed the second soldier, nudging his buddy in the ribs.

And there came into his friend's face the same furious blush.

The bartender set the drinks in front of Jim, then moved back to the soldiers. Jim was glad the soldiers had come into the bar. He began to feel less tense and empty. The whiskey began to run warm through his blood. He listened to snatches of their talk, grew pensive and dreaming, and then would listen again. He thought of the dream he had had the night before, in the bus station where he had slept after searching till dawn for Eiko, saw the dream vividly again:

. . . He was a Japanese sailor on a Japanese warship. The ship had just been hit by torpedoes and the captain had gone from man to man giving each a black pill shaped like a flat disc that they were to swallow to commit suicide and then jump in the water. Jim swallowed the pill and waited. On either side of him seamen were leaping into the water. But Jim was afraid to jump and decided to wait until he was quite certain he was dying. He began to feel weak and dizzy and he was sure that death was not far off. He jumped into the water but suddenly he began to swim, unlike his comrades who all were sinking to their deaths calmly as the captain had ordered. Jim swam strongly, taking long strokes in the water, feeling new strength.

Suddenly before him an enormous ship loomed up. He swam to it and climbed aboard. The ship was deserted and he wandered about the decks but could find no one. The bulkheads were rusty and it looked as though the ship had been drifting for a long time, deserted and neglected. Passing a row of cabins he saw scrawled crudely in the rust of the bulkhead the words: THIS IS A FRENCH SHIP. A feeling of elation filled Jim in the dream. This is familiar to me, he thought, suddenly happy. It's as though I've come home. Now I'll be safe and will live again. I won't have to die. . . .

Jim mused on the dream as he drank his beer slowly. Japanese. The enemy in the war, he thought. Eiko. Her lovely Japanese face. It got all mixed up in his mind. The thought of enemy and Eiko confused him. French ship, he continued thinking. Friend ship. To return to what he had been long alienated from. To go home. A feeling of poignant sadness and longing came over him. He saw the drifting ship as the ship of himself which he had deserted so long ago. He thought of Eiko and wondered what the dream could have to do with her. Was she the stranger, the alien in himself? He did not know and sat perplexed, puzzling over the dream.

The sound of the door opening brought him back. A heavily-built young man wearing steel-rimmed glasses came in with a girl on his arm. She was a thin mousy girl, no more than twenty. Under her coat she wore a dark sweater, and a skirt with a wide kidney-like belt with a silver buckle around her waist. Jim turned a little on his stool to watch them. They stopped at the door, by the jukebox, she, a little hesitant, looking about her uneasily. The young man with the glasses was protective, slightly clumsy and awkward as he put his thick arm around her, steering her to the jukebox and talking to her softly as they decided what songs they would play. He was so broad and heavy and she was so small. A pinched look on her face, as though she had too often gone hungry, or had been ravaged with illnesses all her childhood. A pale pinched face, afraid, but a softness and kindness there. Her thin mousy hair.

Maybe she would blossom—in the sun of the big guy's warmth and protectiveness. Maybe the wrinkled little seed she was would unfold and bloom, in his love, into some soft and dreamy flower, Jim thought.

After making their selections on the machine, the young man led her over to one of the booths in the rear and the bartender went to take their order. The room was filled with soft music coming from the jukebox.

Jim swallowed the beer left in his glass. It tasted bitter and he made a wry face. Green beer, he thought. He had seen the breweries across the river in New Jersey. The big copper cookers gleaming in plate-glass windows four stories high. Green beer, sour, he said to himself, putting down the glass. In the morning, the raw tongue and queasy belly.

A warm whiskey pleasantness filled him. Unawares, without warning, Eiko's face slipped into his consciousness. There was the feeling of warm blood gurgling in his throat, as though he was bleeding, as though a knife had been slipped between his ribs, the blade of it so honed there was barely a sense of pain, barely any feeling except an almost pleasant sensation of inward bleeding and the slow longed-for approach of death, quiet and painless, not as he had expected death would be.

He saw the hands of Doctor Sylvan, reaching down, lifting; hands of life and love to pull him from the mud, from the depths of apathy and deadness. That Doctor Sylvan cared, that he loved him enough to offer hands to bring him back again into life—Jim loving him, and hating him for it because of the pain, the struggle of lifting back into life.

He needed him and, yet, he could not go to him. He felt as though he were ringed in by a magic circle of fire that he couldn't move beyond. He imagined a butterfly flying out of his mouth. He watched it beating at the windows of the bar to get out. The butterfly of the soul taking leave of the body which lacerated it, where it could not abide, where the long wars of the self would destroy it. It took leave of his body and tried to get away, to inhabit another—a body, like a temple—swept and ready to receive it, a clean and quiet place a long time in the preparing for its coming. Come back who has flown, Jim cried in himself, suddenly seized by his imagination, as though a butterfly actually fluttered against the window panes of the bar, its wings splashed with every color of the rainbow. Most delicate feet, so light you never bend the flowers, he continued crying in himself. Most delicate and light, who never wears down the grass— Who has left me, who has flown out in an unguarded moment. I've been torn and don't want to be torn any more. Come back into me that I may be healed, that I may be quiet and at peace. That the green of me shall grow, that I may live again.

"You want another beer?"

Jim pulled himself up.

"Huh?"

"You're empty." It was the bartender standing before him, holding up the brown bottle.

"No— No more," Jim said. He fumbled in his back pocket and brought out his wallet. He took out a bill and laid it on the bar. The bartender went to the cash register, rang up the amount and brought Jim his change. He got up.

"Good night," said the bartender, moving back to the soldiers. "Come in again."

"I will. Good night."

Jim went to the hat rack, took down his coat and slipping it on opened the door and stepped out into the street.

He started to walk uptown, walking slowly, a lightness in

his body. The pain and heaviness in his chest gradually subsided. He began to count the blocks as he walked and then
lost count. He looked at the buildings as he passed and they
were mostly sooty tenements with here and there on the fire
escapes pots of early spring flowers. Children ran past him on
the sidewalk, shouting and laughing in the early evening light.
He passed dimly-lit stores with long links of sausages hanging
in the windows; bakeries with enormous odd-shaped loaves of
bread, bread that he had never seen before. Now and then he
stopped to look in the windows and then walked on. He was
filled with a pleasant sensation of floating. The neighborhood
began to change. The buildings looked cleaner now, more subdued. The streets were quiet. Presently he found himself in a
sedate little street surrounding a small park with a high iron
fence enclosing it. Warm lights glowed behind gleaming windows of the severe graystone houses around the square. The
polished doorknobs shone in the lamplight. Like in a picture
postcard from London, Jim thought tipsily, pausing to look up
into the warm inviting windows of one of the houses.

There was a flurry of movement on the steps of a house
farther down the block. Jim, seeing it from the corner of his eye,
turned and saw three couples hurrying arm-in-arm down the
long stone steps. They were all laughing and in high spirits as
they came down the sidewalk towards him. The women were
dressed in expensive-looking cocktail dresses with furs draped
loosely on their arms. The men were in dark formal evening
wear, white silk scarves tossed carelessly about their shoulders. Jim moved to the curb as they approached, each chatter-
ing and laughing. As they swept by he could smell the perfume
of the women.

He started walking off slowly in the opposite direction, looking over his shoulder at the couples as they stopped at the corner and one of the young men hailed a cab. He felt suddenly

alone. He wanted to go with the young people, to laugh and be as lighthearted as them. But he moved on, away from the tiny park with its heavy locked gates and the tall houses with their black doors gleaming dully in the light of the ornate street lamps. It was all closed to him, in spite of the cheer and pleasant warmth. He had no place there. He continued to think of the blithe young couples. Maybe they're going to a party, he thought. He wondered if Greg, his friend, was giving a party that night. Greg's always giving parties, he thought. He's sure to. It would be some place to go. He didn't want to be by himself. He stood under the street light at the corner, undecided.

He and Eiko had been to a party at Greg's recently. Maybe he had better not go. Maybe it would only make him feel worse, going there and remembering another time with her. Then, too, he knew what the talk at the party would be like, could almost predict it. The pauses and silences with his friends. Had he changed so much? Or had they? Or had none of them changed at all? He felt like an alien amongst them. Especially at Greg's that night with Eiko he had felt that way. He had gotten more and more bored with them, impatient with the talk. He no longer cared. He hit his heel against the curbstone and stared down into the gutter. The street was very still. There seemed no one living in the houses— Only the soft appealing lights. He decided to walk down to Greg's place. If there were lights on he would go in. And if there was a party going on maybe it would not be so bad. I feel like getting seriously drunk, he told himself, as he started walking again, heading back downtown.

As JIM WALKED beneath the bridge and entered the narrow empty street, he saw a knot of people going in at the door of the building where Greg lived. As he got closer he

looked up and saw the high windows of Greg's loft brightly lit
and heard the muted sound of dance music. He hesitated a
moment, then threw back his shoulders and pushed open
the door and began climbing the rickety stairs. When he got to
the top landing he walked to the door and listened a moment.
From the other side came the low drone of conversation and
the music, which was louder now. He pushed open the door
and went in. He stood a moment near the door, leaning against
it for support. The enormous loft was filled with an assort-
ment of people standing and talking, glasses in hand. Most of
the faces he did not know. A new set, he thought solemnly. Greg
was nowhere in sight. Probably passed out under a table somewhere, Jim said to himself. He felt suddenly very clumsy and
even, in his drunkenness, shy. He knew no one. Nearby on a
table were bottles of liquor. He went to the table, poured himself a stiff shot into a paper cup and came back and leaned
against the wall near the door. He sipped at his drink and looked
around. Girls with cork-like faces glided past, flat-chested, their
arms and legs like sticks, held in the arms of young men in
dark suits with pink cherubic faces as they danced. Everyone
looked warm and flushed with drink. An elderly woman stood
nearby, her purple-tinted hair piled high on her head. Her long
clawlike hands thrashed the air as she talked to a young girl
with long braids down her back who was listening avidly. The
old woman had a voice that sounded like fingernails scraping
down a blackboard. Jim shivered, listening to her, and he
turned, slowly and carefully, to survey the other part of the
room.

In a corner three men squatted, huddled close together in a
circle. One had a beard and was dressed in a dirty sweatshirt
and blue jeans, the second was clean-shaven and wore an im-
maculate charcoal gray suit with dark tie, and the third, very

tall and thin, was wearing an extremely narrow suit, the trousers of it, Jim thought, making the man's legs look like drainpipes.

They hunched facing each other, heads together, and passed between them a thin cigarette which each inhaled, holding his breath for as long as possible. Jim watched, fascinated, waiting for one of them to keel over, but the men seemed only to become more loose-limbed and to swim away from each other, a blankness in their eyes as the marijuana took effect.

There was in the faces of the three men a dreamy isolation. Cut off. Not there. No longer a part of the room or of themselves. Separate and floating. Something repulsive in their faces, Jim thought drunkenly. Smug, doped faces, vacuous and empty. It seemed a drawing in upon the self, a casting off of the self and others.

I probably don't look so hot myself, and Jim had to laugh to himself. Too drunk, he thought. Too drunk to think.

There was a girl with luminous blue fingernails, the shapely nails fluttering around the lapels of a young man's coat and she smiling up at the young man, drunkenly. The blue nails swam before Jim's eyes as he watched them move over the youth who stood with a broken nervous grin on his face, staring down glassy-eyed at the girl. Her hands were rough, insistent on his coat. Jim stood spellbound by the blue fingernails which floated before his eyes like cold petals from a prickly flower. He gulped down the drink in his hand and looked around the party.

A girl with soft blonde hair was trying to get through to the other room. The guests were packed so densely she was making slow progress and others called out to her and she would smile and stop to speak with them. She seemed to know everybody. Jim stared at her, his mouth open, taken by her beauty. He looked around for a place to put down his empty cup and set it on top of a bookcase. Then he began edging his way carefully through the crowd, trying not to stumble or fall on anyone. When he got directly behind her, he hesitated a moment, then, taking a deep breath, touched her lightly on the shoulder. She had been talking to a young man with a thin straggly beard and as she turned to Jim her radiant smile dissolved slowly as she realized she didn't know him. The expression on her face became one of amused bewilderment. I must look very crocked and foolish, Jim thought hopelessly. He tried to speak but his tongue seemed too thick to move. Finally he managed to blurt out, "Will you dance with me?"

She studied him a moment, still with that vague smile of amusement, then, excusing herself to the bearded man, she took Jim's arm. He moved a little ahead of her, pushing his way to the other room where there was more space for dancing.

He put his arms about her and they tried a few steps. She felt so soft and light in his arms. She smelled of sweet soap. He stumbled badly and at one point stepped heavily on her toe. He murmured apologies and then stopped dancing altogether. He stood, his hands slack at his sides, his eyes cast down sheepishly.

"I'm sorry," he mumbled. "I'm pretty smashed. I really shouldn't've tried it."

His Adam's apple bobbed up and down nervously and his hands began to sweat. The girl looked at him curiously, as though waiting, her arms still resting lightly on his shoulders. Seeing his forlorn expression, like a small boy's, the look of amusement again lighted her eyes and she began to laugh, a rich and lilting laugh.

Jim looked at her quickly and felt his eyes smarting. He thrust her arms away from him roughly and turning quickly shoved his way through the crowd and out into the other room. As he started for the door he felt his face and neck burning. He stared down as though he dared not look around him. He yanked open the door and hurried out into the hall. As he was about to go down the steps he felt a hand on his arm and looking around cautiously stared into the face of the blonde-haired girl.

"I'm sorry," she said, breathless, a look of concern on her face. "I didn't mean to hurt you."

He made a move to pull away but she held on to his sleeve.

"You looked so much like an awkward little boy at his first dancing party. I didn't laugh to be cruel. Please believe me," she said, glancing apprehensively over her shoulder back to the party.

And she had such a look of genuine apology on her face that he knew she meant it.

"That's okay," he said with a clumsy gesture of his hand, and staring down again. "I better go. I'm just touchy tonight. I've had too much to drink."

He turned from her, taking a step down the stairs.

"Drowning your sorrows?" she asked.

He looked into her face again, mistrusting, a sudden sharp pain in his lungs, and seeing that she was serious, said quietly, "Maybe."

"Really, I didn't mean to laugh," she went on in the same serious tone, her voice almost plaintive as she glanced again into the other room. "But you did look so perplexed. I couldn't help myself."

"It's all right," he said. "I told you that."

He started down the stairs.

"Wait." She opened her purse and drew out a slip of paper and a pen. She hastily scrawled some words on the paper and handed it to him. "Look, here are my name and telephone number," she said, extending the paper down to him. "Call me? I really would like to make amends. And we can't really get to know each other here." She waved her slender arm toward the noisy room.

Jim held the piece of paper clutched in his hand, staring at it dumbly, the handwriting wavering before his eyes so that he couldn't read it. He felt a lump in his throat.

He had an impulse to touch her and reached out, moving back up the steps, and tried to kiss her, but she drew away from him as a noisy couple came swaying out the door and clattered, singing, down the stairs.

"I'm with someone," she whispered close to his ear, glancing behind her through the doorway. Then she skipped lightly across the hall and at the door she spun around and gazed at him, smiling. "You won't forget?"

"No." Jim gripped the railing, standing tense, watching her as she blew him a kiss and ran into the other room. He stood on tiptoe and looked through the open door. He saw a tall dark man with a neatly-clipped mustache approach her. He had on his overcoat and he held out her coat to her as he spoke to her. Jim couldn't make out the words but it was apparent the man with the mustache wanted them to leave. Jim took one last look at the girl then hurried down the steps and swinging wide the front door strode out in the cold night air.

At the end of the block he turned and began walking north. He walked for what seemed hours, block after block, not paying any attention to the street signs or the stop lights. A few times he had stepped out directly into the path of an oncoming car and there had been a screeching of brakes and the driver leaning out the window to yell at him. But he did not care. He walked on as though he desperately needed to keep moving, to not stop for rest. Finally, footsore, his legs aching and his throat parched, he saw ahead of him the dark green trees of the park. The park with its new soft growth looked restful and inviting. At the corner he crossed over the street and entered one of the footpaths leading into the park. The night air smelled fresh and cool and he breathed it in deeply, feeling better now that he was out in the open under the sky, with the dark earth and blossoming shrubs on either side of him. The lights along the path lit up the early spring leaves of the trees and he walked along, his hands in his pockets, looking up at the leaves rustling in the faint night wind. On a bench, in the shadows, he saw two lovers sitting, their arms about each other, oblivious to him as he walked by. The thought of Eiko swarmed up again. The drink had cushioned him, like cotton batting, protecting him throughout the evening from thoughts of her. But now, with the alcohol wearing away, the dull pain of losing her started again in his chest. He tried desperately to thrust thoughts of her away, to force himself to forget, to think of other things— of the fine green leaves fluttering in the wind and, above the trees, the dark sky with its sparkling stars. He trudged along, heavy-footed, his head down, moving across the park. And still, he thought morosely, in the morning I'll remember and it will be worse than ever.

He came to a water fountain and going up to it leaned over and turning the faucet let the spurt of water splash over his face, the coldness of it awakening and refreshing him. He shook his head briskly from side to side, then leaned again and drank long and deep. Finished, he walked on and leaving the park crossed over the broad avenue which skirted it and turned down a side street, heading toward the river. Walking several more blocks he came to a dead-end street which over-looked the freight yards. Two bright red lights gleamed in the darkness on the barbed wire fence at the end. He walked down the dead-end street and stood, his fingers hooked in the grimy chain fence, and watched the trains being shunted below. Over the tracks stood a clapboard shack, its windows glowing soft and yellow in the cold glare of the floodlights of the yard. Big dark locomotives, their diesel engines throbbing in the night, sent up to his nostrils a smell of oil and motor heat. The locomotives were backing up and going forward and there was the chock and slam of the couplings as an engine slipped off or took on a car; then, a hard chugging and sudden swift belch of oil-smoke as the diesel pulled away, the brakeman swinging his lantern in wide slow loops to the engineer, waving his arm above his head, his breath steaming in the cold spring air.

A man went into the shack, closing the door carefully after him, and came out a few minutes later with a paper in his hand. He walked up to another workman and showed him something on the paper. Together they walked down a string of freight cars, inspecting the numbers, then jumped a coupling and disappeared from view on the other side. The night air was filled with the sharp sounds of metal striking metal and the muted thrum of motors stopping and starting.

Jim turned and walked slowly away. He began to cry, surprised at the sudden unexplained tears. He kept walking, his head bent, the tears streaming down his face. Eiko was dead. Somewhere in the night Jim realized it, vividly, for the first time. He felt as though something had broken in him, that a weight had been lifted from his shoulders.

"Eiko," he said softly, tentatively, in the still icy air. The dullness and ache did not arise in him. Eiko was dead and Jim felt suddenly lightheaded. He stopped in the middle of the sidewalk, closing his eyes. "Eiko. My most dear and beautiful Eiko," he breathed. "Good bye."

He walked on, hurrying now, then broke into a run, his footsteps echoing in the quiet street. Glancing back, he saw again the fence of the dead-end street with its two red lights gleaming in the darkness. As he ran, the face of Doctor Sylvan came into his mind. He could call him now. It was all right. He wanted to talk to him, tell him everything.

Rounding the corner, Jim saw an outdoor telephone booth glowing brightly in the next street. He hurried up to the booth and stepped inside. Dropping a dime in the slot he dialed the operator and placed a person-to-person call to Doctor Sylvan. The operator rang and a moment later the phone at the other end clicked and Jim, letting out a long breath, heard Doctor Sylvan's voice saying sleepily, "Hello."

"Doctor Sylvan?" the operator asked.

"Yes."

"Long distance calling. Go ahead, please."

"Hello, Doc."

"Hello. Who is this?"

"Three guesses."

Doctor Sylvan laughed drowsily. "I don't have to. Jim, where are you?"

"You're not playing fair." Jim grinned loosely into the receiver. "You're s'posed to guess."

"Well, I guessed right, didn't I?"

"Oh—maybe. You asleep?"

"Not now. Have you been celebrating?"

"Huh?"

"You sound a little merry."

"I'm not very merry." Jim belched and holding his hand to his mouth, said, " 'Scuse me."

"Where are you?"

"Where am I? I don't know. Yes I do. I was only kidding, Doc. I'm really on the Martha Washington Bridge."

"You mean the George Washington."

"They put a new bridge under him— Call it the Martha Washington. Mother of our country. Get it, Doc?"

"Sure," said Doctor Sylvan. "And the Empire State Building's that way about the Holland Tunnel."

"Yeah," Jim laughed. "That's it. I'm gonna jump off 'er."

"Jump off where?"

"Martha Wash'ing bridge." He put the tips of his fingers to his mouth. "Oops. Can't say it."

"Seriously. Where are you?"

"Damned if I know."

A middle-aged man was standing at the corner, waiting for the light to change. Jim swung open the door and leaning out, called raucously, "Hey, mister, where am I?"

The man turned, gazed at Jim solemnly.

"New York City," he said carefully.

"I *know* that," said Jim. "Whatta you think I am—a *cretin?* I mean, what street?"

"Oh," said the man, lifting his hand and smiling sheepishly behind it. "This is West 72nd Street."

"Thanks!" Jim started to duck into the booth, then ducked out again. The stranger was starting across the street.

"Hey, mister!" Jim called, putting a hand to the side of his mouth. "You want to join me in a drink?"

But the man kept on walking and didn't look back. Jim slammed the door shut.

"Man out there says West 72nd Street," he said into the phone. "Wouldn't have a drink with me. Very rude fella. Hey, Doctor Sylvan, you still there?"

"Yes."

"Oh."

There was a long pause. Jim stared silently into the mouthpiece.

"I don't know what to tell you," he said, his throat tightening.

"It went badly, didn't it, Jim?" Doctor Sylvan said quietly.

"Eiko? How did you know?" Jim hunched up closer over the receiver.

"You're not with her?"

"No. The hell with her."

"You don't mean that."

"No." Jim closed his eyes tight and bit his lower lip hard. "I found her and—not with her any more. Broke a bottle of wine against her wall. Childish, wasn't it? Go on," he said, his voice rising, "tell me it was childish. No, don't," he continued in a pleading voice, like a small boy. "Don't tell me anything. Just let me talk to you." He paused, rubbing his brow hard with his knuckles. "Don't know where I am—I went to a party— Been drinking and don't feel very well—" His voice trailed off brokenly, his head dropped to his chest.

"Come home, Jim."

Jim stirred.

"Home?"

His throat became choked. He could not speak for a moment.

"Home," he repeated dumbly, uncomprehending.

"My door's open to you." said Doctor Sylvan. "You'll always have a home here, with Elizabeth and me. You know that, Jim."

Tears fell down Jim's face. He tried to speak. "Oh," he said simply.

"Shall I come and pick you up?"

"No," Jim said suddenly. "I don't want you to do that."

"Will you be all right?"

"Yes. I'll find the bus."

"And, Jim?"

"Yes."

"When you ride over the George Washington Bridge— If you look north and it's a clear night you can see the lights of the town. Not very well—but sometimes you can see them."

"I'll look. I will."

"I'll be waiting here for you. With lots of black coffee."

Jim laughed and snuffled a finger at his wet nose. "I'll need it." He paused a moment. "Doctor Sylvan?"

"What?"

"You can't walk over the bridge anyway."

"I know."

"The crosswalks're closed. You know—since they're fixing it."

Jim gripped the phone. "I was only kidding about jumping off the bridge," he explained earnestly. "Only sometimes. . . ."

"I know. We'll talk about it. I'll see you soon?"

"I'm going to the bus now." He leaned in close to the receiver. "Doctor Sylvan?"

"Yes?"

"I love you."

Jim clamped down the receiver. The phone rang immediately and he lifted the receiver again. The operator told him how much to put in and he found change in his pocket and dropped the coins in the slot and hung up. Shoving open the door he hurried out into the street and down the sidewalk. An empty cab was waiting for the light at the corner and Jim ran to it and opening the rear door got in.

"The bus terminal, up near the bridge," he said to the driver.

As they pulled away, Jim leaned his head back against the seat and closed his eyes. He slipped his hands in his pockets and in one pocket felt the crumpled piece of paper. He lifted it out and held it between his fingers. In the darkness of the cab the slip of paper looked like the tattered broken wings of a butterfly. He waited until the taxi passed under a street light then hunched over to the window and tried to make out the words. His vision wavered and the neat handwriting blurred illegibly before his eyes. The cab passed into darkness again. Then, out of the confused and blurred happenings of the evening, he remembered the girl with the long light hair and knew that it was her name written there on the paper. The bit of paper became suddenly precious to him. He smoothed it out painstakingly on his thigh with his fingers and folding it carefully in two put it back in his pocket, holding it cupped lightly in his hand as though the scrap of paper was something delicate, fragile, which the slightest pressure of his fingers would crush.

The taxi was driving through the park now which overlooked the river. Jim leaned back once more against the leather cushion and stared out the window. The dark waters moved past them in the night and, suddenly catching his breath, he saw, up ahead, the lights of the bridge spanning the water, the sweeping invisible arc of the bridge disappearing across the river into the blackness of the far shore.

I'm going home, he thought. A feeling of warmth and happiness stirred in him. He saw the red chair in Doctor Sylvan's living room in which, soon, he would be sitting and drinking coffee, talking to the doctor. Then the bright image of the girl swam before him with her light green eyes and soft blonde hair.

Eiko, he called softly to himself and sat stock-still as though waiting for an answer out of the night rushing swiftly by the cab windows. But her name was like an emptiness in his heart. There was no answer. Nothing stirred in him, breathing her name, as it had once stirred him to elation. Her name was like ashes in his mouth, a darkness to him. It was as though she had become in that moment an alien, a stranger. He had left her and she seemed far away now.

The clear green eyes of the girl whose name he held so carefully on the scrap of paper in his hand, moved before him once more. As they drove closer to the bridge, its lights dipping gracefully over the water, Jim propped his elbows up on the front seat. He leaned close to the driver's ear.

"I'm going home," he said happily.

The driver lurched around to look at him and Jim smiled.

"Yeah," said the cabbie, turning his gaze back on the road. "We all get to go home, sooner or later."

✑ THE YELLOW BALLOON

As ALICE AND JIM STOOD at the corner waiting for the light to change before they crossed over to the park, a horse-drawn cab passed in front of them. They stood, hand-in-hand, watching the horse as it trotted by. It was a big black animal. Patches of its coat were dark with sweat. It was old and thick-limbed and pulled the peeling battered old cab with its long quivering neck held high, green foam frothing at its jaws, its head tilted up and back and tossing from side to side, tugging irritably at the reins. The driver, a thin red-nosed man with a dented top hat on his head, held the reins firmly in his fists, his lips pressed tight and his eyes filled with silent anger as though he were furious with the animal.

The light changed but Jim and Alice still stood in the same spot, as though they could not take their eyes from the horse. Crossing the intersection, the horse, in the midst of traffic, suddenly became skittish and, snorting and lifting its hoofs high, began performing darting little prancings to the side, jolting the empty carriage back and forth. An automobile swerved to avoid the leaping horse, the horn honking. The cabman rose in his seat and seizing his whip from its socket snapped the long lash down sharply across the animal's flanks. The horse's hindquarters shivered under the slashings and swinging its big head around, its eyes wide and dark, it whinnied hoarsely at the driver, then slowed its pace and resumed a more normal gait. The cabman stuck the whip back in its socket and sitting down, pulled smartly at the reins, turning the horse in at the curb. They drew up at the block-long hack stand where other horses and cabs stood waiting for customers for the drive through the park.

"Come on," Jim said, giving a tug at the peak of his red baseball cap. "Let's go over and take a look at him."

He took Alice by the arm and led her across the street. Once on the other side they walked down the line of cabs until they came to the black horse who stood restive, kicking at the asphalt with his hoofs and neighing loudly. The cabman was stroking the horse's neck, the dark glossy throat quivering under his touch, and saying gruffly, "Easy, you bugger. Easy now."

"He doesn't look like much," Jim said to Alice.

"But he's got spirit," she replied.

"Maybe he just doesn't want to pull cabs. He looks like he *ought* to want to. But maybe he's meant to be out in the open. Running in fields and sunlight. He's pretty frisky," he said in a louder voice to the cabman.

"He needs more of the whip is what he needs," growled the driver.

A little old lady with blue-rinsed hair who had stopped to watch piped up and said to the driver, "Maybe you should give him a tranquilizer."

"Yes," said the driver sourly. "A sharp crack on the head with a hammer would do."

"Oh my," said the old lady, putting gloved fingers to her mouth.

"He doesn't like the bit," the driver explained.

"Well, I shouldn't either," said the old lady. She minced over to the horse. "Such a spirited creature," she cooed sweetly. "There, there."

She lifted her hand to stroke the horse's nose but the horse reared away, dragging the cab from the curb.

"Get away! Get away! You old busybody!" shouted the cabman, holding firmly on to the horse's reins with one hand and with his free arm flailing out at the old woman. "You'll get him started again with your oo-ing and ah-ing!"

The old lady darted back, her pocketbook raised as though in self-defense or else ready to strike the man. She crinkled her nose distastefully and stalked indignantly away, tossing petulant looks back over her shoulder as she hurried on down the sidewalk.

Jim and Alice burst out laughing.

"That old girl could do with some of the whip herself," said the cabman testily.

"You want to risk your life and limb in a ride with him?" the driver said, turning to Jim and Alice. "I'm insured, you know."

"No thanks," Jim laughed. "We just came over to look at the horse."

"I might as well take him back to the stables. There'll be no more fares with this one, I can see that."

"Oh Jim," Alice whispered, leaning close to his ear. "I want to come back here, at night sometime, and maybe this horse will be here. And we'll ride with him through the park. It's so nice to go under the trees in the dark. Wouldn't you like that?"

"Okay," Jim said. "We'll do that." He kissed her lightly on the tip of the nose. "Right now, what do you say we get over to the zoo?"

They said good bye to the cabman and started back toward the corner. They crossed over the broad avenue. He took her hand and they entered one of the paths leading into the park.

It was a soft spring day with the sun shining and a fragrant smell in the air of early-budding flowers and trees. Jim put his arm around Alice's waist as they walked up the path and came out onto the lake. They strolled over to the edge and stood looking out over the water, the surface fanned finely now and then by an occasional breeze. On the benches surrounding the edge of the lake, people sat reading the Sunday newspapers or dozing or enjoying the sun. There were a few lovers with arms about each other.

The ducks, plump and immaculately white, without a feather out of place, swam listlessly here and there near the shore, ignoring the bits of bread a small boy was tossing out to them.

"Oh, Daddy, they won't *eat*," the boy cried in a worried, almost tearful voice, as he tugged at his father's trouser leg.

"They're not hungry now, son," the father said, rumpling the boy's hair affectionately. "They've had enough to eat."

The ducks swam around in lazy slow circles, their bright yellow bills in the air, keeping a distance from the bobbing bits of swelling bread in the water.

The little boy ran to the edge and leaning over, his hands resting lightly on his kneecaps, called across the water to the ducks, "Come on, eat now. I want to see you eat."

"Poor kid. They're too fat and tame," Jim said to Alice. "They've got it too easy. Let's go see some livelier stuff."

They continued along the asphalt path which skirted the pond, holding hands, as they headed toward the zoo. Old ladies on benches, their parched white faces lifted to the sun, eyed them through drowsy slits with faintly simpering smiles on their faces as they passed.

"Everybody's got a grin on today," Jim said to Alice as they left the path and started over toward the animal cages. "I guess because it's spring everybody's a little dazed and remembering how to smile again."

The zoo was packed. Children ran everywhere, shouting, bright colored balloons bouncing from strings held tight in their fists. Whole families trooped along from cage to cage, the fathers reading aloud, importantly, the latinized names of the animals. It got very warm. Jim slipped off his jacket and hooking his thumb in the collar slung the jacket over his shoulder. He tipped back his baseball cap and rubbed at the band of sweat on his forehead. There wasn't a space left on any of the benches; they had to walk slowly, picking their way carefully through the dense throng.

They passed the seals, their plump bodies sleek and glistening as they sunned themselves on the concrete slabs jutting up out of their pool. Passing the monkey house, a blast of fetid smells blew out from the open doors.

"Phew!" Jim said, putting his fingers to his nose. "Let's bypass the monkeys. I'll lose my breakfast."

"Let's hurry up and get past," said Alice holding a handkerchief to her face.

Beyond the monkey house they came to a sign hanging on a post. They stopped to read it.

       FEEDING TIMES:
       Grizzly Bear—1:30 p.m.

Jim glanced at his watch. "We're in luck. It's 1:25. Come on. Let's go watch them feed the bear."

He took her hand and pushed his way through the crowd, heading toward the bear cages.

A crowd had gathered in front of the cage to watch the feeding and Jim, pulling Alice along, shoved in amongst the people to get a good view.

The grizzly bear, its great head almost as broad as its body, as though it had no neck, lumbered up against the cage on its hind legs, the thick black claws of its forepaws swiping clumsily at the bars. The animal, as though by daily habit realizing it was feeding time, was restless, swinging his enormous bulk from one hind foot to the other and flailing his front paws in a kind of awkward dance.

At the side of the cage an attendant appeared. He was dressed in a dark green uniform with a stiff crowned cap on his head. He was slender and had sooty blond hair and his face and neck were pock-marked. He looked like the kind of guy who works in a gas station. He was carrying a bucket filled with raw chunks of meat. Moving slowly in the space between the cage and guard rail, his face was blank, expressionless, as though he were about to go put water in the radiator of a car.

The crowd pressed forward against the railing and Jim held Alice's hand tightly so they would not get separated from one another. Everyone stood on tiptoe and craned their necks. A stillness came over the crowd as the young attendant set down the bucket of meat and stepped up to the cage. The grizzly was extremely agitated now, jigging roughly from side to side and smacking the iron bars of his cage with such force that his long claws made the metal ring. The attendant leaned one shoulder indolently against the cage and with a solemn and bored expression tickled the rough fur of the animal's chest. The bear thrust back his head and reared up taller on his hind legs, his enormous jaws parting in a wide animal grin. The crowd gasped as the sharp tusklike teeth and dark pinkish under-flesh of the bear's mouth and throat were suddenly exposed. The attendant, with the same bored look on his face, gripped the bear's lower jaw with his fingers and pried the cavernous mouth open still further. The heavy gleaming teeth of the grizzly glistened in the afternoon sunlight, and still he jogged from foot to foot, his mouth grinning wide and eager, and strings of saliva beginning to swing and hang down from his jaws, wetting the matted fur of his under-belly. Then the attendant, his eyes dull and listless, wrapped his fingers around one of the bear's teeth and taking a firm grip on it rocked the beast's great head from side to side. The crowd squeezed in even more tightly. There was not a sound as every eye watched intently and with fascination as the attendant thrust his hand in the bear's mouth, shoving it in and down almost to the elbow into the animal's throat, as though he were trying to reach deep into its belly.

Jim looked around uncomfortably, beginning to feel nervous in the close-packed crowd. He looked about him quickly, his eyes shy and alarmed, then at Alice who stood as though hypnotized, her eyes wide and her mouth open. He moved closer to her, his fingers beginning to ache from the tight pressure of holding on to her hand.

Now the attendant had pulled his arm out a little from the grizzly's throat and turning his arm around, the flat of his palm up, he curled his fingers and began fluttering them against the roof of the bear's mouth. The bear was panting heavily now and still jogging up and down, the saliva dribbling more quickly from its jaws, as the attendant continued to tickle and stroke the roof of the animal's mouth. The attendant's face was slack and flat, without emotion of any kind. Jim saw that the hand in the bear's mouth was sooty, the flesh of the stubby fingers dry and cracked, dirty, as though from the sludge and oil of a motor. He turned away, leaning close to Alice's ear and whispered, "Come on, let's go. It's too crowded here."

He began to feel dizzy and closed his eyes for a moment.

"In a minute," she answered absently, completely absorbed, not glancing at him. "Wait. Just a minute."

The attendant withdrew his hand very slowly from between the bear's jaws and with his fist knocked the grizzly lightly on the snout and stooping down grabbed the handle of the bucket and cradling it in one arm, reached in and pulled out a thick piece of red meat and swung it in between the bars. The bear, now standing very still, his front paws hanging limp at his sides, his body inert and slumped, his fur shivering slightly, snatched out swiftly and clamped his powerful jaws down over the meat. There was a sharp crack as his teeth closed over it and then with a loud smacking noise the animal swallowed the meat whole in one gulp.

The crowd laughed. A few began to applaud. There was a general restlessness as everyone relaxed a little, getting down off their toes and uncraning their necks. They talked to one another in brief hesitant whispers.

Jim tugged at Alice's arm.

"I feel a little sick to my stomach," he said. "It's so close here."

He gripped her hand and moved ahead of her pushing his way through the crowd. Another couple surged forward to take their places. Out on the open sidewalk Jim released her hand and taking out his handkerchief wiped the sweat from around his mouth. He rapidly coiled and uncoiled his fingers.

"Let's walk a little," he said. "I want to clear my head."

"All right."

They walked on, not saying anything. Then Alice looked at him hesitantly, a question in her eyes.

"Do you think the man was cruel to the bear?" she said slowly.

"No."

"I was beginning to think maybe he was, a little."

"That's his job," Jim answered, an edge of irritation in his voice. "That's the way things are."

As they walked along out in the open, Jim began to feel less nauseous and dizzy.

"Oh look!" Alice cried, gripping his arm and stopping in the middle of the path. Jim looked to where she was pointing. In a garden plot enclosed by a low fence at the side of the snake house clusters of brilliant daffodils, their blossoms bowed, swung to and fro in the light wind. They walked over to the edge of the fence and looked down at the flowers.

"They've just opened," Alice said, crouching and stroking one with her fingers. "I bet just five minutes ago."

Jim squatted down beside her, laughing, and tugged at a strand of her hair playfully.

"You know something?" he said. "I bet we must've happened the same time as flowers."

"What?"

"I mean, in school they make how man came about so boring and uninteresting. But I think we must've happened the same time the flowers did."

"You mean me and you?" she laughed, tipping her nose down to a blossom.

"You and me." He waved his arm around. "All of us."

"How do you know?" she asked with a teasing light in her eyes.

"Some days you can just tell. It's in the air. Like today. The first time flowers sprouted up, we must've too."

Alice stood up, smoothing her skirt down over her thighs. "I'd like to think it was that way," she said, and took his arm and they walked on.

They came to a row of cages with fewer people standing before them. They slowed up, moving from cage to cage, Jim's hand resting on her shoulder, as they watched the strange antlered creatures standing or lying motionless behind the bars. The eyes of the animals were so warm and strangely soft. Shy dumb beasts filled with a quiet heavy life, filled with an imperturbability, a solidity.

They can die so easily, Jim thought. They can be butchered maybe without even a struggle. Only a high thin cry.

Lovely passive creatures heavy with a dark life that seemed so alien to him. And yet not so strange. Was he really so different? He gazed about him at the people watching the animals through the bars, watching the silent cumbersome beasts lying on the cold concrete in their cages, animals with queerly shaped horns like old tough wood out in the weather for a long time that has become smooth-worn, silvery and rough; animals whose names he didn't know. The fascination of the people for the animals seemed to lie in the realization that they and the animals were somehow close. There was a kinship, warm and dark and unknowable, a kinship in the deep yellow eyes of the animals, eyes which seemed to look inward upon a world of formless sensations and of passive still power — The yellow eyes of an older time under an older sun, of a darker blood and flesh, of thick rough hides molting into the new thin light hair, and the delicate sweet smells of sparse forests— A world which Jim, and the others about the cages, had forgotten but which still lived in each, it seemed, like some frail remembered life out of another place, timeless, wordless, without hours—solid and sure, as the dark beasts, squat there upon the stones. Their rough coats were thick and long or short and satiny, moving sinuously on the lean muscles of their haunches, their great sides moving slowly in and out as they breathed, unruffled, lying vivid and real upon the concrete, as though taking strength and life from the sun and air and, mindlessly, gently, giving back life to everything about them. It was this thought struck him so deeply—that the animals moved him so because they were also in him— Dark sensual creatures, so strange and, yet, so near, forgotten and yet remembered now, as he stood before them looking into their clear yellow eyes. And it must, he thought, be the same for all those here. Feeding the animals, they fed the shy queer animals of themselves, a giving and a taking back, a recognition and tribute, each to the other. He saw suddenly in the animals and in himself, in the people around the cages, a stolid heavy life, yet, curiously delicate and gentle, that persisted, that went on, that lived, stubborn and quiet and sure, in spite of everything, in spite of sickness and hunger, in spite of wars and murder— Lovely shy and fearful life that lived and stayed strong on the face of the earth in spite of everything that sought to destroy it.

The animals filled him with a sense of quietness. They walked on, Jim's hand still on her shoulder, but resting there lightly. She can walk away easily from under my fingers, he thought. If you hold a thing too tightly, you lose it.

They came to a little stand where a vendor was selling souvenirs of the zoo and pennants and balloons. He bought her a bright yellow balloon and she held it clutched in her hand, pleased and surprised, like a small child, the breeze catching at the balloon and bouncing it from side to side as she held it.

They left the path and walked up a slope and came out

on a broad open area of grass and small shrubs. Here and there the daffodils sprouted. She took his arm and, with an eager smile, led him to the middle of the field. As he trudged along beside her, puzzled, almost unwilling, he looked at her questioningly but she said nothing until they got out in the open where the trees looked distant and the close-packed buildings lining the park seemed far away.

"I'm going to let the balloon go," she said.

"Why? Don't you like it?"

"Yes. But I've always wanted to come to the park and buy a balloon and let it go." She gave him a forlorn little smile. "It's no fun doing it when you're alone."

He shrugged his shoulders and winking at her indulgently, squeezed her around the waist. "It's your balloon. Stick a pin in it if you want."

She extended her arm out straight, her eyes, light and eager, watching the balloon as the slight wind batted it about. She seemed to be waiting for the wind to die down and when at one point it did, the string of the balloon pulled taut and straight, the balloon itself resting motionless at the end of it. She held the string pinched between her thumb and forefinger and when the air was completely still and there was not a sound to be heard in the broad field, she seemed to hold her breath for an instant, a look of radiant anticipation on her face, and released the string. The balloon, as though anxious to be off, rose vertically, veered for a moment, and then, as though becoming some eager and animate creature, dipped in the air an instant and then flew up above the trees straight and swift high over their heads.

Jim tucked his hands in his hip pockets and tilted his head back, squinting his eyes against the light and watched the yellow balloon rising into the clear blue sky. Alice moved close to him and slipped her arm around back of him and, her lips dry and parted slightly, her eyes tense and wide against the glare, said softly, "I've done that. I'm glad."

She glanced around at Jim to see the expression on his face. He was still intent upon watching the balloon, his head craned farther back now on his slender neck, his large Adam's apple protruding and bobbing in his throat. Alice laughed and standing on her tiptoes swung around and kissed him on the Adam's apple. He swallowed quickly, surprised and caught off balance, and taking his eyes reluctantly from the balloon, turned and grinned down at her.

"What'd you do that for?"

"You looked like a flower bending its face up to the sun."

"Ragweed, huh?" he snorted.

"No. Your face was like some bright flower on a slim stem. It suddenly occurred to me," she said gaily.

He bent down and kissed her mouth. "My daffodil," he whispered. He looked up at the sky again, where the balloon was now a barely visible speck of yellow in the cloudless sky.

"Look," he said, pointing up. "It's flying back to the sun."

She gazed up at the sky, spotting the balloon again. "It's flying back home," she said. There was a tremor in her voice. Jim looked at her and saw that there were tears glistening in her eyes. He put his arms about her and she laid her head on his shoulder. Together they watched as the balloon disappeared, going up and up, watched it until they could no longer see it.

"Well," she said quietly. "That's done."

They started to walk away over the field, arm-in-arm, back toward the path. She was silent and they walked on over the grass, moving under trees now and coming to several benches scattered here and there beneath the trees on which people sat, reading newspapers or with arms about each other.

She smiled up at him suddenly and pulling his hand up

to her cheek, held it there. "I won't ever forget you looking like a flower."

"And you—the daffodil girl!"

"The daffodil girl?"

"Yes!" He broke into a trot, pulling her along after him.

"Wait! Where are you going?" she cried, dragging along after him, trying to keep up.

"Come on," he laughed. "I'll buy you a hot dog."

A little farther on was a pushcart topped by a big red and green beach umbrella. A little man in a white cap and white linen coat stood beside it, selling ice cream and bottles of soda pop. They headed toward the cart and when they got there Jim ordered two hot dogs. The little man forked two hot dogs into rolls and handed them to him. Jim paid him and then squeezed mustard on them from a plastic bottle on the wagon.

They sat down on a park bench to eat their hot dogs, Alice holding hers daintily between two fingers. She flipped it upside-down quickly to keep the mustard from running down and then licked the side of her hand where some of it had dripped out between the bun.

"You put too much mustard on," she said, a look of annoyance on her face.

"I like mustard," Jim said unconcernedly, gripping his hot dog firmly in both hands and chomping away on it. He suddenly poked Alice in the ribs with an elbow and when she looked at him he jerked his head toward the bench across the way. A mother sat on the bench, holding in her lap a little girl of about three. The mother was staring vaguely off in the opposite direction, holding the child with her two arms clasped loosely around its belly. The child was gazing open-mouthed at Jim and Alice and idly kicking one small foot back and forth between her mother's legs. The mother continued to peer off at something in the distance and the child, seeing that Jim and Alice had noticed her, lifted her arm and waved to them, curling her tiny fingers back and forth as she did so, and, smiling shyly, revealed two front teeth missing from her lower gum.

Alice smiled at the little girl and Jim, having finished his hot dog, briskly wiped his hands on his thighs and, grinning, waved back at her. The little girl smiled more widely now and the mother, staring now at something behind her, shifted her weight on the bench, pulling the child over to her other thigh.

Jim crinkled up his nose and stuck his tongue out at the little girl. She stopped waving and let her hand drop in her lap and immediately bunched up her cheeks and stuck her tongue out right back at Jim.

Alice threw back her head and shook with laughter, grabbing her knees in her hands.

Jim stuck a forefinger in either side of his mouth and pulling his lips apart stuck out his tongue and crossed his eyes.

The little girl giggled, hiding her face in her hands. Her mother pulled herself around a little more on the seat to get a better look at whatever it was she was looking at behind the bench and the little girl lifted her arms out, steadying herself, until her mother got settled comfortably. Then she looked across quickly to see if Jim and Alice were still watching and, first wiping her mouth with one hand, she put a thumb in one side and her little finger in the other side and stretched her mouth apart as wide as she could and darted her tongue out at Jim. She tried to cross her eyes but could only manage a straight-eyed stare and so just squinted at him.

Jim and Alice threw their arms about each other and laughed out loud until their faces got very red and their eyes began to run with tears.

The little girl began to cough and took her fingers out of

her mouth and folded them daintily in her lap until she stopped coughing, then lifted one hand and waved again, smiling.

Jim stuck a thumb in each ear and waggled his fingers at her, his face twisted in a hideous expression. The little girl aped him perfectly, sticking her hands up to her ears and wagging her tiny fingers slowly and awkwardly back at him. Only she didn't make a face. Her eyes looked off to the side, coquettish.

Her mother gave a tremendous sigh at this point and heaved herself around. The little girl dropped into the hollow between her mother's legs and, with a slightly alarmed look on her face, held her arms out once more for balance and, deciding she was safe, tilted her little bobbed head back and looked up into her mother's face. The mother gave her a rough little peck on the nose and then turned her head to the left, then to the right, looking up and down the path. As though not finding anything of interest, she pulled herself up off the bench, caught the child around the middle and straddling her on her hip with one arm, started walking away slowly. The little girl, riding slowly up and down on her mother's hip, flashed a grin back at Alice and Jim.

Jim made a gun out of his hand and squinting one eye, straddled the bench as if it was a horse and took a couple of potshots at the little girl. She capped her thumb over one knuckle and pointed a tiny finger at him and shot right back. Then as they moved farther on she smiled and waved at Jim and Alice and continued to smile and wave at them until she and her mother rounded a turn in the path and were out of sight.

Alice took out a paper tissue and wiped the tears of laughter from her eyes and blew her nose. She crumpled the tissue and put it back in her bag, then turned sideways on the bench, facing Jim.

"You'd make a good father," she said.

"I would?" He grinned shyly at her and, tipping his baseball cap over his eyes, slid down on the bench until he was resting on the small of his back, his head practically on the seat and his long legs spread wide and stretched out before him.

"She was a cute kid," he said, closing his eyes, the smile still on his face.

"She liked you a lot," Alice said, reaching over and with two fingers taking the peak of his cap and lifting it back from his eyes.

He grabbed hold of her wrist playfully.

"What kind of father you think I'd make?"

"A good one."

"Come on, come on," he urged teasingly.

"Oh," she said, glancing up into the air, "I can see you carrying your little son on your shoulders, holding on to him with one hand, and him with bunched fists grabbing your hair for balance."

Jim swung his legs up and around and onto the bench, his knees bent, and dropped his head in her lap.

"You want to have kids?" he asked.

"Sure."

"How many?"

"Enough."

"How many's enough?"

"Hmmm," she murmured thoughtfully. "Four, I guess. Maybe five. Oh, I want to have lots of kids so none of them'll be lonely!" she cried ecstatically. Then, her face serious, she asked, "Jim, do you think I'd make a good mother?"

"How do I know?"

He closed his eyes and nestled his head against her belly.

"Be serious now. Do you?"

"I don't know. Maybe you'd beat the kids."

"Oh, *you*." She looked away, a little irritated, her mouth pouting. "I'd smack them if they needed it."

"You'd probably try to make them all geniuses and bank presidents," he went on. "They'd all end up with nervous breakdowns because they'd want to be firemen or garbage collectors."

"I would not. Well," she said, glaring down at him, "would that be so bad? The first part, I mean."

He gazed at her.

"You know something?"

"What?" she said, her voice softening.

"You're terrific to make love to."

He buried his face in her stomach again and reached up and cupped her breast in his hand.

"Jim," she said, taking his hand firmly and pulling it down and holding on to it. "People are watching."

"They are?" he said in a muffled voice, his head still buried in her dress. "I don't see anybody. It's awful dark up against here."

She began to laugh, a soft and lilting laugh.

"You're awfully silly. You look very Irish today. Did you know that?"

"No," he said, turning his head around and smiling up into her eyes. "Do the Irish look silly?"

"Some do. You look Irish, but you don't look silly-Irish. You look like a nice young lad—a little roguish. You look like a charming young pub-crawler who has a way with the ladies."

"You read that in a book. Hell, I'm American."

"I love you."

She leaned down and kissed his mouth gently. He reached up and put his arm about her shoulder.

"Let's go home. Let's go home and make love," he breathed softly. There was an edge of urgency in his voice.

She smiled wistfully. "You are a rogue."

He sat bolt upright and swung around and grasped her hands.

"Come on, Alice, let's go. Now. Let's run all the way home," he said eagerly.

"Can't we ride?" she moaned.

"A bus! A taxi! A helicopter! Anything you want. But let's go."

He pulled her off the bench with such force she flew up from her seat and fell heavily against his chest. He wrapped her in his arms and kissed her nose, her throat.

"Jim," she protested in a small pleading voice, trying to push him away. "Wait till we get home, at least. I don't like people watching us."

He kissed her on the mouth once more, then took her by the arm. "All right," he said. "Come on."

They started down the path, Jim pulling her by the hand, she running along beside him to keep up. At one point, laughing, he slowed his pace so that together they ran, hand-in-hand, over the grass, heading toward one of the exits leading from the park.

WHEN THEY GOT UPSTAIRS to the door of her apartment, Jim took the key from her and unlocked it. She went in ahead and he closed the door behind them. The rooms were dim in the late afternoon sunlight and in one of the open front windows Jim caught sight of a pot of tulips, their leaves and pink petals fluttering in the breeze.

Alice took off her coat and threw it on a chair. She came up to him, pushing strands of her hair back over her shoulders and said, "I'm going to take a shower."

"Why?" he asked in a soft whisper and putting his arms about her waist. "Don't. Don't wait to take a shower."

He lifted her off her feet, holding her high above him. She rested her hands on his shoulders and laughed down at him.

"But I have to. I'm all hot and sticky. Don't be impatient. Make yourself some coffee. Or have a beer. There's some in the refrigerator. I'll be through in a minute."

"Promise?"

"I promise." She leaned down and kissed him on the forehead.

He carried her down the hallway to the bathroom door and there set her down.

"You want to wear my cap in the shower? It's waterproof."

She looked doubtful a moment, then said, "Okay."

He whipped off his baseball cap and put it on her head at a jaunty angle.

"There you are," he said, standing back to look at her. "You look like a first-class pitcher."

"I'll tuck my hair up in it. I don't want it to get wet."

"Go on. Hurry up." He turned her about by the shoulders and steered her into the bathroom. She went in, closing the door behind her.

Jim took off his jacket and flung it beside hers on the chair. He undid a few buttons at the throat of his shirt and stuffing his hands in his pockets went to the front room and looked out the window. He put his nose to the tulips on the sill and smelled the blossoms. Then, restless, he paced about the room flipping the pages of magazines on the low table near the sofa and, going to the bookcase, pulled out one book after another from the shelves and slid them back into place without reading the covers. Whistling, he went out to the kitchen and opening the refrigerator door, stooped down, his hands resting on his thighs, and spotting a can of beer, took it out and slammed the refrigerator door shut. He looked around in a drawer for an opener, found one, and punched open the can.

Drinking out of the can, he walked to the bathroom door and listened. He heard water rushing in the shower and Alice quietly humming as she bathed. He took a swallow of beer then knocked on the door.

"Hey. I have to go to the bathroom."

"Well, come in then," came Alice's voice calling over the sound of the water. "I've started already."

He opened the door and went in. The room was warm and steamy and filled with the fragrant odors of her cologne and lotions. He lifted the toilet seat and unzipped his trousers.

"Are you in here?" Alice called from behind the curtain, her voice muffled.

"Uh-huh," he shouted back, turning his head and looking over his shoulder at Alice's shadow silhouetted against the plastic shower curtain.

"I can hardly hear a thing in here," came her voice over the rushing water.

Jim kicked down the toilet seat and gave a tug at the chain and there was the loud suck and roar of water swirling down the bowl.

He adjusted his clothes but did not leave. He stood gazing at Alice's shadowy outline against the curtain. He went to the mirror to take a look at himself but the glass was steamed and he saw nothing. With his finger he drew a circle on the misty glass, poked three dots inside it for eyes and mouth, stood back a pace and gazed at it, then drew on some sugar-bowl-type ears and scrawled some straggly lines over the top of the head for hair. He looked at the comic face once more and, satisfied, turned and went over and stood near the shower, putting his head close to the curtain.

"Hey," he called.

"What?" There was a pause. "I thought you were through and went out."

"I'm combing my hair. Hey."

"What is it?"

He paused a moment, then scratched his ear. "You want me to wash your back?" he said, speaking closer to the curtain.

There was a brief silence inside the shower. He cocked his head, listening intently.

"That might be nice," Alice said carefully. "But you might get all wet."

He shifted from one foot to the other.

"I'll risk it."

He heard her turn off the shower and stepped back a pace, clasping his hands behind him. Alice's glistening wet face poked out between the curtains as she clutched the plastic bunched around her chin, the red baseball cap on her head and water dripping from the peak of it. She smiled at him. He smiled back, a delighted smile, seeing her wearing his cap.

"Now you know what a pervert I am," he said and scuffed the toe of his shoe against the tile wall.

"No you're not."

"How's the cap?" He began to laugh at the sight of her.

"Pretty good." She dipped her head to let the water run off the cap then let the curtains go and as they parted she turned her back and handed him outstretched over her shoulder a soaped cloth.

"Here," she said. "Rub good."

His heartbeat quickened, seeing her slender body pink and luminous from the bath. "I've never done this before," he confessed with a catch in his throat, taking the washcloth from her gingerly. "I mean, to a girl."

"Only to boys?" she asked with a teasing lilt in her voice. She flashed an impish smile at him.

"Well," he stammered, "at camp—and school and all. You know. Horsing around. Where do I start?"

"At the top of the shoulders, you dope." She swung her head about to smile at him again, encouragingly. "Go on."

He began washing her shoulders carefully and gently.

"Harder."

He spread his legs apart, getting a good footing, then leaned to the task, rubbing vigorously between her shoulder blades.

"These are the beginning of your angel wings," he said, prodding a blade as he scrubbed.

"They must be frost-bitten," Alice laughed.

He lathered the sloping curve of her spine. The line of it struck him as so lovely he bent over and kissed it through the suds.

"That wasn't the cloth," Alice murmured.

"You have a very nice back," Jim said, returning to his scrubbing. He washed the small of her back, her flesh glowing rose from his efforts.

"Gee," he said, suddenly stopping and looking down at himself. "I'm getting kind of wet."

She turned to see.

"Maybe I better take my clothes off too."

A sly soft smile came over her face. "Well, maybe you'd better."

He handed her the cloth. "Be with you in a minute."

He went to the toilet seat and sat down and pulled off his shoes and socks. He stood up and unbuttoned his shirt and let it fall to the floor. Unbuckling his belt, he let his trousers drop and stepped out of them, then he pulled his T-shirt over his head and slipped off his shorts.

He went over and stood with one hand resting against the shower, suddenly quiet and hesitant, a shyness in his eyes.

"Is there room in there for two?"

She extended her arms, touching the tiled walls with her fingers. She held out her hand to him.

"I think so."

He took hold of her fingers and she looked at him and smiled, then dropped her gaze.

"Turn on the water," he said, stepping into the shower with her and pulling the curtain shut behind him. She turned on the faucets a little and gentle warm water shot down lightly over their bodies. He put his head under the spray and shut his eyes tight, snorting.

"God, that feels good."

Alice pulled her head back, away from the water, saying, "I'm trying not to get my hair wet."

"I dry hair pretty good," he said, his long arms clasping her about the waist. "You don't have to worry."

He reached up and took off the baseball cap and her long light hair spilled down over her shoulders. He hung the cap on one of the faucets. She quietly laid her head against his chest.

"Let me finish the job," he said, taking up the cloth again from the rack, his eyes keen, his voice tremulous. He rubbed soap in the cloth so hard the cloth disappeared in his hand in a cascade of white suds. Then he carefully washed her brow, dabbed gently around her eyes and nose and mouth. He washed her throat and shoulders, and her breasts, kissing each lingeringly as he washed them. He held out each of her arms and slowly and softly ran the cloth down the length of each. He washed her stomach, getting one of his ears full of soap as he rested one side of his face against it briefly. Crouching, he washed her thighs and legs, and turning her slightly, kissed the gentle slope of her buttocks, ran the cloth down the backs of her legs. He kneeled on the shower floor and taking her foot in his hand washed it, first one and then the other.

He stood up and kissed her on the mouth.

"All finished," he said quietly.

He reached over her shoulder and turned the water on with a little more pressure. He stood back against the tile watching her as she turned herself around and around, the warm heavy suds falling from her, like snow melting, Jim thought, as he watched her turn, slowly, with a quiet grace, her eyes gazing down. She turned down the water, leaving a fine mist falling over them. She took the cloth from his hands and turning him about began to wash him, starting at the shoulders and working down his back to his lean buttocks, his long thin legs. Her touch was sweetly soft to him and like a gentle caressing. He felt tense and shy at first and then let himself go, felt himself relax, yielding to the comforting slow rhythm of her hands as they moved over his skin, cleansing him. A warmth of desire flowed in him and he turned his head into his shoulder and closed his eyes. She had crouched to wash his feet and he took her by the shoulders and brought her up to him and kissed her quietly.

"I feel clean now," he said, his voice husky and subdued. "Let me rinse off."

She nodded and stepped from the shower. He turned the water on full force and stood under it, the water beating down hard on top of his head and running down swiftly over his body, flooding the soap away. He turned off the faucets, shook his head quickly from side to side, and stepped out.

She stood, smiling, gazing at the funny face he had drawn on the mirror. She was holding up a big bright green towel spread loosely in her hands. He took it and dried her body, then taking the long strands of her soft hair in the towel, he began drying it briskly.

"You dry hair like a man," she said. "Like my father used to."

"How's that?" he grinned, rubbing away, the slender muscles in his forearms taut.

"Rough. But nice."

When she was dry she went to the back of the door and unhooked a robe hanging there. It was a soft flannel robe with short sleeves and open down the front. There was a flap to keep the back of the neck warm. He helped her on with it.

"Go lie in the bed," he said, burrowing his nose in her hair. "I'm going to dry off. I'll be in in a minute."

She went out, the robe gathered around her, the robe so long the hem of it almost touched the floor.

When he had dried himself he went out and down the hall to the front room where Alice lay on the bed, the robe pulled around her, opened slightly at the throat. She smiled up at him as he lay down beside her. He took the top of the robe in his hands and parted it. He kissed her breast and moved close to her, his hands trembling as he stroked her skin beneath the cloth.

He took her roughly, with a quick urgency and excitement and, after, held her close and still, his head resting in the soft hollow of her neck. She held him clasped lightly in her arms and they lay silent without speaking.

He began to doze and dozing dreamed that he was walking under trees in bright sunshine, the branches of the trees heavy with buds, as though the trees were about to burst into leaf.

When he awoke the room was in darkness. Dusk had fallen while he slept. He turned over on his back and looked out the windows, seeing the black roof tops against the light evening sky and early stars hanging heavy and low on the horizon. He held his breath. Through the upper wrinkled pane of one of the windows glowed a soft quarter-moon, glowing duskily in the sky like an orange slice. He turned his head to look at Alice and saw she was awake, her face pale and indistinct in the shadows, her face pensive as she stared out the windows as though she had not slept but had lain awake for a long time.

"Do you see it?" he said softly.

"Yes."

She had that lost and wandering expression on her face, a look of poignant melancholy. Jim propped himself on one elbow and stroking the flesh of her throat said, "What are you thinking? You look so sad."

"I was thinking of the yellow balloon."

Jim chuckled softly and, a chill evening wind blowing in at the windows, pulled the sheet up about her.

"It must be very lonely up there with all the stars," she said.

"But we're not." He held her close.

"No," and she tilted her head up and kissed him on the chin. "I'm so glad to know you," she said quietly.

He felt his throat tighten and tears start to his eyes. For a moment he couldn't speak. Then he said, "It's good not to be lonely any more."

"Yes," she whispered. "But let's not talk about love."

"No."

"Or the yellow balloon?"

"It's all right. It's gone home. Remember, Alice?"

She turned her head on the pillow and gazed at him. "It's enough that we have each other. Now. Just for right now."

"Yes."

They lay quietly side by side, holding hands, watching the sky as it darkened, watching the moon as it lost its orange hue and became more bright. Jim leaned over and glanced at the clock on the desk.

"I've got to go."

"I know. I wish you didn't have to."

"I'll miss the last bus."

She sighed, letting her hands fall at her sides, clenching her fists. He leaned over and kissed her tenderly, then slid out from beneath the sheets and started to get dressed.

"Walk me to the subway?" he asked, buttoning his shirt in the darkness.

"Yes."

She got up and went into the bathroom while he finished dressing. When she came out her hair was combed and she had put on make-up. She was wearing a light green dress. She held his cap, smiling.

"Ready?"

"Yes. I'll get our coats."

She went to the chair and came back, holding out his jacket and cap to him. He laid them down and helped her on with her coat, then put on his own, and taking his cap put that on, too.

"All set. Let's go."

She turned on the hall light on the way out and he opened the door for her. They went out into the hall, Jim making sure the door was locked behind them. They went down the stairs and out into the street, Alice taking his arm as they headed in the direction of the subway station.

They were silent as they walked. Jim felt pleasantly drowsy and at peace with himself. He felt quiet and at rest, his body filled with a new strength, as though, in giving himself fully to her she had given him back a full measure of delight and strength. He felt imbued with a still and wordless power. He sensed this in her too; that there was no need for words, that what had passed between them in the darkness had been a wondrous giving and receiving, an expending in the yielding which gave back to each a power and sustenance each held for the other.

The evening air was mild and marvelously fragrant. There seemed a softness over everything, even the harsh buildings, and the pinched winter-whitened faces of the people who passed them, took on a gentleness like a softening of hard edges, a gentling and coloring of the bleak and drab. Winter's dying, Jim thought. He remembered his dream and felt a warm light over everything and gazed back over his shoulder at the piece of orange moon.

When they got to the subway she tucked her hands in her pockets and stood before him, her head bowed, silent. He took her face in both his hands and lifted it and looked into her eyes a moment before kissing her.

"Good bye."

"Good bye, Jim. Call me?"

"Yes."

"Soon."

She turned and began walking away. He started down the subway stairs slowly, watching her as she walked across the little park. He wondered if she would turn to look back and dragged his feet as he descended the stairs, wanting her to turn and maybe wave at him. But she continued to walk on, her back to him, her hands in the pockets of her coat, her slim body held erect with a certain poise and quietness. He had reached that point where the stairs went underground; his eyes were level with the sidewalk and he paused a moment, his hand resting on the metal railing, not able to take his eyes from her as she moved away from him. He wanted to shout to her, to get her attention, wanted to call some last word, to see her face again, see her smile. But he kept silent and lingering a moment longer, watched her go, deciding it was better that way— To see her leave with her hands tucked in her pockets and her long light hair luminous in the gathering darkness of the street. She turned a corner and was gone. Jim hurried down the stairs and through the tunnel, heading toward the turnstiles. He put a token in the slot and pushing through the stile walked out on the platform to wait for his train. The station was almost deserted as though a train had just departed. I'll have a few minutes to wait, he thought. He gazed down the darkened platform.

A woman, in her late forties, her back to Jim, stood talking to another woman who was dressed in black. They seemed strangers to each other. The one woman was explaining to the woman in the black dress that she didn't see very well and that that was how she had cut her leg. Jim looked at the woman again, then down to her legs. One of her stockings was badly torn and there was a long gash around her calf, the wound surrounded by dull blue bruises. The woman was explaining in a quiet but hurried voice—the voice of the lonely, Jim thought, who stop to speak to strangers out of desperation—that she had taken the subway downtown to go to a movie, "to have a time for myself," as she put it. She explained that she had tripped against something and had cut her leg.

"I'm blind as a bat," she said. "I even have to sit on top of the screen practically," she added, with a shy little laugh that seemed to say, Don't pity me— Please don't. I only want to stand here for a few minutes and talk to you and be your friend.

"Now I'm so ashamed," she continued in a hushed voice, moving closer to the woman in black. "My ripped stocking must look awful. I only want to get home as fast as I can."

She turned, as though to see if anyone were watching. Her eyes were crossed, the left eye crossed very badly and bulging slightly out of her head. These were behind thick glasses. Jim, seeing her face for the first time, felt a sudden sharp pain of revulsion in his heart for the woman and made to turn away. The woman, seeing that he was watching her, turned her back quickly, a little flustered, and moved closer to the woman in black, tilting her head sideways slightly, as though to watch him.

Jim didn't want to but he forced himself to look into her face again. Her eyes made her ugly, comic. She had tried to make up carefully, plucking her brows and arching each with a mascara pencil in a thin coquettish curve. Her lips were deformed, pulled down to one side, and she had tried, with her lipstick, to make them appear straight, but the lowest hanging part of her lips, the part which made it look as though her mouth were torn, was unpainted and stood out beside the brilliant scarlet of the lipstick the tinge of pale dead flesh. She had crimped her hair and it stood out in dry frizzy strands about her head. She was dressed in her Sunday best—a pale blue light coat faded at the shoulders, and a dress that looked worn and out of style. She clutched a big peeling patent-leather pocketbook in her hand. Her dark high heels were scuffed and run over at the heels so that her legs leaned to either side, and the bulge of her toes could be seen squeezed into the tip of each shoe. She continued to tell the woman about her accident. The woman in the black dress seemed not to want to listen, there was a look of impatience and distaste on her face, as though she wished the woman would go away. The cross-eyed woman repeated again her main concern, with a kind of dumb misery, to get home as quickly as possible, she was so embarrassed by the torn stocking and the cut in her leg. She unconsciously kept tugging her coat down as though trying to cover that part of her leg, hide it from view.

Jim's throat went tight and tears came to his eyes. Why does that have to be? he thought. Why does she have to be so ugly? Maybe she was hoping some man, somebody, would love her. And no man would. No guy could ever love her, Jim thought. Why does that have to be? And she had dressed herself up and made up, maybe hoping to find somewhere a little love.

Jim wanted to go over and put his arm around her. He wanted to tell her it was all right, not to worry about her ripped stocking and cut leg, not to worry about taking such pains to make it look as though her lips were straight, not to turn her back in embarrassment and shame when she caught him looking at her. What else to dress up nicely for but for love and not for shame. He wanted to go and put his arm around her and kiss her, tell her not to wear make-up, to let her face be as it was, her ugly face which seemed at moments strangely beautiful and shy, lit by the light of her suffering and loneliness, her longing. He wanted to tell her not to be embarrassed and ashamed, to not worry about her torn stocking, to go on to her movie and have "a time for herself." He wanted to kiss her and tell her this and then walk away, just to kiss her once, to let her know that someone would want to kiss her.

He knew that this was foolish. She would probably scream for a cop. He went behind one of the iron pillars so that no one would see him crying. He did not want her to see him crying. Maybe she would think that he was only pitying her— And perhaps he was, but he didn't want her to see that, he didn't want to make her self-conscious and maybe ashamed.

Not to pity her, he thought. Pity was a one-way street, static, and eventually a killing of feeling for both the pitied and the one who pities. He thought perhaps his feeling was the obverse of compassion—perhaps a savage brutality that really wanted to laugh at her, mock her to her face, hurt her cruelly, perhaps even press out with his thumbs those hideous cross-eyes which so offended him and made him feel guilty for wanting to jeer, and even cry, at their ugliness; guilty because of his straight and clear ones, his "lovely eyes," as Alice called them. He wanted both to caress the woman and to strike at her, to laugh at her and speak to her tenderly, reassuringly. But he could do neither. He could only lean against the cold grimy pillar of the subway station and cry, crying because she could never know what it was to have someone kiss her, to hold her hand, make love to her. Would never know things that he himself knew—the pleasure of being wanted, of being desired. He thought of Alice and of her love for him and his heart constricted with tears. He wanted so badly that the woman should also know these things, and knew at the same time it was impossible for him to ever share these things with her and for her to ever know them.

The train pulled into the station and the doors slid open. He waited to see which car the woman got into and then stepped into the car behind that one. He tipped his baseball cap low over his eyes and sat down in a seat in a far corner of the train. As the doors closed and the train lurched out of the station he looked up and saw sitting a few seats away, facing him, a young girl with a calm and pretty face. She was sitting very erect with her head held high and her long legs primly close together. She was gazing down at a single daffodil that she held in her lap, clasping it about the stem with her shapely fingers. The blossom bobbed and shook with the jolting of the train. She held the flower delicately and carefully, as though protecting it. Fascinated by the flower, she did not seem to want to take her eyes from it. She lifted the daffodil to her nose and smelled it. Then, aware of Jim's eyes upon her, she looked at him, a steady, clear-eyed gaze. Jim smiled and tipped his hat to her and nodded toward the flower as much as to say, That really is a lovely thing—and so are you. She smiled back, flushing a little and self-consciously shuffled her high heels prettily and, lowering her eyes, gazed down at the flower again.

Jim rested his head back against the wicker seat and closed

his eyes. He felt pleasantly tired. The balloon flying up to the sun and the clusters of bowed daffodils swaying in the wind, Alice's bright lovely face, smiling, and her long blonde hair, merged and moved vividly in his mind. It had been a good day, he thought happily. A yellow warmth of light glowed in him.

✑ THE LOVING

Jim SAT CLASPING his hands tightly, sitting on the
edge of the chair as he looked out the open window. He was
watching for Alice to come up the drive. After she had gotten
off the bus, she had called him from a little grocery store in the
center of town. She had stopped on the way to his house to
"buy a few things" for their supper she had told him on the
phone. He wanted to come meet her right away, but she said not
to, she wanted to cook a surprise supper for him and didn't
want him to see what she was buying.

He sat tense now, waiting. Outside the windows the trees
shone bright in the early afternoon sunlight. A drowsy late
spring afternoon, warm and quiet. There was a murmurous
hum of bees in the still air. Now and then the grass in the broad
front yard rippled in the slight wind. Far down the yard, beyond a clump of tall pines, was the street. There was the occasional slap of tires on the hot asphalt as an automobile passed.

216

Cindy, the landlady's dog, lay dozing under the shade of one of the pine trees.

Jim began to daydream, having powerful memories of the girl, remembering her eyes, the line of her neck and the slenderness of it. Her white teeth. Remembering her body, he desired her very much. He leaned back in the chair, less taut, his hands resting on the arms of the chair. He couldn't wait for her to be there with him, to put his arms around her, to kiss her, hold her close to him. The memory of her had persisted through the week, since the last time he had seen her, the memory of her loveliness, the fullness and beauty of her.

Cindy roused herself from beneath the tree and gave a sharp bark. She leapt up and ran off down the driveway, still barking. Jim was up like a shot and, pushing open the screen door, ran out into the yard.

Coming up the drive, with Cindy barking and dancing around her, was Alice. She was wearing a light green dress that swirled nebulously about her. She walked quickly toward Jim, her long blonde hair curling down softly at her throat, strands of it flying back from her shoulders. She was carrying an enormous paper sack in one hand and a small overnight bag in the other. As Jim ran to her, she smiled and called hello. He met her halfway to the house and flinging his arms about her, kissed her on the mouth.

"I'm so glad you're here," he whispered eagerly, taking the paper bag from her. "What'd you do, buy the whole store?" he laughed suddenly, feeling the weight of the bag in his hands. "Why didn't you let me help you? What's in it?"

"None of your business," said Alice, with a teasing smile. "I told you— It's a secret," and she rapped playfully at his knuckles as he attempted to open the bag.

Before they got to the door, Alice stopped and looked at the house. "What a nice little place," she said. And then gazing about the yard, said, "It's really a lovely place you live in, Jim."

"Come on," he said, taking her hand. "There's lots more I want you to see. We'll go inside and dump this stuff and I'll take you around. Oh—" he said, looking into her face and his voice changing. "But maybe you're tired from the bus trip?"

"No. I'm anxious to see what the place is like."

Jim held the screen door open for her and she went in ahead of him, setting her overnight bag down and looking with curiosity about the room.

"So this is your home," she said, turning to him with a smile.

He stood by the door, a look on his face as though he were anxious for her reaction, that she be pleased.

"You like it?" he asked.

"Oh," she said, clapping her hands together and gazing around. "It's so big and cool and homey—like a farmhouse. Just as you described it."

"I cleaned the place especially," he blurted out. Then in a more quiet, slightly sheepish tone, "Since you were coming."

"How sweet of you," she laughed and running to him, kissed him on the cheek.

"Out here's the kitchen," he said, and led her through the room and out back.

Following him into the kitchen, she ran with a light step to the windows and looked out at the green fields sloping far off beyond the house to the pond. The branches of the pine trees lifted and fell easily in the light wind.

"I can't tell you how much I like it," she cried, spinning around to him with a bright and ecstatic expression on her face.

"I knew you would," he said. "I'm glad."

He nodded down to the bag in his hands. "What do I do with this?"

"Give it to me," she said, running over and taking the bag from him. "I'll take care of everything. Now you just go in the other room and I'll put all my surprises away. Be with you in a minute."

"Aw, come on, Alice. Let me see," he said, a hangdog look on his face and tugging at the top of the bag, trying to peek in.

"No," she said, laughing, and snatched the bag away from his grasping fingers. "When I set the dinner on the table, then you'll see."

"Can't I show you where to put things?" he asked, as though with one last desperate try.

"I can manage," she said, and turning him around, kissed the back of his neck and pushed him toward the door.

"Don't be too long," he said over his shoulder, watching her walk to the table as he went out, lingering for a moment, fascinated by the movement of her full hips in the green dress. Her shoulders were slender and softly rounded, like a little girl. He saw that she had high heels on. That she was wearing high heels pleased him. And that she was wearing the filmy green dress pleased him, too. It was as though she had dressed especially for him. Had wanted to look nice. As he walked into the other room, he smelled the lovely aura her perfume had left there, and as he walked to the window he breathed it in, as though he were breathing in a part of her, wondrous and yielding. He listened to the sounds she made in the kitchen as she put the groceries away—the refrigerator door being opened and slammed; the rattling of paper packages as she put things in the cabinet. The house seemed less empty, the rooms seemed to have taken on a brightness, an aliveness since she had come into them. She had dressed up for him and the thought of this gave him a pleasant elation.

"I'm ready." It was Alice standing in the doorway.

He turned and gazed at her.

"I've brought some low shoes," she said, coming into the room. "It'll only take a minute."

She went to her bag and snapping it open, brought out a pair of practical Oxford-like walking shoes. Kicking off her high heels, she stepped into them, then went to Jim and put her arms about him, laying her head on his chest. He breathed her sweetly scented hair.

"See? I'm ready," she said, rubbing her nose against the buttons of his shirt.

He held her tightly for a moment, closing his eyes.

"How good it makes me feel to have you here," he said.

Then he took her hand and pushing open the door, they stepped out into the yard. Cindy, who had been lying near the step, as though waiting for them to come out, became suddenly alert and, with ears and tail pointed high, trotted after Jim and Alice as they rounded the corner of the house, Alice pausing and stooping to sniff at the iris and late jonquils which grew in narrow beds beneath the windows.

The air was fragrant with the scent of blossoms and the smell of newly cut grass. Behind the house there was a larger garden and at the end of it was a grape arbor. Picking their way among the flowers, Jim led her into the arbor. They sat down facing each other on the low rough-hewn benches which ran along either side. It was cool and sweetly damp beneath the vines, a cool shade. Out at the front of the arbor they could see the broad sweep of the Hudson. The sun was hot, so hot it made a mist over the river. Far back, over the broad field of grass, was the pond. Their hands touched and Jim watched Alice's face as she lifted her head and looked at the river and the pond, then above her at the leaves and blossoming grapes. Like the fox grapes in the woods at home, Jim thought.

Cindy lay in the shade near the entrance to the arbor, panting heavily, her tongue lolling, her tail occasionally brushing at a fly on her haunches.

The place was dark and they were surrounded on each

side and overhead by a roof and walls of old splintered vines from which the new leaves and tiny buds of grapes emerged— As by some magic from those gnarled cracked vines that seemed to have no life in them at all, and yet from which the new green leaves were sprouting, and the blossoming grapes—as out of some old and wonderful dark miracle and mystery.

Jim reached across and touched her, caressed her face and hair. She sat quietly, her hands in her lap, her head turned slightly towards him, smiling.

"It's lovely," she breathed.

"Yes." He cocked his head to one side, studying her.

"That's your best side," he said.

"What?"

"The way your head is turned now, it presents your best side."

She laughed. "I've got to remember that."

There was a silence as he gazed at her. Then he said, "You're very beautiful."

Her throat flushed and an added warmth came into her eyes. "Thank you," she said, dropping her eyes and smiling.

"Lift your hair."

"What?"

"Lift your hair. I want to see your ears."

She began to laugh. "Why do you want to see my ears?"

"Because they're funny elfish ears."

She laughed outright and threw back her head and bunching her long blonde hair in her hands, pulled it back.

"They're lovely little ears," he said. He leaned forward, his hand tremulous, and his fingers brushed one ear lightly, tracing the delicate curves of it.

"Funny ears," he whispered.

He kissed the ear, then put his arms about her. His body stiffened with awe as he saw, over her shoulder, a snowy egret come floating slowly, dreamily, out of the sky to alight soft and easily as a feather on the waters of the pond.

"Look," he breathed quietly, as though, even from that distance, the slightest sound would startle the bird and put it to flight.

Alice turned on the bench and looked in the direction of the pond, her hand moving to her mouth at the beauty of the bird. They couldn't take their eyes from the egret as it stood long-legged in the shallow water near the shore and ducked its head beneath its wing and cupped its wings about itself, then stretched one wing down, long and rippling, the broad sweep of tip-feathers barely brushing the water. Then, as though gathering itself into itself, it stood tall and erect, its neck looped slightly down, and stalked easily, with grace, through the water.

Jim held his breath as he watched it, then gave a start as a shot rang out on the still afternoon and an abrupt spray of water fanned up near the egret's stemlike legs. The bird, frightened, took long jigging steps in the water and, with head darting back and forth, its wings began to beat slowly as with rhythmic, unhurried ease it lifted from the water and flew up into the air.

Another shot crackled sharply in the stillness, but the bird, its long wings beating swiftly now, flew safely high above the trees and was gone.

Jim grabbed Alice by the arm and pulling her after him, bolted out of the arbor. Cindy leapt up and chased after them, barking.

"What is it?" cried Alice, trying to keep up with him as they ran over the grass. "What were those shots?"

Jim, his face tense, said nothing. When they got to the pond, they saw, at the far end, three boys, two of them with .22 rifles in their hands. On seeing Jim and Alice approach, they quickly propped their guns against a tree where several fishing poles were also leaning. At the base of the tree was a heap of knapsacks. One boy squatted quickly at the pond's edge and began prying stones out of the mud and with a blank face of nonchalance began chucking rocks in the water. The other two looked at Jim, unsure, waiting to see what he was going to say. Cindy pranced around the boys, barking and snorting eagerly.

Jim came up within a few yards of them and, hands on hips, said, "What did you want to shoot that bird for?"

"What bird?" said one of the boys, glancing innocently at his companions.

"We didn't see no bird," said the one who had been throwing rocks, as he straightened up, rubbing his muddy hands on the thighs of his dungarees.

"We heard the shots. We saw the bird fly away," Jim said, an edge of anger in his voice. He took a few steps forward. "Get your gear together," he said with a brusque motion toward the rifles. "Get off this property. You don't belong here."

"We were only trying to scare it a little, mister," said one of the boys who had not yet spoken, rubbing the toe of his shoe in the mud. The other two glared at him.

"You got no business doing that," Jim said. "Now get out."

The boys, with surly faces and hanging heads, muttered amongst themselves and went to the tree where the guns and knapsacks were. Jim turned and went back to Alice and took her by the arm.

"I'm glad they didn't kill the bird," she said, and gripped his arm. Her hands were trembling.

"It's all right," he said, squeezing her gently around the waist. "They're going now."

"Who are they?"

"Just kids from the town. They wander in here once in a while."

He led her along the edge of the pond until they came to the flume where the water rushed clear and cold and became a stream running off through the woods. Taking her hand and going first, Jim helped her hold her balance as they crossed on the stones and short sections of log set in the flume. Cindy splashed after them, pausing in the middle to duck her head in the water and drink and then trotting on. On the other side Jim found a dead tree limb fallen across the water and he pulled at it and broke it loose and heaved it off in the brush.

"You see," he said, putting his arm around Alice and pointing, "You get a better idea how big the place is from here."

They gazed across the pond and over the wide field with its pine trees. Far up the field, toward the village, Jim's small white clapboard house shone so brightly in the sun it almost hurt their eyes to look at it.

Cindy began barking fiercely in the low bushes nearby, ruffling the plants with her movements, darting around in a circle, her head down, as she yipped at something in the grass.

"I hope that's not a snake," said Alice uneasily, glancing over her shoulder toward Cindy. She took Jim's hand and held it tightly.

"Come on. Don't be afraid. Too early for snakes," he lied.

They walked over to where Cindy was still barking and circling about, her tail wagging furiously, and came out onto a flat patch of ground. A muskrat lay dead at Cindy's feet.

"Get away, Cindy. Away, girl," Jim called, and the dog slunk off a few paces, low growls coming from its throat.

The muskrat was lying on its back in the grass near the water, a small bullet hole through its chest, not a speck of blood, the wound was so neat. Jim and Alice stared down at the dead animal quietly, Alice standing a little behind Jim and peering over his shoulder.

The soft rich fur of the muskrat glistened in the sunlight. Its thick tail, dry and scaled like a whipcord, tough, tapered off to a slack curling tip. The hind legs lay crooked and sprawled a little to either side. The dark feet were webbed, the thighs muscular, well-developed, strong back legs for swimming. The fore paws were short and tiny, the paws like small black hands, the fingers curled slightly upon the fur of its chest. The eyes were closed in the sloping head, and protruding from the upper jaw, its two front teeth hung down, long and sharp, looking like thin hard kernels of corn. The teeth were clamped over its small chin and it seemed as though the animal was never able to get them into its mouth.

It lay as though sleeping quietly in the bright afternoon grass.

Jim looked away. Across the pond, he could see the three boys gathering their guns and knapsacks and fishing lines together.

"Jim, don't say anything to them," said Alice, tugging at his sleeve. "They're going."

"Come on. Let's head back to the house," he said.

They crossed over the flume and started back in the same direction, towards where the boys were. They passed a clump of long-stalked milkweed pods, dead and leaning in the slight wind with a dry swaying. Jim stopped and pulled one up by the roots. Alice suddenly dropped his hand and running ahead, caught the low branch of a tree and swung herself up and forward and landed a few feet from the boys.

They paused a moment, hesitant. Alice stood watching them, an uncertain smile on her face.

"Hello," she said.

The boys mumbled hello back and went on with their packing. Jim came up behind her, watching the boys and waving the long milkweed stalk in his hand.

The boys halted in their packing and watched, and Alice turned, too, as the gentle swinging of the stalk in Jim's hand released the tight-packed seed feathers from the pod and they flew up, soft and winking in the light and were carried away slowly in the wind.

"That's just a' ole leftover skunkweed," said one of the boys, heisting his knapsack on his back.

"Yeah," grumbled the other two disparagingly, and taking up their lines and guns, trudged off single file down the path toward the road.

Alice was fascinated and couldn't take her eyes from the plumed seeds drifting from the burst pod. Jim turned from the departing boys to look at her face. Walking, he continued to sway the stalk back and forth before him, the dirt-clotted roots of it dragging behind him in the grass.

Cindy went chasing after the seeds and snapping at a few caught them in her mouth. She began to sneeze and stopped abruptly to rub her nose in the grass. Snorting and coughing, swiping at her nose with a fore paw, she trotted back to Jim and walked several feet behind him.

They moved off, away from the pond, and Alice ran before him, her cheeks red from running. Laughing, like a child, her slender arms reached up and all around her as her fingers tried to catch the feathery seeds which now filled the air and swept, snowlike, amongst the branches of the trees. Jim walked slowly, smiling, himself fascinated, and watched her face. The sun was sloping down over her shoulder and the white puffy seeds floated about her and then up above her, sparkling and delicate in the clear light, as though, by some magic, they were flying back to the sun. She caught one and holding it carefully between her fingers, touched it to her cheek and brushed her lips with it, and all the time her eyes were alive with a childlike light, and the smile of a child as she touched the seed to her nose and then brought it to her lips and kissed it before releasing it to the air.

Jim threw his arm around her and they went back to the

house, laughing and talking, the stalk, slung over Jim's shoulder, still sending off a smoke of feathered seeds sweeping off to either side and swirling about them.

BACK IN THE FRONT ROOM, sitting on the sofa, Jim realized how different Alice was, like another girl from the one he'd met for the first time at the party. Then she had seemed wandering and lost. There had been that indefinite smile on her face and she had seemed so out of place, as though she had nothing to do with the party around her. She had a way of speaking and then looking away, her eyes taking on a remote and veiled look as though she were suddenly some place else, some place he could not enter, as though she had shut him out, not harshly or offensively, but always it seemed in the most gentle way. It annoyed him, and troubled him. He did not like the feeling it gave him that she was turning away from him, excluding him from some private inner feeling she would not share with him. It made him feel strangely alone, as though she were no longer there for him. She seemed like that now—in her eyes there came that remoteness and inner-pensiveness, her eyes cast down, staring at the design in the carpet.

"What are you thinking— When you turn away from me— Like now— When your eyes get that lost and wandering look?"

She gazed at him slowly, puzzled, not understanding, as though being pulled back unwillingly from another world.

"I was thinking how happy you make me."

He grinned. "But you looked so solemn."

"I didn't feel solemn. It's a very nice feeling."

She nestled closer to him and he realized now, seeing her alone in his house, that she became vivid for him. There was still that sense of wandering and lostness about her, but it was not as strong or as apparent. Sitting beside him on the couch, she revealed an oblique and quiet sense of humor. He realized a practical and purposive nature in her, and a gentleness he had not known was there. And she liked him. This made him feel very good, very sure of himself. All of his earlier apprehensions were slowly vanishing as his old preconceived image of Alice subsided and she gradually revealed herself to be someone totally different, soft and appealing, very desirable.

He gazed at her face from the corner of his eyes. Her face was round, an open and generous face; in the delicate green eyes there was a light of humor and good nature. Her mouth fascinated him, he loved to watch her mouth as she talked or smiled.

"Such a lovely dress," he breathed, running his fingers gently over the fabric. She smiled, pleased, and he put his hand beneath her chin and kissed her. His heart beat fast and as he caressed her arms, he whispered, "Let's make love. I've thought of nothing but making love to you all week."

Her eyes took on a warmth and she nodded quietly and getting up, crossed the room to the bed. He watched as she sat and took off her shoes, slowly, carefully slipping down her stockings. She lifted her dress over her head and let it drop on a chair, the gauzy dress shimmering lightly in a heap, like green water. She took off her underclothes quickly and lay down on the bed, reclining on her side, smiling at him, a sudden voluptuous smile.

Jim came to her and sitting down on a corner of the bed leaned over and kissed her. Then he began unlacing his shoes, his throat suddenly dry, constricted, with desire. He stood and took off the rest of his clothes and threw them on an armchair close by.

Going from window to window, he drew down the shades making the room dim. As he pulled down the last shade, the cool spring air rushed in the open window and whipped delicately about his skin. He shivered and crossed his arms over his chest, cupping a shoulder in each hand, delighting in the coolness of the soft breeze on his body. He went to the bed and lay down close beside her. He took her hand and put his face against her cheek. With his other hand he traced the contours of her body.

"You have such a lovely belly," he whispered gently, a bemused smile on his face. "I want to lay my head there. I want to put my ear there and listen."

In the near-darkness he could barely make out her face and he saw that she was smiling. Her small hands reached for his face and clasped it between her fingers lightly as she drew him down to her. He kissed her nose and eyes, gently bit the soft flesh of her throat. Her breath quickened and she held him to her tightly. She was such a different woman in the darkness. In his mind, as he kissed her, there leapt up the image of daffodils—she had that same brightness and freshness of the flower— Her vivid green eyes and the soft yellowness of her hair which spread out wide and soft now over the coverlet. There was that brightness about her, in her face and smile; it thrilled him as the first flowers of spring shooting up amidst patches of snow in a field thrilled his heart and made him feel glad and intensely alive. She was that, with a sweet warm smell about her, but she was also a darkness, another woman now, different from the girl, the daffodil girl, he had seen in the light. There was in her the deep rich darkness of the iris, like the black iris with their brilliant yellow throats which grew outside beneath the windows. He thought of her and the iris, thought of the flowers humming and burning with a dark life out there in the shadowy stillness of the afternoon—burning darkly as she seemed to now, a mysterious warmth and yielding in her that stirred him deeply.

He laid his face against her stomach, listening, listening to the life and darkness beating in her, feeling in himself the same trembling vivid life. Her flesh was soft and sweetly amorous beneath his cheek. He kissed the softly scented skin and moved up to her breasts, brushing their firmness with his lips. Turning her head slightly on the pillow, he moved to the soft nape of her neck, then to her mouth which was warm and yielding, waiting.

A breeze blew in at the windows. The leaves rustled on the trees in the yard. Down on the street the tires of an automobile whined past. For him the moment was poignant, held motionless. The powerful odor of flowers filled his nostrils as he moved over her in the darkness.

ALICE WAS SLEEPING softly beside him, curled up, her knees close to her chin, her hands clasped, as in prayer, and resting under her cheek. Jim got quietly out of bed and slipping on his trousers went to the screen door and looked out. He watched the deep iris growing under the windows, their centers a vibrant tawniness— Watched them as though they were alive, as though, in some indefinable way, they were about to become animate: dark petal-like creatures dancing in the grass.

He pressed his head against the screen door. There was the soft afternoon still, a softness over everything. The fields stretching off beyond the house were softened and in himself he felt a quietness. He gripped the edge of the screen door, saying in himself, Let it come back. Please, let it come back. The softness of the day and in himself a softness and quietness; in himself the remembering, the lost years. His illness of two years had been like rooting in mud amongst pigs for what little garbage of sustenance that seemed all that was left in the world. Living in mud amongst pigs. How had he wandered there? He saw that he had been mistaken, that he had been ignorant and afraid, afraid of all that was tender and warm in him, all that which made him human. Burying his heart, his feelings, he had buried himself, deeply, remorselessly; a suffocating deadness that was not death. Then if he had had to go there, to the mental hospital, to learn that, it was well learned. If only it was not too late, to begin again, to dig further out of his buriedness, to get completely back into life now, back amongst living things.

Maybe now, after all those years under the mud he would succeed in stretching out his roots and push himself up and out into the Jim that he was, the hidden and unknown Jim. The hurt, the pain—flowers do this—they are lovely, and dangerous, he thought, just as in ourselves, those flowerings.

It was like when, as a child, he had been kept in the house two months with scarlet fever and the morning the quarantine had been lifted he had gone out the front door and stood quietly in the early morning sun. Across the street, the trees in the woods were fine with the soft new shoots of spring. He had taken a few cautious steps forward and then had begun to run, and lifting his arms wide, he ran among the trees, laughing happily. Flinging his arms around the slender trunk of a budding sassafras, he pressed his face against the rough, sweet-smelling bark. Birds flew up, filling the air with their cries, and he looked up to watch them, tears running down his cheeks. There was the sky, as now, a light and impenetrable blue, and the early sun, warm and soft over everything. He had stood, clasping the thin tree lightly in his hands, and bent his head and kissed the bark. Slipping to his knees, he laid his face against the roots, vowing in his heart to love all things forever and ever.

Now, tears fell on his hands and he lifted his hands and kneaded them together. The fields outside the screen door became blurred with his crying. I want to get well, he said over and over to himself. I want to get back into life. I want to live again.

He felt a hand on his shoulder and turning looked into

Alice's eyes. She saw that he was crying and put her arms about him and held him close. Jim laid his face against her breast, his thin shoulders shaking.

"I didn't mean to wake you," he said.

She held him more closely and whispered into his hair to be still and rocked him gently back and forth in her arms.

His tears were like a melting of all the gray cold lostness and terror that had been in them the past two years, and his eyes, stricken though they were, became warm and alive again, a melting of the grayness and deadness of his fear. He felt his fingers reaching out to her, as to heal, to touch, in himself, and, hand upon hand, make him well again. He stood with his arms around her and his head on her breast. He could hear the beating of her heart, feel the warmth of her. He suddenly felt very awkward and shy. He saw the rains of love, like oil, over parched and tired skin; the rains of love that are bitter tears, that are soft delicate words from the heart. He saw the broad fields of himself suddenly fine with green buds of innumerable possibilities, the self generous and abundant with the possibilities of life. He was a lean, intense and vital being. He had burned and would burn again. It was in his nature to be this thing. In his feeling was his strength, in his heart was his strength. He wasn't alone now. There was the possibility of seeds of himself sprung within him, the grasses of his own broad fields, now mostly flinty and rocky, the soil thin and cracked and parched— His feelings and words as rain, her feelings and words as rain falling on the taut, dried fields of him. And the seeds of him leapt up, eager, the way a fish, hurtling, a silver flash in the air, leaps up out of a river.

Rain coaxing the unwilling earth, arose slowly in his mind.

They stood for a long time in the doorway, she still holding him, and he grew quiet. Gazing down at her, he touched the side of her face with his fingers. She dried his tears with her hands, then loosened her arms about him and stepping back, rested her hands on his shoulders.

"You must be hungry," she said quietly.

He nodded, smiling, and as though happy to see him his old self again, Alice pecked him on the nose and ran across the room and started to get dressed.

"I'll start dinner," she said, dropping her slip over her head. "It won't take long. You stay put. I don't want you in the kitchen."

She put on her dress.

"But can't I help?" he asked.

"Yes. Move that table out from the corner and set up two chairs. Do you have a cloth?"

"I'll find one."

"Good." She smoothed her dress down over her thighs with the palms of her hands, then blew him a kiss and was gone into the kitchen.

Jim put on the rest of his clothes, then pulled out the table as Alice had directed and drew two chairs up to it. He poked around in the bottom drawers of an old chest and found a faded table cloth. It was a little wrinkled so he shook it out, giving it a couple of smart snaps, and threw it over the table. Up on a ledge near the door he found the dusty old candle in a metal holder that he used for whenever the lights went out. He blew the dust off the candle and made a clucking noise as he saw that it was chipped around the middle. It'll have to do, he said to himself and set the candle in the center of the table.

He went to the doorway to the kitchen and holding a hand over his eyes, called, "Hey, Alice."

"Get out of here!" she cried, good-naturedly.

"I'm not looking. Hey. I got some sort of nice dishes the landlady gave me—they're in the sideboard here. And some old heavy silverware. Shall I set the table with that?"

"Fine. Yes, that will be a great help."

Jim went back into the front room and over to the side-board and bringing out the plates and cups and saucers, began to set two places at the table. That done, he rooted around in the sideboard again and found a pair of wine goblets at the back of the closet. One was cracked, so he set that in the place he figured he would be sitting. After carefully lining up the knives and forks and spoons, he stood back a step, surveying the table, looking satisfied at the job he had done.

He felt drowsy and going to the chair near the open window, sat down, resting his head against the back of it. He closed his eyes. From the kitchen came the first delicious odors of dinner cooking. It gave him a sudden sharp pang in his stomach. He hadn't eaten for hours. He had been too excited about seeing Alice, too busy cleaning up the place, and had forgotten to eat. He listened as she moved about the kitchen. Stretching out his long legs, he sank deeper, more comfortably, into the armchair. The sweet-smelling wind blew in at the window and he began to doze and, dozing, dreamed:

. . . He was on a ship going through a narrow passage. He was lying flat on his back in the foremost part of the prow, his feet against the bulkhead which sloped off to either side, his hands folded over his chest, keeping as still as possible, while the ship, with barely an inch of space on either side to scrape past, edged slowly through the narrow strait. . . .

It was as though in the last few years he had been going through a pass, as, in the dream, a moving through a tight place, and he had to shrink in upon himself, hunch his shoulders and draw in his head and, crouching, make himself as small and still as possible so that he and the ship, the ship of himself, could get through— As a seed must, sleeping gathered into itself in stillness and buried around by the weight of its darkness

— It had been like that, as though he had had to withdraw, pull into himself—a recoil before he could again become open, could move again in his life and in the life around him.

He felt a hand gently shaking him on the shoulder.

"Wake up." Alice was bending over him, whispering. "Dinner's ready."

He opened his eyes, stared at her stupidly a moment, as yet unawake, then rubbed fiercely at his eyes with his knuckles.

"Shall I throw a pitcher of water on you?" she laughed.

"No, I'm awake now," he said, and leapt up out of the chair.

"The surprise is ready," Alice whispered, smiling, and taking his hand led him over to the table. She pulled out a chair and made him sit down.

"You've set the table very nicely," she said, giving him a quick kiss on the ear. "Only you got the silverware all backwards."

"Well, you can't have everything." He smiled up at her.

"Be back in a minute," and she turned and hurried out of the room.

The candle was lit and near it was a vase of deep purple iris. Jim leaned forward and smelled the blossoms, thinking, She must've picked them while I slept.

Alice came back in from the kitchen carrying a huge three-inch steak smothered with mushrooms on a tray.

She laid the tray on the table, a shy expectant smile on her face and Jim leaned forward in his chair and breathed in deeply, grinning and closing his eyes in pleasure at the aroma.

"Smells delicious," he murmured.

She gave a pleased little laugh and went out to the kitchen again and returned a moment later. In one hand she held a dish of rice, brightly yellow with saffron, and in the other a green salad, the crisp leaves curling up out of the wooden bowl.

She set these down and hurried out again and came back carrying a trencher piled high with roasted ears of corn. These she also put on the table.

"There, I guess that's everything," she said, folding her hands loosely at her stomach. There was a fine bead of sweat over her upper lip and her full cheeks were flushed. A strand of her hair, slightly damp, had fallen over her brow.

"This is really a fine supper," exclaimed Jim, his eyes wide with delight as he surveyed the food.

He leapt around and slid behind her and reached for her chair and pulled it out for her.

She smiled, a little flustered and, thanking him, sat down in the chair, turning her head to look up at him.

"Is it safe to go in the kitchen now?" he said. "I've got some wine in the icebox."

"Yes, it's safe now," she laughed.

Jim came back in a moment carrying in one hand a metal corkscrew and in the other a slender bottle of red wine. He stuck the screw in the top of the bottle, then held the bottle between his thighs and turned the handle slowly and the cork slid out easily. He put his nose to the wine and took a sniff, then picked up her glass and filled it to the brim. He poured wine for himself and, holding his glass aloft, said, "I propose a toast to the cook!"

She began laughing, putting her hand to her mouth.

"But you haven't tasted the *food* yet!" she protested.

"That's true. But even so, I want to propose a toast at least to the delectable *odors* of the food."

She laughed again, a merry flushed little laugh and she touched glasses with him and they drank together. Alice took a small sip and looked at him with expectant eyes over the rim of her goblet.

They began to eat, she taking dainty little forkfuls and

casting her gaze up surreptitiously every now and then from her plate to see what his reaction to the meal would be. Jim ate with tremendous gusto and could barely keep himself from wolfing the food down. In between bites, his mouth full, he kept telling her how delicious it was. She relaxed in her chair with an expression of quiet pleasure on her face as she watched him eat.

There was not a shred of anything left when they had finished eating.

"And now," Jim said, wiping his mouth heartily with his napkin, "now that we've eaten—I propose a toast to the excellence, on all counts, of our beautiful hostess, and chef! Alice, it was really very good."

"You sound like you're in a movie," she giggled.

They clinked glasses once more and drank. Jim sat back, his hands rubbing his stomach, an expression on his face as though Alice could expect bubbles of contentment to come burbling out of his mouth at any moment.

The wine brought a look of merriment to her features. He watched her face, watched her eyes, her mouth move, wanting to kiss her, wanting to touch those funny ears of hers. She was so soft and he was afraid of her softness. With such a woman he must be very tender; he must have feelings equal to the softness and tenderness, the beauty of her.

"I'll make coffee," she said.

"I'll help clear the table."

"No. Sit and smoke. Let me do that."

She got up with a light quick movement and held him in his chair by placing her hand on his shoulder. He looked into her eyes and put his hand over hers and then took her hand from his shoulder and put it to his lips and kissed it.

She smiled and looked aside, as though not knowing what to say. She brushed his hair back with her hand, and said, "I'll clear the table now and get the coffee going." And she moved away from him, stacking the dishes slowly and carefully and taking them out to the kitchen.

"It's such a nice night," he called after her. "How about going for a walk down to the river? We can have our coffee there."

"All right," she answered from the kitchen.

For dessert she brought in a bowl of chilled fresh strawberries. Jim whipped the cream. His wrist ached by the time he finished but he felt a sense of pride seeing his accomplishment: the cream standing up in firm snowy whorls in the bowl.

"I'm never able to get it just right that way," said Alice, admiringly. And flushed with pride and the wine, Jim kissed her.

She topped the strawberries with the whipped cream and they ate the dessert, Jim crushing the icy berries with his tongue against the roof of his mouth, delighting in the surprise of their tart chilled sweetness. She watched him doing it and did the same, both of them laughing as some of the bright red juice ran down her chin. Like a child, Alice saved her cream till last.

Outside, over the trees, the full moon was rising.

THE LIGHT was just going out of the day as they started down the hill, hand-in-hand, Jim carrying the two mugs of coffee in his free hand. Cindy jogged along behind.

They could see the white hulls of the boats bobbing gently on the water. Watching them, Jim thought of wings, of butterflies, souls of boats beating on the darkening water. The lights of small towns across the river were coming on, small clusters of warm orange lights here and there and long stretches of black empty shore. Launches were returning from the day's outing, their spars tipped with green lights, and moving slowly, quietly, over the water towards the pier to tie up for the night.

In the east, the moon, at first a milky blur, emerged from behind a cloud—full moon glowing brightly over Tappan Zee.

Jim and Alice sat on the flagstones of his landlady's dock and watched a boy dive and swim from the dock next door. Cindy ran farther down the beach and splashed into the water and swam about in wide circles, her head pointed skyward, her mouth wide in an animal grin.

The night and the silent dark-running waters of the Hudson moving past them in the dusk evoked in Jim night journeys and the thrill of departures—change, and new places, the thrill of beginning again. Now new moon over the waters, Alice's soft voice speaking to him in the darkness, Jim listening and not listening, the river slapping against the wall of the dock— There was in him a sense of a great silence, each gesture and movement accurate and held: the boy poised for an instant standing in the half light on the white railing of the pier, for an instant his body tensed and lovely before the plunge— Explosion of white foam in the darkness.

Dark freighters passed, moving out to sea—Jim dreaming, in the seaweed toss, of new journeys, new beginnings, wonderful sun-drenched mornings and the green hills of a sea island. How alone in his death he had been, and now, dreaming on the flagstones still warm from the day's sun, surrounded by night, his hand holding her hand, his heart, again, after so many years of buriedness, stirred by all the evocation of moon and waters. Clouds parted and stars flooded through. He felt the run of the earth rushing backward from the sun. There was the darkness and mystery of hills on the far shore, the heart straining in his breast, an ache, of wanting to go, to be off—the night journey beckoning, the magic of the evocations of the night stroking and stirring his heart, and Jim wondering if it would lead to nothing more than the same old thing, the emptiness and disenchantment, and the incredible loneliness of his lost years.

Put an end to desire, the heart speaks. Wondering if his death would come again, wondering and imagining a black carrion bird crouched in the corner near the pilings, its rough feathers scratching the wood as it moved, waiting. Trembling, he held her hand more tightly and thought of himself and the girl, wondering if it was at all possible, saying in his heart, My wife, my wife, I love you very much.

Now, after the heat of the day, after the sun burning, a torpor over the river, over everything, now the cool night and full moon down the old village street; lulling waters of Hudson ashine with the light of it, and the black boats sliding by, green and red lights, far out in the channel— And in Jim, a stirring, as of something broken and of something lifting, emerging, deep within him, a small stirring like a new life, fluttering and delicate. He sat perfectly still, feeling the new desire and longing, the life in him that was old and now new again, the ache in his heart to be off, to be moving again, and in his pain the old doubts and fears storming in. What will be? And in him there was no answer except the delicate stirring of desire and new longing in his heart.

"Where are you?" It was Alice's voice coming softly out of the darkness, gently chiding.

"What?" He looked at her as though suddenly remembering she was sitting beside him, as though being pulled back to himself again.

She leaned over and stroked his hair.

"You seemed so lost," she said, smiling and smoothing his hair back gently with her fingers. His throat tightened and he put his arms about her and kissed her. Close to her, he felt wrapped around in a kind of peace and contentment, felt held and central in himself, softly rested. He felt like a man who had strayed and slumbered and been lost those many years and in whom now another part of him was rising, as the morning, clean and still.

"It's a lovely night," she breathed, resting her head on his shoulder.

Jim kissed her lightly on the throat, then stood and taking her by the hands, pulled her up.

"Where are we going?" she asked.

But he only smiled and led her to the ladder at the edge of the dock and climbing down the rungs first, he reached up and helped her descend to the beach below. At the last few rungs he lifted her in his arms, she laughing and clasping him about the neck. The tide was high and he carried her under the pilings of the pier to the other side where rocks were piled up against a sea wall. He walked across the beach to the water's edge and there set her down. Squatting, he ran his fingers over the sand, searching for stones, while Alice watched him, a smile of curiosity on her face.

Small waves curled whitely up the shore.

"Got some," he said, grinning and standing up straight.

"Got what?"

"You'll see."

Bouncing the stones in one hand, he gazed out over the water. The stones made a chocking sound in the quiet air.

"Look there," he said, taking her by the shoulder and pointing to where the bright band of moonlight cut across the water. Then, selecting a flat smooth stone from the heap in his open palm, Jim took a long step back in the sand and crouching slightly, he flung back his arm and shot it forward, sending the stone skimming over the water; the stone glinted dipping and rising in the swath of moonlight as it skipped over the rippling face of the river.

Alice clapped her hands and turned to him, laughing gaily.

"Did you count?" he asked, smiling with the eagerness and pride of a small boy.

"It jumped six times!" she exclaimed, and laughed again.

"Watch this," said Jim, and taking another stone sent it flying across the water. The stone hit the surface with a quiet ping, sending up a tiny spray, then swiftly rose and fell for such a long distance in the moonlit trough of waves that it soon disappeared from view, still hopping and jumping over the river.

Alice was jumping up and down ecstatically. "I counted twelve times!" she cried, clapping her hands. Cindy pranced to the edge of the waves and barked at the other shore.

"It's probably still skimming to the other side," Alice laughed, delighted. "It'll probably skip up on the beach on the other side."

"Well, I don't know now," said Jim, smiling quietly and looking across the water. "It's a *wide* river, Alice."

"Oh, I'm sure it will make it!" she cried, and flinging her arms about his neck, kissed him.

"Look," said Jim.

Alice turned and they both watched as on the far shore a passenger train, gleaming long and silver in the moonlight, moved swiftly down the track, a far soft hum near the water's edge, its windows, tiny from the distance, burning brightly in the night.

"That stone should just about be there by now," said Alice softly in his ear. "It might break one of the train's windows."

Alice began to laugh at the thought of it, and Jim laughed, too. They stood laughing quietly together, their arms about each other, watching the train as it gathered speed and vanished in the distant darkness.